Praise for Tariq Godd[...]

FOR *HOMAGE TO A FIRING SQUAD*
Auspicious and audacious, a triumph of philosophical enquiry with earthy gory action.
Independent on Sunday

FOR *DYNAMO*
Original, clever and accomplished, a wonderful premise for a novel, which he pulls off with a flourish, a smart, engaging novel from a refreshingly unusual voice in British Fiction.
The New Statesman

FOR *THE MORNING RIDES BEHIND US*
Large-minded and deserving of a wide readership. It is hard to believe that there is a more promising novelist under the age of thirty working in Britain today.
The Scotsman

FOR *THE PICTURE OF CONTENTED NEW WEALTH*
An ingenious take on the Gothic novel that forsakes cheap thrills and chills in favour of something much more interesting – a lucid exploration of good and evil and the meaning of faith.
The Daily Mail

The Message

The Message

Tariq Goddard

Winchester, UK
Washington, USA

First published by Zero Books, 2011
Zero Books is an imprint of John Hunt Publishing Ltd., Laurel House, Station Approach,
Alresford, Hants, SO24 9JH, UK
office1@o-books.net
www.o-books.com

For distributor details and how to order please visit the 'Ordering' section on our website.

Text copyright: Tariq Goddard 2010

ISBN: 978 1 84694 879 4

A CIP catalogue record for this book is available from the British Library.

Design: Stuart Davies

Printed in the UK by CPI Antony Rowe
Printed in the USA by Offset Paperback Mfrs, Inc

We operate a distinctive and ethical publishing philosophy in all
areas of our business, from our global network of authors to
production and worldwide distribution.

Tariq Goddard was born in London in 1975. He read philosophy at King's College London, and Continental Philosophy at The University of Warwick and the University of Surrey. In 2002 his first novel, *Homage to a Firing Squad*, was nominated for the Whitbread (Costa) Prize and the Wodehouse-Bollinger Comic Writing Award. He was included as one of Waterstone's 'Faces of the Future' and the novel, whose film rights were sold, was listed as one of The Observer's Four Debuts of the year. In 2003 his second novel, *Dynamo*, was cited as one of the ten best sports novels of all time by The Observer Sports Magazine. *The Morning Rides Behind Us*, his third novel, was released in 2005 and short-listed for the Commonwealth Prize for Fiction. In 2010 *The Picture of Contented New Wealth*, his fourth novel, won The Independent Publishers Award for Horror Writing, and he was awarded a development grant by The Royal Literary Fund. He lives with his wife on a farm in Wiltshire where they run zer0 books and have an organic herb business. *The Message* is his fifth novel, and he is currently writing his sixth, *Nature and Necessity*.

To John and Sarah

'What is a woman that you forsake her,
And the hearth-fire and the home acre,
To go with the old grey Widow-maker?'

Rudyard Kipling

'Life is beautiful but the world is hell'

Harold Pinter

The Holy City of Qom, Iran

Now

'Who are you anyway?' was a question Dr Mahmoud Golem usually asked his wife when he had drunk too much and been guided into bed, her eyes alien catastrophes that bore no relation to those he rediscovered over breakfast every morning. For the sake of consistency this ought to have been a question Golem levelled at everyone, and as Deputy Director of the Ministry of Intelligence and National Security of the Islamic Republic of Iran, there was a sense in which he did. But his enquiries only took him as far as what people pretended to do, stopping short of uncovering the mystery of their being, a shortfall which left him with a thirst that had not gone unnoticed by his superiors. Though his cheerful scholarship, worn lightly, and war record in the Revolutionary Guard meant that there were still several cigarettes to smoke before he got cancer, or so he liked to joke after a discrete bottle of arak, all was not well. Gifted theologians with photographic memories were tolerated, even ones that had a tendency to look a little too deeply into questions of no political consequence, but Golem's decadent irreverence was undermining his office. The summons for an audience with Grand Ayatollah Jafari seemed to herald his dismissal or worse, but that was last night's thought, the product of sleeplessness and air-conditioned sweat. Mornings had their own logic, and as he crossed the outwardly bland courtyard he thanked God for sparing him for reasons he could neither understand nor be worthy of. Life was not finished with him yet, or he with it. Beside him students mingled in purposeless swarms, their turbans and clerical gowns evoking a timelessness that he had once enjoyed the English variety of, watching Middlesex bowl out Hampshire at Lord's as an exchange student.

'Stayin' alive, stayin' alive', he hummed noiselessly, 'ah, uh, uh, stayin' alive.'

Jafari's chamber was located under the "Shia Vatican", away from the heat amidst a catacomb of prayer rooms, lecture halls and interrogation chambers. Golem preferred natural light and fresh air, the narrow corridors and arid decor of this subterranean world horribly claustrophobic, its model most likely the Pentagon, whereas he yearned to serve in a Muslim St Paul's. Vowing to remain calm in the face of any eventuality, Golem did up his top button and waited for the green light to come on, the watchful eye of the Chinese CCTV camera having replaced the need to knock and announce his arrival.

Jafari was sitting cross-legged on a cushion, Cheshire cat-like, his bearded double chin twitching greedily. Although he was only four years older than Golem, the physical difference between the two men could have been measured in light years. Jafari's face resembled nothing so much as an overturned plate of humous with red currants and an oil slick in the place of eyes and a mouth.

'Ah, on time,' he groaned softly to himself. Cynicism and underground living had spoiled his shape, creating a body within a body, his vitality struggling under layers of kebab-induced neglect. By his side lay a plate of moist buttery cakes, and with an affectionate shove of his hand he offered Golem one. Winking indulgently Golem politely declined. As a keen footballer, with a tendency to catnap whenever he could, Golem retained a freshness the late nights ought to have cheated him of. His eyes looked forward to what they would see next and his taut physique retained something of the hungry frontiersmen he was the cerebral descendent of.

The grand Ayatollah wheezed and coughed something into a tissue, 'God be with you, I did not ask you here to incriminate you with temptation.'

'Incriminate me?' Golem froze.

'My sweet tooth,' he pointed at a box of halva, 'sloth is one of the deadly sins. Rabi brings in these goodies from Lebanon every morning and by lunch I'm set to explode. They just keep disappearing, I don't even notice myself doing it any more…but I have something serious to ask of you brother.'

Golem tried to hide his relief, 'name it.'

'Shimba. The name will not mean much to you, it is not a *necessary* country.'

'On the east coast of Africa, below Tanzania, or Uganda?'

'Exactly, until a few months ago it would have made little difference. The West and China could fight over its raw materials, our African section had tried to distract us over this, but I had warned of the dangers of overextending ourselves; let the superpowers quarrel over King Solomon's Mines I say, we have the middle east. We should try and live within our means. And then this happened.' Jafari held up a photograph of a lithe black man carrying a machine gun.

Golem, who at this moment wished he knew a little bit more about Shimba than he did of the English Premier League, cleared his throat to buy a precious second, 'Julius Limbani,' he said, a concrete memory forming, 'leader of one of the small rebel factions trained in the Congo. The Americans want him indicted for War Crimes. I recall it gave you the opportunity to lecture them on double standards…hasn't he just converted to Islam? In fact, haven't we been covertly supplying him with arms?'

Jafari sighed patiently, 'good but out of date. This is the man who was Julius Limbani but who would be Muhammad Al-Mahdi, twelfth Imam, ultimate saviour of mankind and descendent of the prophet Muhammad.'

Golem looked to see if Jafari was joking, and deciding that there was no way of knowing, asked 'I beg your pardon?'

'No, this is, as your English friends say, "one of those funny little bits of information that carries a wallop"', Jafari grinned unpleasantly, 'it could be as serious for us as the "War of Holy Defence" against Sadaam. Think about it, Khomeini himself said our guardianship of the faith lasts only as long as the Twelfth Imam remains in hiding...'

'Which is where he has been since 868...and will be until the day of Judgement and the end of history.'

'Exactly, and now, for reasons best known to Allah, he has decided to appear in the earthly incarnation of a middling African warlord...thus ushering the final battle between righteousness and evil in an apocalyptic contest that will end in his stewardship of the world for several years under a perfect and spiritually enlightened government,' Jafari paused to wipe a stubborn crumb from his bottom lip, 'until the return of Jesus Christ, which I'm glad to say will turn the problem over to the Christians.'

'But he must be an impostor?' No one can take a war criminal seriously...as a religious figure.'

'Thousands have, he's gobbled half the country in the last two months, and now threatens the borders of Shimba's neighbours, inciting Muslims everywhere to join his banner. We've deliberately blocked the story from all our media outlets. Only our foreign desks know of the developing situation. And of course, aside from our supporting his rise, the most disturbing aspect of this is that he says he is a Shia.'

'Africa is a desperate place, he's taken advantage of people's hunger, of their hopelessness...he can only have weeks to go before he implodes like those Somali courts keep doing..'

Jafari smiled coyly, 'only if you believe that he *is* an impostor, don't you trust the teachings of the Shia, Mahmoud? Why ought we all to follow theological instructions when they remain just that, theology, and yet the minute we are asked to trust a real life miracle we become the arch practitioners of agnostic common sense; really, you surprise me, I thought in you the regime had at least one true believer?'

An awful doubt struck Golem, might this whole business be a bizarre test he was in danger of failing? 'I only meant that the story struck me, in my capacity as an intelligence chief, as unlikely, as much the product of self- deception as the will of Allah. Such people exist everywhere, the only difference is in the scale of Limbani's claim.'

'Quite. Self deception, it begins in childhood when we pretend the tree we climb is in fact a space ship, then continues into adulthood as we convince ourselves that those we love, love us in return, and the ones we obey value our loyalty...'

Golem noticed Jafari's eyes glaze slightly. 'I'll speak frankly, our revolution is old and in denial,' he said. 'Nations that do not acknowledge human frailty or human weakness allow both to thrive. The masses tolerated our double standards and severity for as long as they were thought to work, but every day the petrol queues grow longer and our village girls sell themselves to buy the stockings they hide under robes. We call America the new Rome, but it could just as easily be us. And now these protests, Tunisia, Egypt, Libya, the Greens, everywhere and every day these protests, how long do you honestly think we can last?'

'I myself have had a hand in putting those down,' said Golem a little uneasily, it had not been a task he relished, 'the regime has been shored up.'

Jafari adjusted his cushion, 'don't try and contradict me, I know there's not a word of this you haven't said yourself at your drinking parties. So take the three together, our, shall we say, erratic President, this heretic who rises from nowhere, and us, at the moment of our greatest weakness, sitting atop a degenerating keg of discontent' Jafari pulled out a folder he was sitting on top of and thrust it at Golem, 'here, it's all in here, everything you need to know about the usurper who challenges our authority as defenders of the true faith.'

Golem took the folder. It was not very thick. 'Why me, I'm internal security, wouldn't an African expert be more your man?'

Jafari chuckled, 'why you? Because you once asked, "is it always in God's interest to have people who believe in him running the world?" Your intellectual background and enquiring mind is worth more to us than a hack with a grasp of Swahili. We need you to find out if Limbani is who he says he is and if he *is*, is he capable of carrying such historical responsibility on his own?'

'You mean we should help him?'

'Not help, *investigate*, it is the priesthood and not the prophet that makes the world fit for religion...interpret the situation as you see fit but do not take this lightly, if this man is a pretender then he must be exterminated with extreme prejudice. If he is not, then leave on good terms, and we shall try and make Shimba our Israel, an outpost for our interests in Africa.'

'Still, I've never been south of Egypt.'

'And? I ask you not just because of your mind, but on account of what you'll become if you stay here. A frivolous and trivial man, wasting his days with long walks and pointless gossip, and who knows, perhaps even a danger to yourself. There were many who thought you a natural figurehead for the Green revolt, even that you might share the demonstrators' sympathies. You need to travel, to get out of here. Some people have a way of growing into themselves, others fall the other way, it is your destiny to leave here and find your way again in Africa,' Jafari concluded waving a hand in the air in what might have been a blessing.

'I see.'

'They will be expecting you, and will regard you as a friend sent to advise them from their "older" Islamic brother. But remember Mahmoud, whoever our "Mahdi" really is, the one thing we are told he is sincere about is his wish for Islam to rule the world. This must not be allowed to happen.'

'Why?'

'Because the capital of Islam is here,' Jafari tapped the floor, 'not Shimba. Now go.'

CHAPTER ONE

Who Dares Wins

The two officers were stationed in a corner of the country that could have been West Germany in the seventies, or possibly, though neither of them could think how, a place even less unique. It was England, but not the England they would see in their mind's eye as they died for their country. The more martial of the two, Sean Pagan, was silent and full of the dread of waiting for something bad to get worse. He had made the wrong life decisions, seen that he had, and failed to act on the knowledge. At the time it had seemed easier not to. This was his general malaise, the spiral staircase of regret he returned to when specific problems abated for a happy moment or two. Justin Elder, his friend in the cot next to him, was concerned with problems of a more specific kind.

'I wonder where we'll go?' he asked, his castrato voice too fraught for his lined face, pockmarked and round like the moon, 'go next, eh Sean?'

Pagan ignored his earnest friend, a vision of the wife he loved imperfectly writhing lasciviously across the ceiling. So imperfectly that he amended his theory of love to one in which imperfection was as good as love got. A change that had left the way open for a randy actress who enjoyed sleeping with SAS men, the brush of her imaginary hand causing his cock to fire up a stage. Jumping her was like joining a pornographic troupe that had been on tour since the beginning of time, his contribution full blooded and unoriginal. It was difficult to tell whether he had enjoyed it though, for a steady desire for oblivion ran beneath everything he did, dominating hungover Mondays such as this. In all probability his life had been invented as an excuse to

8

disguise the problem of being alive, each successive crisis a covering story for the primary existential wound he returned to.

'I hope it's not Afghanistan again, it's like holidaying in the same place every year. It would be good to mix it up a bit, see somewhere else.'

'Right.'

Elder, in a way that not all of his colleagues found endearing, had retained a naivety that eight years in the service had done nothing to lessen, his middle parting worn long and shined shoes a throwback to a more trusting time. His enthusiasm betrayed a thirst for irrevocable acts, his military service up until now neither dangerous nor fraught enough for his liking. Next to him Pagan was a middleweight boxer approaching round four, a tense frown hanging protectively over a face one meal short of anorexia. Only his small nose with a flat end was peculiarly delicate, his hair cropped too close to his scalp for an officer and his tattoo even less becoming a Captain.

Without forewarning there was another person in the room, slightly excited and exchanging glances.

'Christ Beasley, haven't you ever heard of knocking?'

Beasley was a rangy Sergeant in his early forties. Almost uniquely in the Regiment he retained a moustache, worn on a face that emanated feral disobedience. When not communicating in obscenity, innuendo or riddles, he was one of the most experienced non-commissioned officers still on active service, a fact he often had cause to fall back on, for he was not the most agreeable of men.

'The Headmaster wants to see you both, and I can tell you off the bat, we're not going back to bandit country.'

'Going nowhere would be the next posting I'd recommend you for. I don't know what you're trying to prove hanging on here at your age' Pagan got off the bed and slowly bent down to fasten his laces, 'and didn't NCO's call officers Sir when you first joined up way back in 1914?'

Beasley's eyes hissed like coals dipped in cold water, 'retire, you say, been in service too long, is that what you're saying Sir?'

'We're reasonable men, or at least Captain Elder is, you could rely on him for a good CV when you start your minicab firm...'

'That would sort of leave you short of someone to save your life; neither of you are cautious lads, no disrespect to your public school combined cadet forces intended my good sirs, but you'd be tackle out without me to tuck you back in.'

The piss take was Beasley's life and the last word always his to dispense. What it might have been like for him to show a superior respect, no one knew, as the turnover of officers in the SAS was too swift for Beasley ever to arrive at such an evaluation. Elder and Pagan would have to content themselves with having risen higher in his esteem than most.

'At least he's never called us Ruperts,' said Elder as they crossed the parade ground to the Headmaster's office.

'Yes' said Pagan dryly, 'that would be really bad.'

The Headmaster, Peter Skellen, commanding officer of the Regiment, looked relieved to see them, as though some niggling irritation had lifted and been passed to someone else. His office was an unprepossessing place, low key being the Regiment's touch word, yet both Pagan and Elder could not help feeling that a little more razzmatazz would not go amiss. Even in an uplifting era, which theirs wasn't, the office of Director of Operations appeared to have been designed for the dark times. The decorative had been sacrificed to the utilitarian, dowdy accoutrements found in the office of any public servant were punctuated by photos of unsmiling faces in uniform, the odd flag and a portrait of the Monarch-to-be. The only properly military touch was an Airfix model of a Boeing Chinook that doubled as a paperweight.

'How now to begin?' said the Headmaster mockingly. He was a stooped and thorough man, with sandy hair and crooked teeth who, having done something brave once, was now sitting behind his desk because he had to. Occasionally he let on that he had been betrayed by politicians, which though true was only part of the reason for his decline into bitter indifference towards most things. Like so many men in the Regiment, to press him any further would be like asking an artist what his paintings meant or an alcoholic why he drank; one would receive an answer but it would not be the truth.

'Balance is what this thing is about, in practice as well as the idea of it. Balance and imbalance' he muttered.

Pagan looked at Elder who seemed, somehow, to understand. There were days in which Pagan found concepts disabling. This was one.

'We are currently experiencing a profound imbalance in Africa, so if you've heard that you're not going back to Afghanistan then you heard right because you're not.' The Headmaster got up and pointed at a stained old map that had never before, to their knowledge, been used for its intended purpose. Tapping it almost made the Headmaster look like he was about to say something interesting, 'Shimba gentlemen, I've a story for you that may remind you what you got into the service for. It's certainly woken me up from the doldrums.'

And so he sketched the outline of a former British colony, bought low by a maniacal warlord who believed he was the descendent of the prophet Muhammad. 'Which is of course no concern to us,' he concluded, with a flourish.

'It isn't?' Elder blustered too readily. Some part of his life had always involved intense fantasy, but contrary to his hopes, the army had put a temporary stop to it. This news, however, raised the welcome prospect of a destiny he had day dreamed of since he was a boy, Elder, Lion of Shimba and Saviour of a Continent. It had a ring to it. 'Sir, we've waited years to hear a story like this, and now you say it's got nothing to do with us?'

'Easy now, that wasn't quite what I said.'

Pagan was less sanguine. Stories like Limbani's raised the prospect that for all he knew this man was no different from himself, not what he seemed, maybe not anything at all, just a few odd decisions he didn't realise he made, ending in his deification by a pack of starving morons.

'So if we discard history and the religious stuff, what's our angle in Sir?'

For once the Headmaster did not look as though he were eagerly anticipating retirement, 'officially Sean? Shimba was part of our East African Empire, we have a moral duty to prevent humanitarian disaster, or at least, that's the rhetoric our liberal imperialists will use on the news.'

'And unofficially?'

'Cadmium, cassiterite, manganese, geranium, wolframite beryl, columbo tantalite; at ease, I don't expect you to know what they all are, they're our lesser interests, but Shimbite? That might mean something to you, ring any bells?'

'It's a sort of rare stone isn't sir?' said Elder, 'like tanzanite, big in the seventies and eighties.'

'That's its elder brother, the stuff they're mining these days is smaller, more precious, brown caviar they call it now.'

'It's taken over from iron ore and logging as their main interest and become some kind of magic ingredient for technology, according to the Christmas edition of the Economist,' offered Pagan hesitantly, embarrassed by his reading and loathe to play the call and response game favoured by senior officers.

'My, my, I should loan you two to MI6. Yes, it's to technology what butter is to cooking. Every mobile phone in the country contains the stuff. What's worse, it's perfect for pilfering. Tiny enough to be packed into suitcases, handbags or pockets, shoved up the arses of mules, any which way you like. The stuff is pouring out of Shimba every day. And it doesn't need any clumsy apparatus of electrolysers, smelters, refiners or any messy infrastructure either, so forget rickety railways, road haulage and quaysides. No wonder every bugger and his chum is at it like billy-oh.'

'Including Julius Limbani our Mahdi, I suppose.'

'Especially our mad Mahdi; in fact, it's helping the man fund a war that will do away with an elected government that has been a friend of Britain and member of the Commonwealth ever since independence. Which is where we, or I should say you, come in. You see, it's not just our business interests at stake, though of course they are; this man is something of a menace in his own right.'

'I take it then, this isn't a peace keeping mission we're embarking on?'

'Correct Justin, quite the reverse. It won't have escaped your notice that we've been asked to do far too many "conventional" jobs that should have gone to the infantry, these past few years. In effect, we've become a superannuated arm of the regular army. This is different; it's what we're about, what Stirling formed the Special Air Service for.'

Pagan noticed a sadistic glint in the Headmaster's eyes. 'A full briefing will come later, but in a nutshell, we need you to locate the Mahdi, apprehend him alive and hand him over to the Congolese who'll take him to Kinshasa where he's wanted for war crimes. In doing so you'll deprive a burgeoning movement of its figurehead, and, God willing, restore some balance to a very unhappy part of the world. Certainly so far as our trading relations with a free and prosperous Shimba are concerned.'

'Crikey!' Elder cried, 'you couldn't make it up could you?'

'I couldn't but you'll have to Justin,' replied the Headmaster, 'make it up as you go along in the finest traditions of special operations. And you can drop that downcast melancholia Pagan, it's a poor act, I know you're dying to get back into the field. They'll probably make a film out of this one, I know any number of young officers who'd bite my hand off to get this assignment, but I'm giving it to you because this will be your last run out before you return to your former regiments and,' he paused for effect, 'because you're the best we've got. It'll be difficult, the word is that the Iranians and even the Chinese may be involved, there's even talk of a small detachment of British mercenaries helping the Mahdi, so God knows, the stakes are high. The whole show couldn't be any more delicate. We're calling it Operation Wild Geese. You're both the same rank, but given his experience Pagan will lead. Any questions?'

'Many thanks for providing us with the piece de resistance of our careers sir' said Pagan. Elder and the Headmaster grinned as one as a hint of sunlight edged into the room.

'What are you thinking Sean?'

'Nothing, nothing yet Sir.' It was a lie, though better than telling them of his ruminations on time moving in a forwardly direction, thus forcing even the most stubborn of men on.

Elder had started to ask questions.

With a swift exertion of will, Pagan forgot his wife, the actress and their illegitimate child, and began to listen to words, exact and precise, simple and concise, words, and at the end replied with five of his own; 'we'll do our best Sir.'

* * *

'So what do you reckon Sean?' asked Elder, finishing his cigarette with a flourish, 'I mean he's not joking is he, the Headmaster, when he says this is the kind of gig we signed up for?'

Pagan was stood with his hands in his pockets staring at the men on their way to the dining hall.

'It's hard to take in,' Elder continued, 'compared to other jobs this is like reinventing the wheel, I can't even remember the order everything is supposed to happen in...'

This was a prompt, for Elder needed a storyboard before he could grasp his role in unusual missions.

Pagan feigned a smile, 'in a nutshell Justin, we go to Africa, we find this fucker, kill or capture but probably kill him and leave whatever's left to the worms or a criminal court. Capiche?' Pagan's expression had turned jolly, the frown easing off his forehead, 'of course, it's a sequence of events that's going to gain everything in the doing. We're never going to be so alone as we'll be on this one. The Shimban Jungle, I mean for Christ's sake, it's supposed to be the size of France.' The thought seemed to have cheered him up and as he reached for one of Elder's cigarettes, Pagan decided that he remained a mystery to himself, or at least able to take himself by surprise. 'Yeah, it'll turn ugly no matter what happens' he chuckled, 'this bloke isn't going to come quietly, it won't be like the West African Militia, they were just kids, this Mahdi is a bona fide jungle pirate. No helicopter back up or regular army to call in, could get tricky Justin, very tricky.'

Elder held a lighter up for him, 'don't like the way you're stressing that part of it, bit morbid.'

'We screw up out there and we won't even get a mention on the World Service. Trust me Justin.'

Elder checked Pagan's face and as usual had no idea whether his friend was joking or not, 'it's not like Britain to leave her own hanging out to dry, however unfashionable the idea of our country actually representing something might be.'

'Come on, the Yanks are on to something calling their CIA "the Company". Your country, anyone's country works like a corporate business, it rewards its staff for loyalty and produc-tivity but the day you stop bringing in the bacon or embarrass it and you watch what happens. The whole fucking lot of them will walk to the other side of the room and pretend never to have heard of you. Just like a real company. On our own Justin, no one will hear us out there. As you say, classic SAS.'

'Insane' said Elder, his head awash with antiquated notions of glory, and current day ones of death, 'when I joined up I thought we'd be doing things like this all the time, we never have and now, well, you never know do you, one of us might even get the big one...'

Pagan winced.

'A Victoria Cross!'

'There'll be no one there to see' said Pagan, 'but if I die, recommend me for one, and then you can have mine.'

Laughing uproariously, never afraid of enthusiasm making a fool of him, Elder grasped Pagan's shoulder and said, 'really Sean, you're the only one I can talk to like this, anyone else would think I was a wanker wanting a medal. It would just be good, you know, to have some proof that all this happened.'

Pagan could have said all the proof he needed was the memory of a Geordie Private crawling out of a minefield without his legs, but instead replied, 'I'm hungry, let's get to it.'

* * *

Elder's confusion over his mission objectives were next to nothing compared to Golem, who had left his meeting with Jafari trying desperately to read between the lines. His wife was now fast asleep and, forgoing his usual nightcap, he had lain awake, going over the morning's conversation, sometimes remembering subtle nuances, more often inventing them and retreating further from objective fact, which in any case was no guarantee of ultimate truth. At one level his brief was simple, to travel to an ostensibly friendly country where he would be welcomed as an experienced authority on Islamic Revolution. Add to this that all he had to do was assess whether this friendliness should be reciprocated or not, and then come back with the good, or bad news, and there really was nothing to worry about. So why was he still awake?

Any level of meaning had a tendency to slide into a murkier one, a realm that he had lived in long enough to recognise the stench. This was the place they expected him to delve, and in doing so prove his loyalty by finding, and this was the thing, by finding what *they had already decided was the truth*. Anything he saw and reported on in Shimba would have to match whatever policy had already been agreed upon back here in Tehran. If it didn't he would be marked as a heretic, little better than the Mahdi himself. Yet if this man was a useful proxy to fighting Western interests then heretic or not, he would be required to groom him...wasn't that what Jafari really wanted, a client state in Africa, their own little version of Israel on another continent, only this time they would own it and not the Americans...

Outside the last of the Green protestors were shouting anti-regime slogans from the rooftops, clothed in the same religious language as an ordinary call to prayer but different somehow, more desperate, closer, dare he admit it, to how he himself felt. Golem fell asleep wishing that his opinion was, and would always be the same as that of the regime's, so that the problem of having a mind of his own would be solved forever, for his sleeping wife's sake, if not for that of his long lost soul.

CHAPTER TWO

Out of Africa

Nataka, Northern Shimba. One month later

Foy Fox-Harris wanted to exist for a reason. The only reason compelling enough to support the conceit of her existence was to do good, yet she worried that she had not done enough of it. Had she ever really escaped from herself into that realm where one acts for others, rather than indirectly for one's own desires? Every African she wept for, tramp she gave an ineffectual pound to or sponsored run completed in record time, had been made in relation to herself. And therefore invalidated in the context of the lives of those she sought to help, or so she feared. Her father, a free thinking accountant, had made the point that no one, using her criteria, could be regarded as good and that the suffering millions would be just as complacent in her position, and she would be no more morally exalted if she lived in theirs.

Sometimes Foy accepted that she had done more for the world than the other girls in her year at Saint Helen's, if only because their socialisation acknowledged no reality greater than lacrosse, snogging at Balls and the inevitability of a scripted wedding to someone in the City. She, at least, had tried to break out of this cycle of life-denying madness, though her attempts were stymied by egotism. The stint as a youth television presenter investigating homelessness was marred by an ignoble desire to appear on the small screen. Her subsequent flirtation with Trotskyite politics had been no better than joining a third rate cult, motivated as she was by shallow and immature posturing. Even collecting signatures for charity petitions was a waste of her weekends, as was the patronising and unhygienic Christmas spent in a soup kitchen. These endeavours had not only failed to do anyone any good, the motivation to do them was wrong. But still she resisted the lure of her own kind, and the opportunities bequeathed by privilege.

With some intent, Foy chewed her way through her straw and eyed the Marlboro Light balanced between her fingers as though she intended to write with it. Smoking abroad seemed healthier than at home, not counting as much. And doing something purposeful with her hands made her less nervous of prying eyes. For not even her outgrown crew cut, retro sunglasses and ill-fitting African maternity smock could disguise the obvious. That in jodhpurs and thigh high boots, Foy Fox-Harris would secure over a million hits an hour from Internet masturbators the world over. This lanky Englishwoman was a flamingo out of water, and everyone from the café's other patrons to the taxi driver who had brought her there, and still watched her from his toot toot, knew it. Foy put down the cigarette and tried to ignore her immediate surroundings.

What had attracted her to goodness? The same thing that had taken her to Shimba and stopped her from using her first in English to join a publishing house and commission mid-list authors. If she could not do something significant herself, like write poems or sing on stage, then goodness was the only excep-tional route open to her, and from what she had heard, there would be plenty of opportunities to practise it in Shimba.

To her relief her African adventure, sponsored by Trade Aid and discouraged by her friends, had not been an unqualified disappointment. True, the orphanage she was sent to was riven by corruption, and some of the boys, including very young ones, were ungrateful and lecherous. Worse still, her co-volunteers were a mix of self-righteous lesbians, Canadians and dysfunc-tional Christians, yet there was a moment every day that transcended the hand she was dealt. Sometimes it was a sunset or an unfamiliar scent from the bush, though mostly it was a human incident; successfully persuading a teacher to give allocated food to children and not the black market, or a high five with a leper she was scared of touching. Gradually her fear of becoming a cliché disappeared and with it her exaggerated awareness of her motivation and sense of self. Africa, or unambiguous raw experience, was slowly working.

The war had not made much difference to her at first, everywhere in the region was in (or had just left) a conflict of some kind, often civil and usually some distance away. The aid workers who fled had overreacted and shown they were there for the wrong reasons, she proudly surmised, as to her amazement, she realised she was not in their number. The children grew closer to her and even protective as she noticed she was more assured with them, communicating directly with the big charities, assessing information, being asked for her own opinion and practically taking over the place. Back in England her family were terrified for her safety and privately she enjoyed their fear, it proved she was doing something worthwhile. Also she knew there was nothing really to be scared of, she was not being brave because there was no danger, only a Western media that loved to exaggerate ordinary misfortune.

This was two weeks ago. In that time the last two of the gap year girls in the district had been robbed and raped at gunpoint on the main road, the children had melted away, and she could not hold eye contact, let alone receive a straight answer from the remaining Trade Aid representative, an Egyptian named Steve. All he could tell her was that Oxfam were on their way out and Medicines Sans Frontiers were coming in, and that the wounded soldiers arriving from the north in Trade Aid lorries expected to sleep in the empty dormitories she was pointlessly locking. For the first time she was scared. That night she accepted the American film crew's offer of a lift to Nataka, the coastal town popular with tourists she had avoided thus far. On reaching it they discovered a bona fide disaster in progress. To their horror the road behind them had filled full of rebels, who had surrounded the Peninsula, cutting them off from the rest of the country. Shattered from their drive the crew had told Foy to meet them at the café for breakfast to discuss taking a boat down the coast, but it was now lunchtime and there was still no sign of the Americans. Not only that, but for once, none of the locals had come near her, not to serve, sell or even make conversation, only watch with a collective expression she could not decipher. So thank God for the Websters, a family whom on good days she could probably have done without, but on one like this were the cavalry and a bedtime story rolled into one. They were odd alright, taking off to go to the toilet together and having no plausible reason as to why they were in Shimba, but at least they were English, from Ipswich in fact...and she would need people who were a little rough around the edges to get out of a spot like this.

Foy's lips held the lit cigarette without help from her fingers, its dry chemical sand filling her mouth and reminding her that she had not cleaned her teeth that morning. Well what of it, it wasn't as if she was going to have to kiss anyone today...

* * *

Just six miles north of Foy Fox-Harris Golem asked 'can these really be Muslims?'

Artay, his assistant, who was even more shocked by what he saw, but by inclination more inclined to conceal it, whispered a quiet prayer. Relations had not been good between the two men. Golem's tendency to read Western novels on the long sea journey to Shimba upset his pious companion whom Golem, at his most paranoid, believed to be a plant sent to spy on him by Jafari. The pretence of having to be merchant seamen played to Golem's strengths but Artay had alienated himself from the crew, complaining that it would have been just as low key to fly first class to their destination and masquerade as businessmen. This, and his high-minded religiosity, made them an unlikely partnership, the younger man's superiority complex suggesting that he was answering to one far higher than his nominal commander in the field. Unlike Golem, Artay, barely into his twenties with the gait of a tipsy giraffe, was a product of the revolution and had been fast tracked into the religious police from his seminary. This trip was intended to be his blooding, which was just as well, as it was all Golem could do not to break the boy's nose. Especially as he had disturbed his sleep with his five o' clock prayers, a duty Golem was sure the Prophet would have excused him of in the circumstances.

'I've never seen such...colourful youngsters, soldiers. Not since our revolution. Tehran was full of sideboards and polyester flares in the late seventies.'

Coming up the road towards them was the first wave of the Mahdi's assault guards, the storm troops of his army. A thin line of men, all wearing wellingtons and replica Arsenal tops, shuffled forward warily, followed by something even more unusual. First in pairs, then in swarms, came boys dressed in looted wedding dresses, high school commencement gowns and wigs. Behind them were girls covered in grease with clay faces and war paint, worn to ward off enemy bullets and shellfire.

'They can't really believe that, not as Muslims?' said Golem, his question not a rhetorical one, 'and women, what are they doing so close to the front line?'

'Muslims of a kind, Shimba kind' replied General War Boss, the Mahdi's Chief of Staff in this sector, 'the girls fight good too, stop the boys from missing home, their mothers, sisters, girlfriends.'

They were sitting on top of a goods vehicle watching this display of martial prowess with the high command of the Army of the South, whose leading lights were General Murder, General Rambo, General Amnesty and Sergeant Scrappy, an ugly looking Nubian in an Iron Maiden t-shirt. Despite their camp airs, and garish appearance, Golem did not doubt that he was in the presence of serious people, an honour he extended to anyone who was in a position to kill him and get away with it. War Boss grinned from ear to ear, some Arab blood evident in his pigmentation, 'they think if they don't eat pumpkin, screw, touch lime or take a bath, the bullets will miss. The muck is in case the first set of precautions fail,' he guffawed, 'in the north the Islamic courts try to set these youths straight, make them pure, but here it's as before. Shimba is not Iran.' War Boss exhaled deeply on his joint and passed it to Murder who was wearing a gas mask with a dog tail necktie. Golem winced, thinking better of watching this man's method of inhalation too closely, 'they try to give these children proper Muslim names, stopping the Bongo, their music; it works sometimes, in the north, but not here. They need an army, so long as we fight well they give us no trouble. The Mahdi, he is a great man, he tells the courts to leave us as us. We have always fought, our people, before we fought and did not know why, now we know.'

'Child soldiers dressed in mink and American clothing' Artay pointed to the next formation, in trainers, shorts and baseball caps, 'I thought your Mahdi taught low self esteem was a moral good, not to dress as *jendeh.* '

Golem, who had no wish at this stage to antagonise his hosts, mistranslated the Persian for "whores" as '"dirty". 'My young friend,' he continued hastily, 'who has little experience of not washing five times a day, would rather your soldiers were in pressed uniforms of the kind ours wear on parade. Dirt makes him nervous.'

Turning quickly to Artay, Golem snapped, 'we are here to understand, observe and report on what we see, not to insult or antagonise our hosts.'

War Boss snorted and readjusted the patch he wore over his left eye, 'only Allah knows a clean war my friend, Allah and them.'

Just below where they stood were four young men in loose white robes and facial hair that looked like it had blown off the back of a moulting Lurcher. They shared the intensity of a computer programme that had learned its religion by rote, and were muttering furiously to themselves, their prayers barely audible over the carnival din. 'The African Taliban' laughed War Boss, 'Somalis mostly, and a Sudanese, all Sunnis like their hero Bin Laden; the Mahdi tolerates these fanatics because we need men. I say they're more trouble than they're worth; they bring American rockets on our heads, kill merchants with their human explosions and drive us crazy with their lectures. But the Mahdi says we must have some amongst us. We are a worldwide family.'

'So you have Al Qaeda funding?'

'We take from whoever will provide.'

Golem frowned, Artay less so, trying to ascertain where they would stand with these men, in case of an emergency.

'Sunnis you say?' asked Artay.

'Muslims, we are all Muslims, they came without being fetched.'

'It's like burning down the house to roast a pig, General, if Al Qaeda influence these crazies your country is doomed. Look how they turned the world against us in Iraq, be careful, they count beyond their numbers, it only takes one man with a death wish to kill a thousand,' warned Golem, 'these fools have their own strange ideas.'

'We have nothing to fear from any man,' countered War Boss, 'the Mahdi is God's elect; no human hand can smite him down.' By the glint in his one good eye it was difficult to fathom whether War Boss believed this or was merely repeating a party line, like a tour guide on an open bus cruise of familiar sights.

Artay bristled; he was struggling to control his agitation as more teenagers in fright wigs and Donald Duck masks passed the truck, their swaying bodies more redolent of transvestite psychopaths than an army of God. He was aware enough of the purpose of their mission to hold his judgment until they had met the Mahdi, but this circus was already a provocation too far. 'We've heard many stories, that your Mahdi is the anointed one, that he is a descendent of the prophet, a reincarnation of Ali and so on, but are any of them the truth?' he asked, with an pomposity born of inexperience, 'when the Iranian nation sends you money to build your army I hardly think this is what it has in mind.'

'There is opposition in you' smiled War Boss fingering a whip fashioned out of a bull's penis that hung from his waist, 'thirty years ago a woman gave birth to a baby not far from my village that spoke on the very day it was born, the baby said *in English* that the next Mahdi would come from Shimba. It is not wise to pick a quarrel with your hosts...'

'What happened to the baby?'

War Boss patiently bowed his head to General Amnesty, who alone amongst the High Command, was dressed in a formal olive green safari suit, a Guards tie and, despite the heat, a tin helmet, 'I was that child,' he said.

'You yourself?'

'Yes, that is who I usually mean when I say me.'

'You could speak English as a baby?'

Amnesty looked almost apologetic, 'I had many gifts I misused, in my youth I was "Jungle Wolf", I disembowelled many women and was made a General in the government militia when I was fourteen. I told my men I would send them all to college once the war against the north was over, then one day the Mahdi came to me in a dream and sat me at his right hand.'

Artay glanced at Golem, singularly failing to disguise his sneer, 'and what then?'

'Then I saw everyone I had killed, face to face, sitting in a room round a table. There were 43 of them. I was there too. But no one was talking, only looking at me. And when I turned round the Mahdi was there, the Koran burning in his hands...'

'And he hands you the burning Koran to purify your sins?' interrupted Golem.

Amnesty nodded, 'it is so.'

'The Mahdi claims to have had just the same dream, except in his it's the Prophet himself who hands him the Koran' added Artay, stroking his small goatee sceptically, 'isn't that so, General...*Amnesty*?'

'You must not mistake our pseudonyms for childish play-acting; they give us new identities and help with the emergence of a new order. And yes, the Mahdi saw the prophet as I see you now. Why should this be so strange? The basis of our religion is shared revelation, voices, angels and holy visions. Must such things stop just because we live in the age of machines and television sets? You have established your religious order on earth, we bow to your example, now it is our turn, yes?'

Golem scowled. He was enjoying the parade and their proximity to action; Artay could easily spoil both. 'A very valid view' he answered, 'and very well put, eh Artay?'

'Yes, I suppose so.'

'There are many stories and dreams like this in Shimba,' said War Boss checking his watch, 'and they are all true. Now we must follow the soldiers, the Disco begins in an hour. There we will show you how Shimbans fight and die.'

'The Disco? I don't understand.'

'I believe he means the battle they would like us to watch' said Golem helpfully, dearly wishing his colleague could distinguish between a debating chamber and a war.

'Yes, the bridge over the Ongolo River that leads to Nataka, and from there to the capital,' called War Boss, who had leapt off the truck and was in the process of squeezing into a Toyota Land Cruiser with the rest of the High Command, 'we shall brand them on the snout!'

'God willing' said Golem wishing he could swap his black military fatigues and professional detachment for the panoply of colour that was on its way to paradise, via the "Disco" on the Ongolo River.

* * *

'I was beginning to wonder what you could all be up to!' Foy gasped. The Websters had spent the best part of twenty minutes embarked on a family trip to the lavatory, barely a yard away. It was long enough to raise doubts over her new friends' status as trustworthy human beings, but the reassuring sight of three smiling East Anglian faces quickly banished these.

'That was a bad case of Deja vaar love' quipped Mr Webster, five feet two of fading muscle, a floppy hat covering his sun-blistered pate, 'takes me right back to when Nelson,' he punched his much taller son in the hip, 'was just a daisy cutter, deja vaar, 'cos it was deli belly all the time with you wasn't it boy? Weak stomach and no bowels, gets it from his mother's side.'

Nelson Webster tried to roll his eyes and tip his head back in a move that resembled a man attempting to break his own neck. He was skinny for his height, shaven headed and with a despotic upper lip that could probably catch a coin. Although Foy tried to ignore it, his armpits, exposed in his Swastika-emblazoned t-shirt, reeked of amyl nitrate. Still, she was sure he had his good points.

'Never could hold his food in the place it should stay, every-where we took him as a boy he needed the crapper, Majorca, Margate, The Isle of Wight, you name the spot, he had the shits. Told him he shouldn't have troughed that goat what do you call it last night, the stew they all eat here, alright for them, they're bought up on it, but him? Well I couldn't leave him on his own to pebble-dash the paintwork, what with these khazis having no locks an' all these dangerous looking hop heads snooping around. I had to stand guard didn't I?'

'You're a nosy old man' said his son, 'one who can't let go, him. Once he starts on and on he goes. That's what he does.'

'Don't exaggerate for the pretty girl!' Webster punched Nelson lightly and wiped the sweat off his shaved scalp, 'he's been like this all holiday, as soon as we meet someone interestin' on the road, as soon as he's got an audience, he starts to make stuff up about his old man. And he always has, kids would come round to the house and he'd pretend I was a Lord and we had this great big mansion, hidden out in the country that we used to go to on weekends and holidays, weekends and holidays I tell you! What arse, what's in the kitten's in the cat I say, and that boy has never changed.'

Nelson looked as though he might blush. Instead he looked at his father affectionately and shook his head like someone much older, 'don't listen to anythin' he says, he's a compulsive liar, compulsive, just lies because he enjoys it is all, no reason, gets a bang out of not telling the truth.'

'What is truth?' Webster asked rhetorically, smirking at Foy. The smirk, Foy felt, was beautifully inclusive, so what if these Websters were larger than life, wasn't that a whole lot better than being smaller than life? For all her talk about wanting to grow as a person, formal acts of kindness, charisma, performance and spontaneity embarrassed Foy. The Websters were like an old music hall show, beautifully two-dimensional and this was the point, where was the harm in existing on colourful surfaces? The prejudice towards depth, in life and fiction, was simply unrealistic when there were people who really were lucky enough to take life as they found it. After the worthiness of the foreign aid gang, the Websters were a welcome relief. Foy checked herself, of course, they were not here for her amusement, they were here for themselves, which only made their kindness towards her all the more touching.

'Not a lie,' replied Nelson flatly, 'the truth is not a lie.'

'A philosopher he is, I could have found him in the Bible, bless, don't know where he gets it from. Not his Mother. Christ, we hardly know you and already you're gettin' the whole life story. Apologies Miss Fox-Davies...'

'Fox-Harris.'

'Miss Fox-Harris, but it's a family trait, openness, not stuck up like some, what you see is what you get with us, however borin' that might be for others.'

'Put a sock in it Dad, can't you see she's just bein' polite.'

'Hmmm, I hadn't thought of that,' Webster laughed, utterly unconcerned if that were indeed the case, 'that is always a risk of expressin' yourself, is it not...borin' others.'

'Don't mind him, he's a good man really.'

Foy nodded agreeably. She envied them their intimacy; her family would never have talked to each other with such startling candour.

'Taps don't work' said Tawny Webster barging past her brother, catching him with her shot putter's elbow, 'no hot or cold, no water at all. Have had to use those baby wipes.' Incredibly she was even less easy on the eye than Nelson, being a woman helping her not one wit, her aboriginal nose wildly out of place on a white and vein-blasted face. The rest of her was hidden like a satellite station over-grown with space moss, black curls pirouetted in tangles over her shoulders, down to the folds of her ample waist. It was obvious Tawny was no conventional beauty, Foy decided, but she must have a big heart to keep a body like hers going and her muscles showed agility.

'All the two of them talk is toilets, same as they do at home, me waiting for my turn and them talking toilets like they'll never see one again. An' now we're here it's the same, them going on like they do at home,' she paused, her voice was high and pretty, 'lots of ways this place reminds me of home.'

Shimba was like no kind of home Foy had experienced though this was no time to split hairs. She would agree with any observation, general or particular, that the Websters cared to make, whether she understood it or not. What the Suffolk clan lacked in the decorative art of presentation was more than made up for by character. Which was not to deny that they confused her. From what little she could gather Nelson Webster had been living in South Africa playing bass in his Oi tribute band, "The Belsen Boys", and had unfairly earned a reputation as a white supremacist, when all he was really into was the music. Visiting his father, who was either laying pipes in Tanzania or erecting rope round golf courses in Kenya, the two joined Tawny who had been setting up Broadband connections in Shimba, or was it all the other way round? Obviously none of it now mattered. The Websters had a car, a battered old Mercedes, and had been streetwise enough to scare off the local crook they hired it from, who was now skulking on the steps of the HSBC, hissing and tutting to no effect. And not just him, the entire street, normally shuddering with life, was keeping its distance from the Websters, either out of respect or...fear? Even the most indifferent of Europeans liked to boast about their relations with Africans, whether as friends or masters, yet the Websters, who had brought a whole thoroughfare to a halt, barely seemed aware of their hosts.

The only thing they did appear to care about, once they heard Foy's tale, was how best to whisk her off to safety. Salt of the Earth, that's what people like this were; they may be puzzling and use Lynx as aftershave, but their values towered over those of her University gang. In her arrogance she thought she had come to Shimba to interpret, pity and save, not realising that it was she who would need rescuing. Foy could even forgive Mr Webster his political incorrectness that was so wilfully out of date it could be neither serious, nor taken seriously.

'Best we rock 'n roll or else end up in Sambo stew, eh Nelson, your master race merchant mates wouldn't like that, would you lad!'

'Nor will she,' said Nelson pointing to Foy, 'an' I don't like the sound of those,' he continued pointing now to the end of the road that ran through Nakata. The distant plopping of mortar fire was getting closer and more regular, as was the rattle of the small arms response to it.

'That all your things, treacle?'

'Yes, everything else got left at the school, we had to get out so quickly and there was so little room because of all the camera stuff, equipment I mean…because I was with a camera crew who had all this stuff,' replied Foy breathlessly, aware that her urge to over qualify suffered next to Nelson's free wheeling economy with language. The skinhead and his sister were already packing what appeared to be golf bags and guitar cases in to the boot of the battered old Mercedes.

'Where are we going?' she called, as their father picked up her ethnically embroidered haversack and gave her a friendly pat on the bottom by way of encouragement, 'I mean, what's the plan?'

'North,' grunted Nelson, 'we're goin' north.'

'North?' Foy stopped in her tracks, she did not want to appear ungrateful, especially as her need for them was greater than theirs for her, but this was alarming, 'but isn't that where the war is? I only just came, escaped I mean, from that direction, shouldn't we head to the sea or go south?'

'So?'

Foy felt like one guilty of over-familiarity, her new found bonhomie evaporating in the time it took Nelson to say, 'you an expert on this country all of a sudden?'

'No, I didn't mean to imply that. Only the north is where the danger is, surely?'

Webster put her bag with the others and closed the boot, 'may look mad but trust us girly, I'm one of those blokes who knows more than he lets on, and it might not look like it but I care about people and care about gettin' things right, trust eh? Give a nice old man the benefit of the doubt.'

And Foy did, deciding that of all her values, choice, especially at moments of necessity, was easily the most overrated. Taking her place next to Tawny in the back, she watched the café recede behind them, the car speeding out of the city towards the roar of incoming fire.

CHAPTER THREE

An outpost of progress

Fifty Five Miles away

The boy on the screen gestured to the camera playfully and pointed to his Nike Air Force Ones, 'we want consumer goods boyeeee, but without hassle of industry!' and lighting a match threw it at a leaking petrol pump, igniting the forecourt behind him. The tape stopped and Francis, adjutant to the President of Shimba's son, drew the blinds to reveal six men dressed in fitted green t-shirts, combat trousers and boots, sitting in a line. They could have been roadies with a travelling rock band, or action man look-alikes at a fancy dress party, nothing could be stranger than what they were, Englishmen who had come to a country they had never been to before to kill people they had never met. A basic and standing absurdity never lost on their leader, Captain Pagan.

'As you can see,' said the man who had provided the voice-over to the film that had just finished, 'Limbani was still very much the young American then, in love with hip-hop, basketball boots and crack cocaine. To my knowledge this is the first time he was captured on film.'

'How old is the footage?' asked Pagan.

'It was taken fourteen years ago by a team of CNN journalists,' replied Hector, the President of Shimba's eldest, 'and to our great shame has remained the most best known and most watched footage of this country in existence, especially now in the era of You-Tube. I cannot tell you how much this misrepresentation annoys us; it serves so many agendas that are hostile to Africa. Whenever the world's press want a caption of a mad African they reel it out, a photographer even won an award taking a picture of the burning pumps. I draw solace that it must be as embarrassing to Limbani now, our self styled religious leader, as it was to our tourist industry this past decade.'

Hector undid his top button and loosened his tie, the air conditioning had broken down and he was giving off the air of a harassed trader at the end of an undone deal. Patches of his Lauren hound's-tooth suit were stuck to his well-fed frame and his friendly eyes bore the marks of conjunctivitis. What on earth, Pagan wondered, did this Winchester and Oxford educated student of History think he was doing returning to Shimba to become his father's head of security?

'Fourteen years, so Limbani must have been, what, nineteen maybe twenty?'

'Perhaps a little older, by as much as five or six years, he's always looked young for his age. At that stage he was still known as Funeral Executioner, influenced by the ritual killing rites derived from our tribal secret societies, that of the Leopard, Alligator and so on. Missionaries had effectively shut them down but by the time Chuck Norris movies hit Shimba they were up and running again. Limbani embraced an unholy synthesis of the old and new.'

'What was his break?'

'He came to prominence boiling and eating the "main machine", that is the heart, of "Bush Shaker", his main rival who ran a gang of teenage thugs on the Nataka interstate. No great loss, Bush Shaker was an inveterate idiot straight out of Hogarth. When he wasn't fleeing into the jungle to castrate his victims he was pillaging the countryside for drugs, palm oil, women, you name it. In the circumstances people viewed Limbani as an improvement.'

'Where was the then Government in all this?'

'Struggling, my father had yet to be recognised by a single Western country, they could not forgive the fact that he obtained his doctorate in East Berlin.'

'I suppose the political climate in Shimba must have been a hell of a school for Limbani, an ideal place for him to scratch up on the dark arts.'

'It was, there was nowhere lower. Cannibalism was rife, his people were the worst, and the nastiest part about it was that they were our children, every city was held to ransom by the teenage fighters who had killed their commanders and struck out on their own. Villages were surrounded by check points, the youths crazy, many of them would have mascots, a wild pig for example, drunk on local beer, if the pig grunted it meant you were a Muslim and could be shot on the spot, if not you lived; so you prayed the pig was asleep. Other gangs had monkeys and god help us, I even heard of a duck.'

Elder, who had been studiously taking down notes as was his way, put his pencil behind his ear and whistled. 'So what's his road to Damascus conversion, how does he go from gangster to man of the cloth, because at the moment, I don't see the logical progression.'

Hector shook his head, his plump face endowed by a sad passion, 'you are not the only one, regrettably none of us know. It seems, in the great tradition of conversions, to have arisen from precisely nothing. Doubtless you'll have heard the same stories as us, but as to what actually happened...no one knows for sure. It's on record that he left his group and disappeared over the border to the Congo some time in the late nineties, on a kind of spiritual quest, though at this stage his own confederates didn't know whether he was in earnest. He had gone over the lake for diamonds apparently. Once there the Americans trained him up as a preferable alternative to the Warlords, which was what my father, their great ally, had become to them by then...'

'And they neglected to tell us, their great ally, about any of this,' interrupted Elder.

'Too much autonomy isn't to be encouraged Sir,' said Beasley who up until then had been staring at the ceiling with his usual air of inattention, 'unless of course it's for a filthy job like this one.'

'Beasley, please.'

Hector wiped a red tear off his eyelid, Francis, his assistant, quickly providing him with a fresh handkerchief. 'We all know what it is to play second fiddle to the heavy weight champion of the world,' he whispered, 'thank God I was lodging on the Cowley Road in Oxford as this nightmare played itself out…most of what I tell you I learned second hand from those I refer to as the survivors. All of this, everything I have talked about, is far, far worse than I can successfully convey.'

'It's not over yet Sir,' said Pagan. 'Limbani, the Congo, you were saying…'

'It was in the Congo that he had his vision, or the first of several, in which he discovered his "true" identity and vocation. That much we do know, though God knows what secrets that jungle of a place keeps. For Limbani the Congo- Shimban border is his Jerusalem, Mecca and Vatican rolled into one.'

'So you believe he means it, is sincere in his belief that he is the Mahdi? Our intelligence is quite keen on the idea that he could be playing up, if you see what I mean, that he might be a fake and all this Mahdi nonsense is just that, clothes borrowed from the toy box to create an impression on the impressionable.'

'Yes, it is curious that he's chosen Islam and this specific prophecy; maybe politics and a fortuitous encounter with a Shia Muslim influenced him, but there is no doubt in my mind, or those of his fellow country-men, that he believes he's a gentleman of God, just like the last American President in fact. And like Mr Bush it is the devil whispering in his ear making him believe it's good he's doing and not its opposite. Limbani and his followers are the victims of a perfect delusion.'

'But as far as the facts are concerned Limbani came back, organised and united the gangs into a religious militia, and trounced all that stood in his way?'

'Surprising the Americans in the process. For them he was only ever one of three or four options, never their main concern. No one foresaw his movement's explosion in numbers or success except for Francis here,' Hector beckoned to his aid. 'Francis was the first to join Limbani and the first to defect, unlike any of his other leading commanders Francis knew him before the conversion, knew him well. It's why I can think of no one better than him to guide you to Limbani and debrief you on his ins and outs.'

Francis smiled weakly; it was a shield of a greeting. The thin line of upper facial hair and thoughtful eyes could have made him a convincing dictator, they belonged to a face that Pagan could imagine turning very angry indeed had it not looked so refined. He tried to think how the man would appear if they had met in another, less indoor context. For Francis too these Europeans presented an amusing spectacle, so different from the various landowners, engineers and men from the IMF he had met before, a casual equality emanating from their informal and brusque manner that he felt immediately at home with.

'Francis is a first class man so long as you point him in the right direction, a typical Shimban, and also a little more than that. He has educated himself to a high degree and has experience of all that I have talked about, the two together making him rare. In a poor country you can find anyone to wear a uniform. Our new army has mainly been recruited from camps where our people fled the rebels. It was easier than leaving them in the villages where they may have been forced to join Limbani. The trouble is these farmers don't have a great hunger for war, only for UN food handouts,' Hector pulled open a window that overlooked a swimming pool full of soldiers being baptised, 'that is why it's been necessary to invoke a religious dimension of our own to this awful business. If we lose, Shimba will become the Afghanistan of East Africa. It was my father's belief that the hunt for Bin Laden should have taken the form of a police operation and not an invasion of a foreign country. That's why we have no hesitation in agreeing to your government's desire for a percentage of our natural wealth as the price for taking Limbani out of the equation; if he's allowed to remain we won't be worth our weight in Shimbite.'

'Police operation is a very good way of looking at it sir. We've no need for numbers, I have all I need here with me in these five men. Captain Elder's record you're familiar with...'

'Yes, his work in Sierra Leone, Iraq and Afghanistan was most impressive.'

'Well, no more to say about that then, Sergeant Beasley was with us in those places and just about everywhere else you can think of too. Corporal Walter is an expert in jungle tracking and Privates Hightower and Kingston were trained specifically for a kind of mission our country never sent them on, but yours has given them the opportunity to attempt. I think we can bring this to a successful conclusion within the month, complicated as it may seem at the moment. After all, Limbani is hardly in hiding is he?'

'Quite. He is lingering behind his Southern army on the Lower Ongolo River. The bridge there is the gateway to the rest of the country, one's days drive north of here, an excellent opportunity for you all to make his acquaintance and he yours. But I warn you it will be difficult, especially if you are serious about taking him alive to the criminal court. To be quite honest with you Captain Pagan...' Hector looked at Elder inquiringly, 'I understand that although you are both of equal rank Captain Pagan, to all intents and purposes, will be in command for the duration of "Operation Wild Geese.'

'That is correct.'

'Then to be honest Captain Pagan, although British help, any help, is greatly appreciated, of that let me be emphatic, I and my father were still quite, no very, very surprised when your Government suggested it, for it was they, and not we, who first devised this plan, if it be that.'

'You don't approve of the plan Sir?'

'The opposite. If it comes off then we'll all be on champagne for breakfast, for you'll have answered our prayers. No, its not that, only the sheer impracticality of what is being suggested, the vagueness of how the thing will actually be done, the difficulty in navigating and fighting on terrain you have no prior knowledge of, I could go on. I know your Government does not have the highest opinion of the African fighting man, but if it was so easy do you not think that we should have tried it? And we have! Assassinations, the bribery of his inner circle, aerial bombing with the help of American satellites, what have we not tried, and what makes you so sure that you'll succeed where we have failed?'

'Bloody good question,' grunted Beasley.

'There are no guarantees Sir. Though what can I say is, I've got a good feeling about it.'

Hector looked at Francis and laughed, not unkindly.

'My father and I had rather thought that this was a dangerous gesture on behalf of Britannia, her raising her trident to show that she can still be a world player and deliver us from evil on her own. I hope your lives are not going to be used in vain.'

'We'll have to see about that' said Pagan.

'And so what if they are Sir,' Elder cut in, 'we're soldiers, this is what we wanted, why we're not mechanics or computer programmers.'

'Quite so.'

'Best get your factor fifty on then lads' said Beasley, 'the sun's not scared of white skins.'

'His way of saying it'll be rather hot Sir' said Elder, the raging orange ball they were referring to spilling through the curtains and blasting its immoderate glow over them all.

* * *

The journey toward the lower Ongolo had indeed taken twenty four hours, the symmetry of the thing appealing to Elder's pattern-finding tendencies. Or was it twenty-four, it seemed like they had been in the jeep for weeks; which was the problem with patterns, they only worked when you knew what you were looking for. It had already got to that point of the trip where home no longer existed for him, only the long bumpy track they were driving along, punctuated by the steady splatter of insects flying into the windscreen, other realities fading into an indistinct memory.

'Does anyone have the time please?'

Their Land Rover Discovery put Elder in mind of an aged reactionary collecting his grandson from prep school; camels or Bedouin mares would have struck a more appropriate note, but Elder was not churlish. He could only play the team in front of him and history provided each actor with the tools necessary for each task. At least they were not walking. Trying to close his eyes, Elder resisted the urge to place himself in the hierarchy of Imperial heroes with even less success than usual. Danger was bringing him closer to a belief in destiny. If he were to be completely objective, he knew he ranked below Lawrence and Gordon, Clive was not really comparable, and Kitchener and Roberts, well why not them? They were "celebrities" worthy of the honour, not immoral little metrosexuals advertising their genitalia on the side of a bus. Elder twitched uncomfortably, he was grateful that his companions could not hear his innermost longings. Whereas his not being able to share his values once made him lonely, it now guaranteed his inclusion. In as far as these men were aware of his peculiarities, and Pagan was more aware than most, they considered him a whimsical romantic, rather than what he was, a man at war with his own time. To cultivate the approval of his peers in a world he found bafflingly shallow, it was necessary to disguise his uncommon soul and mutate to survive. Indeed, it had always been so, ever since he had learnt at boarding school that his preference for military bands and Gilbert and Sullivan over Pink Floyd, invited ridicule and not respect.

Much as he had tried to concentrate on the memory of an old war film, to usher in sleep, the honking on the road and Beasley's constant chatter made it impossible. He turned to peering out of the window, his hand cupped against his own image so as to see through to the passing vegetation. It was neither the Africa of his imagination or the one old sweats like Beasley had told him about in lurid detail, more like the one he had seen on Nature documentaries over the years; indeed, it still felt as though he was watching it on television. The main characters were all there, humpbacked cattle, roadside shacks and of course, a fair few black people, who were mostly very thin. And yet it was still the same flat reality he encountered, not thunderbolts or lightning, just the world as it was anywhere else, but with slightly different things in it. Nearby, though drifting now, he could hear Beasley explain how to strip down his machine pistol to Francis. Beasley described the gun lovingly, a tender wistfulness entering his drawling Somerset burr. And then a brilliant starry consolation took hold of Elder, and he saw his father holding his hand outside the Royal Tournament at Earl's Court, the years falling away like the flat pack tents he could never open...

There was cramp in his leg. Perhaps he had fallen asleep, though nothing had occurred to mark the occasion. He rubbed his eyes, wishing that for once he could remember his dreams. Half-hearted fingers of light were exploding in grey streaks over the heads of the hawkers and soldiers lining the roads. Nudging his side, Francis offered him a large hard-boiled egg.

'Breakfast sir? It's a double yolker.' The soft diction he spoke in was the kind taught in dusty African classrooms, not the back streets of Peckham. Elder checked himself yet could not help it. He preferred "the African" in what he took to be his natural context, though whether the same could be said for "the African" he could not tell. He might have regarded himself as a dyed in the wool traditionalist but he had met enough differing opinions at University to know that many thought him a naïve racist. Francis's responses to those few questions he fielded earlier were so succinct that they felt like short stories when what he required was a long meandering novel. There was so much he did not understand.

Blinking, he stared into Francis's dark eyes. They revealed nothing. What of it, the man did not exist for his diagnosis and had only offered him an egg, a kindness unheard of in his own non-coms.

'Easy with that ostrich dropping Sir, I wouldn't even trust a banana from this country.'

'Nor would I,' said Francis, 'the ones from Tanzania are better than ours.'

'Good lad, good lad,' laughed Beasley. Elder joined them in scratchy chuckle, they had obviously bonded over the journey which is more than he had achieved in the same circumstances. He envied Beasley's ability to win people's confidences, perhaps because he cared so little and would just as soon be held in contempt. Elder's stomach tightened, they ought to have arrived by now.

'Not for me thank you.'

Elder would have preferred yoghurt and a piece of fruit, a rare concession to modernity. Pockets of sun were prising apart the murk of early morning. A girl was sat atop a mound of earth that could have been an open grave, her mouth covered in flies. There was something wrong with all this.

'Francis, tell the Captain what your name was, when you were a tearaway dead end kid fighting with Limbani's mob, his first lot before the God Squad.'

Francis lowered his eyes but it was obvious he would not take much encouraging.

'Hannibal Rex.'

'Ha ha, and he had dreadlocks down to his arse as well! Just like those fellas out there.'

Francis frowned but not at Beasley, 'these are President Wondwossen's special guards, they should not have dread-locks...' he said gravely.

In the front seat Walter was snoring and their driver fixated on the truck ahead. Elder wanted to ask where exactly they where.

'The special guard have shaved heads, like mine,' Francis ran his hand over his scalp, 'and the officers wear helmets...'

'They look like a load of hooligans, like our chavs, only with unluckier personal histories.'

'Ingenious people all the same Beasley, could you imagine sending the Devon and Dorsets into combat in flip-flops? This lot make more out of less. Incidentally, I hate to draw you on something so practical, but have you been following our route?'

'Come on,' Beasley continued ignoring the question, 'the dice was thrown centuries ago; what do you want, to apologise for them suffering for their descendents' underdevelopment and our grandparents' greed?'

'The route Beasley, do you know where we are?'

They were interrupted by Francis shouting in Swahili at the driver and it was at that moment that Elder realised that they were being followed not by a Land Rover Discovery, manned by Pagan, but by a Toyota Land Cruiser with a pair of unfriendly looking locals and a bazooka sticking out of the back.

He glanced at Beasley who had noticed the same thing and was putting together his machine pistol, 'think I'll have to finish that rant another time if it's all the same to you Sir.'

Elder nodded, a delicious spasm of fear sprinting up his spine, 'prepare to repel borders Sergeant, we're about to get some of what we came for.'

* * *

The Ongolo River

SAS or nothing. Could a life predicated on something as lousy as a tag line for a film Pagan could not even bear to watch be considered worth it? Why had he chosen the SAS and not a safe job in fashion photography, a fate he was equally qualified for? There was no denying that the ratio of nut jobs to chicks, bad smells to good ones and comfort to loss, fell on the side of the path not taken. Oddly the answer to this question, one Pagan usually avoided asking, was analogous to his relationship with women, which was something else he had begun to think of in the mornings. Unlike other basically moral men, Pagan could commit an act that his conscience, or perhaps something else, would tell him was wrong, and not be troubled one bit by the knowledge. This was better, he said in his defence, than committing an act and not even knowing it was wrong, though to his surprise most people thought his knowing made it worse. Being committed to two contradictory sources of action, marriage and infidelity, preserving life and taking it, never posed a problem, but if these opposing deeds did not undermine his ability to commit them, where exactly was the contradiction? Certainly not in his mind, the only place that would have mattered because that was where one got caught or killed; no, the contradiction appeared to belong only to the event, the brute fact that what happened did. And who cared about facts apart from logicians, soft cocks or divorce lawyers, especially when his ability to perform both sides of the contradiction had never been called into question. In truth the media and his ex wife's obsession with truth and transparency got on his nerves, denoting a weakness that would not keep the country safe at night. If he wanted something badly enough there was no point troubling his soul with the horror of what that thing might mean in itself, past what it meant for him. Killing a random shooter who deserved to die and hugging his daughter, fucking a floozy and then going shopping with his wife, it was all of a piece. It was why he was SAS or nothing, why his life was the tag line of an appalling film and why, awful as his loneliness was, he could at least wake up in the morning proud of the skin that held his flesh together. Being a cliché seemed a small price to pay for such tremendous job satisfaction, he would joke, to men who for the most part did not even recognise the cliché.

'You reckon Captain Elder's jeep's broken down Sir?'

'No way of knowing Kingston, he's not going to break radio silence for a flat.'

'What about a flare Sir, reckon he could still see one in this light?'

'Come on, this kind of work is like a wank, everyone knows we do it but you've got to do it without getting caught.'

'We could try his mobile?'

'Not good to, bad for our image, sometimes works, but I doubt you'd get a signal, especially if he's under trees. You got one now?'

'No, no as matter of fact, not since we left the city.'

Thinking of Elder always got Pagan on to the subject of motivation. Elder thought him inexplicably ruthless, whereas he found that Elder encouraged something tender in him, gentle even, the opposite of wanting to kill. Contrary to what his friend thought, Pagan had no trouble understanding Elder's boyish love for an England that for all he knew may really have existed. The trouble was it increased his friend's chances of getting killed. It made him too eager to volunteer for a risky patrol or hang back and rescue the other fellow from a burning truck. Being first out of a plane short of its drop zone was not how Pagan wanted Elder to be remembered, though increasingly, this was how he had started to act. Pagan liked to think that he was too grounded to have a death wish; he was one of life's survivors, a still point in a turning world... he shuddered at the self-dramatising way he viewed his life whenever he lapsed into silence, it was the kind of crap Elder would leak after a few beers. At least this time it wasn't his fault Elder had got lost, they ought never to have agreed to Hector's suggestion that they accept his drivers, especially as their own one had as good as admitted to never leaving the capital city in his life. It was always the same, the pressure to be nice to people leading to major fuck ups, so here they were, at their starting point, one jeep short of a mission, all because he had not done what he knew was right in the first place. Their mission was already, if he were to be honest with himself, far too full of imponderables without getting caught at the outset like this.

Humorously, as if on cue from central casting, drums began to beat on the other side of the river, whoops and shots fired into the air breaking up their rhythm and lending these old African tropes a modern quality. The thin line of soldiers they were standing with reacted badly, stiffening and fingering their triggers. Lines of reinforcements were heading along the riverbank, pointing their mortars and heavy guns at the bridge as if for an exercise, which the whole event was in a way, thought Pagan. An impression offset slightly by the restless stares of the soldiers suggesting that something more final was in the offing.

'Right, we've an hour or two before the President's men launch their attack, and that's if the Mahdi's lot don't come over first. Either way, that's our diversion for getting across and finding our man, Elder knows where we are, even if he doesn't know where he is, and if he can't reach us this morning at least he knows what and who we're all looking for.'

Pagan looked into the fresh faces grinning at him, Hightower, a flat faced shelf stacker who would have volunteered for chemical warfare tests if it meant having a past worth talking about and Kingston, a cautious boy from Belize, both of them trained in man hunts and as yet untried on SAS operations. Pagan had never spoken to either for long enough to have anything like a handle on what made either of them tick, though of late, he had started to feel that it was not necessary to. These men existed for him only inasmuch as the task they were assigned to required them to have personalities. It was a mechanistic universe they had entered, though Pagan was not at all certain that these two realised it yet. Their trusting postures belied what they had come for, their need to believe that there was someone with them who really did know what he was doing and would get them all home safely, even be their friend. It wasn't impossible, thought Pagan checking his watch, however unappealing the prospect might be. For there was a sickness growing in him that had been there for a while, an indifference to whether he saw home again, his life reaching its dark fulfilment in a grassless foreign field.

'Well not long to go' he sighed to himself, the sunlight breaking across the water like tracer fire. There were things he did not understand as a child but he grasped physical extinction well enough, theological adumbrations to one side. That and that some deaths take forever.

'Cheer up Sir, you look like someone who tries to kill himself every Christmas,' quipped Hightower pulling a large hard-boiled egg out of his knapsack, 'try one of these, set you up for the day.'

Pagan smiled in a way he hoped would not be taken for a grimace, the nihilistic pattern of his own thoughts as exhausting as the effort to stay awake, 'thanks, I think I will.'

CHAPTER FOUR

Where the wild things are

Two hours later

There was no kind way of saying it, so thank God she did not have to, far less tell them. Foy had never come across such fucked out eyes as those stuck in the Websters' skulls. All three sets were lost yet calculating, in for the short term, not long. And what a bitch she was for noticing it especially as they were taking her to a place of greater safety. She had not really expected too much from the brother Nelson, and had not been disappointed. To his credit he appeared to know which direction to take the car in, but had spent most of the time since in an arcane discussion with his father over which East Anglian team was least likely to face relegation from the football league in the upcoming season. Their interest was partly sporting, that is if betting could be regarded as a sport. Guiltily she had tried to avoid eye contact with Nelson in the rear view mirror, which was not hard, as they saw each other several times without the slightest sense of one life acknowledging another. Rather his yellowy eyes had peered, started and occasionally popped, but not reached hers with even an imitation of warmth. His father was kinder, occasionally offering her a knowing wink, though the twinkle in his eye was all surface, masking the same calculating shallowness she detected in the son, again so contrary to their civil and decent deed. Usually she would have risen above it all but as neither had made any effort to talk to her she only had these strained impressions to go on which was too little to judge them on. It was not what she had expected from the horseplay in the café, yet knowing she was too judgmental did not appear to help on this occasion.

This isolation ought to have meant that she was grateful for her conversation with Tawny, sitting in the boot, though she could not honestly say this was so. Like many people subjected to hardship when young, Tawny had an adult face superimposed over whatever her own would look like had she enjoyed Foy's advantages. Her high voice was horribly squeaky, the rolls under her lashes an old woman's and the eyes themselves, which on first impression seemed pretty were anything but. In fact, the generosity that supposed they were was nothing more than the worst kind of hypocrisy. The reason Foy attributed beauty to ugly people was not down to woolly-minded benevolence, no, that would be too kind to her. It was that the reality of what she perceived disgusted her, the fact that a person could be born and live with no superficially appealing characteristics. So whom was she trying to fool? Certainly not the Websters, who were utterly at home with their fucked out eyes and peeling skins, or the bored Deity who must have tossed them off for reasons of contrast. Her deception was necessitated by her self-image. The unwillingness to admit she was an elitist had allowed her to keep up the charade of pretending to be interested in the sensitive and subtler points of people who lacked either. All Tawny had to say about her African adventures were complaints about being overcharged for food, transport and pirated DVD's. Worse, it was pretty clear that Tawny was not particularly fussed about Foy, or any experience she wished to recount from the school, interrupting her half way through sentences and after a while not bothering to ask her any questions at all. Why then, Foy asked herself, should she care about Tawny's sketchy monologues, tiresomely returning to money, diarrhoea and African thievery? Far from antagonising her, this made the Websters decency all the more pure. It was touching that they wished to help Foy because she was human and not a leggy chick with a crop. And that sadly was the problem, for Foy liked her distinguishing characteristics and did not want them to be so little regarded.

The concentrated essence of it was that she *was special,* and could probably count on one hand the occasions others had not regarded her as such, whatever her own doubts or reservations might be.

'I tell yer, the Canaries are never going to amount to jack with Delia. They need a Russian or Arab to come in for Mother Smith.'

'Tractor boys'll be fucked if they stick with Roy, the Irishman needs a kitty or he's as naked as the day he were born. Look at what happened with Sunderland, he jumped ship as soon as the goin' got tough. Hardman my arse, media hype is all.'

'You like football?' Webster called to Foy, in a voice that made her think he already knew the answer to that question.

'I can't pretend to know very much about it.'

'You support anyone though?'

'The England team at International tournaments, the club stuff confuses me.'

'England?' Nelson groaned, 'don't get me started.'

'Like Talk Radio these two' said Tawny, 'except in their case no one's listenin'.'

'Well, it'd be boring if we were all the same,' said Foy without conviction, for she could have used a few more people like her at that moment.

'You believe that Shimba actually has a team, the Mangoes or somethin', that's their nickname that, think they got thrashed by Nigeria in the qualifiers of the African Nations Cup, didn't make it to the finals.'

'What they need is an English manager.'

'What England need is an English manager.'

'No, what England needs is a Shimban manager.'

'You what?'

'Just checkin' if you were listenin' boy!'

It was embarrassing, they had only been in the car for an hour or so, barely a mile from the Ongolo Bridge, and she had started to crack. To put it simply she wanted Africa to disappear, click her heels and find her way home, in the manner of Dorothy Gale of Kansas. Home was a thought Foy could be sustained by, a nice pair of Ugg's, Ski Sunday and Surrey in the pouring rain, without a yam, large hard-boiled egg or Webster in sight...if only and with just herself to blame.

'Nah, forget the International game, the Canaries are the fighters of the two, out of them and the Tractors, you wait 'till Christmas...the table doesn't tell a lie.'

Foy awoke in stages, the first few of which were profoundly misleading. She believed she was with a girl she slept with in her faux lesbian phase, walking through the New Forest, stopping behind trees for passionate kisses. The girl was trying to say something to her, an important utterance..."words are so much less than the experiences they describe, you know?"

"Yes!" cried Foy, "that's what I learnt in Africa, people say so much with a look!"

Baring her teeth the girl bent her head, coming in swiftly for another lick of Foy's tongue...

'Hey girly!'

No such luck, the air in the car was foul, she could taste the smell of Tawny's tracksuit bottoms, the polyester finishings of which were particularly unsuited to the Shimban climate, and her face was stuck fast to the seat. To make matters worse Nelson was breaking wind like a flock of carnival whistles as his father belched sympathetically with this Mexican wave of vulgarity. Foy tried to open the window, succeeding in getting it halfway down and gasped.

'Pull that up and get your head in girly' growled Mr Webster, in a way that was about as friendly as possible given that this was an order and not a request. 'You just keep your head down and lips sealed and let us handle this. You don't want to mess up at checkpoints, that's a golden rule of foreign travel.'

'Sorry.'

It was ridiculous, they were going the wrong way, they absolutely had to be, this time Foy was sure of it. By the looks of things they were driving through the remnants of a battle, surrounded on all sides by excremental piles of military technology and abandoned uniforms. Soldiers and civilians were everywhere, some in the turbans and the cloaks of Islamist militia, waving the Websters through their checkpoints, on to the wrong side of the Ongolo River. Little wonder she gasped, these were the very characters that had it in for Foy and any other Westerner they could kidnap, ransom or kill. And was Nelson really barking a few words of Shimbali at them? It couldn't be but it was, the guards nodding and obeying him just as the hawkers had at the café a few hours earlier. What could be going on?

Peering out of the back Foy watched a boy in a tribal gown and trainers raise his arm and, with the strange pathos of novelty salute, then change his mind and clench his fist, before settling on beating his chest. A collective wail began; part war cry part lament, signalling the start of another battle, of that she was certain, but it would be taking place behind and not in front of them. How naïve of her, the Websters were smart cookies, so far ahead of the game they had lapped her. Everything was in hand, just not hers. God only knew how they could do what they did, but she wasn't going to waste time doubting it, these people were fixers of the highest order. They had got her out of one mess and now they were getting her out of another, in them she would have to trust.

* * *

Golem did not notice the battered Mercedes being waved through the checkpoint, far less the pretty white girl struggling with the rear window. He was angry with Artay, mad enough to scold him like a member of his own family and punch his thorax. It had been a long time since Golem suffered a fool at this close proximity, one so arrogantly self-righteous as to wear his ignorance like aftershave. The revolution had produced a generation of sexually frustrated pests, necessarily male, ready to reduce every personal disagreement to a politico-religious argument. Dare he point out the obvious, that at the dawn of a new century these wiry bearded virgins would have to marry the first girl they wanted to kiss, thereby enjoying even less freedom than a Mesopotamian goatherd who was at least free to go whoring, if he knew where to look. Golem saw it all, for his background had been anything but typical of a student of the revolution. He had read Freud, Lacan and Bataille too, Allah had not been his first port of call, religion had come later, once the Ayatollahs had subsumed the revolution and given it a properly Iranian flavour. Instinctively he had joined them, a desire for authenticity trumping his personal predilections that seemed superficial to him at the time. Moreover he really did see God's hand behind everything, even his flirtation with dangerous European thinkers could be regarded as a test. The irony was that he had not escaped decadence, as Artay was only to keen to remind him, because it never left him, one's first loves rarely do, he reluctantly concluded. Should he be more ashamed of himself than he was? It was hard to know as neither part, the religious nor the secular, felt truer than its warring twin.

Since the rise of Ahmadinejad, Golem had, for the sake of his family if not out of conviction, tried to avoid taking a political position, which was not hard as there were so few to choose from. Such politics as he had were embodied in his off duty dress, sense of humour and other unconventional passions, be they William Faulkner or Fleetwood Mac. This retreat into the personal was the very thing official propaganda castigated the "ironic West" for, but for Golem it was driven by more than just taste. By learning to find politics boring, he survived the various in-house fluctuations that signified nothing of consequence to anyone not directly affected by them, treating his security tasks as purely functional. Espionage had always been something of a game, arresting dissidents no more than his duty, and denouncing opposition to the regime a reflex chore. He did all he could to interpret religion neutrally, regarding it as a public good divorced from political bias, and those less savoury tasks his job entailed as necessary police work. Golem reasoned they would have to be performed under any responsible regime, and this helped him find a kind of peace. Alcohol helped toward this end too, though he contrived to overlook by just how much.

Yet something was amiss. The ideology he strove to ignore was buried so deep into the conditions of his life that he could no longer feel its hand up his arse. Hypocrisy permeated his veins; his path to God had made him a liar and to make matters worse he had not even got away with it. Artay took his many evasions as a political position, and chided him for precisely what he had gone out of his way to hide. As Golem held Artay's intelligence in no great esteem, the fault must lie in him, that his idea of subtlety was anything but and that he was not as clever as he thought. The best he could say for himself was that he acted as he did because he thought it would do good, even though he no longer believed in its truth.

'In your position I would have insisted on an audience with their Mahdi before taking a ring side seat in this circus. Jafari may have thought your wayward methods would mix easily with these clowns, but these Shimbans need challenging, not humouring. You saw how their women were, not even in Holland would you see such brazenness, this movement is already in process of degeneration, I don't need to see more to know that. And you grin away like their ringmaster. You should say something, remind them of what they purport to be; I would myself but I don't want to be seen to undermine your authority. We are not here as spectators, our orders were to influence events if we could...'

'And can we? What do you see, a troop of school children

eager for their first lesson of the day Artay? These people could kill us any time they like, we're not at home now, no one is going to call out the Revolutionary Guard to rescue us, out here we walk a thin line between being esteemed elder brothers or meddlesome outsiders, say the wrong thing and you cross it. At the moment they don't know what to make of us, that's to our advantage. You've never left Iran before, shut up, listen and watch.'

'I've been to Yemen...'

'Shut up and look.'

Golem pointed at a mixture of child soldiers, covered in garish war paint, and solemn looking teenagers wearing scraps of white cloth tied round their arm, the religious commissars sent to watch their younger siblings, 'do you see anyone there ready to discuss doctrine with you? They're all, if they have any brains, in fear for their lives, people are going to start killing each other in a minute.'

'That's my point! They should know what they're dying for and be ready to meet Allah in a way befitting soldiers of Islam.'

'As they say in England there is a time and place...'

'You pay too much attention to what they say elsewhere, your years in the West have played havoc with you.'

'I'm getting tired of having to remind you of the basics, of who is in charge here. We haven't been charged with the simplest of missions, a lot will depend on our judgment, what we see on the ground. How we choose to see things in other words. At the moment you're only as much use as half a person, full of your own prejudices, I'm relying on you for clarity, instead you're making a tricky job harder.'

A mortar shell landed on the marshy riverbank like a wet self satisfied fart, causing Artay to spin round hastily, 'what was that!'

'What do you think?'

'They said they'd tell us when they were going to start the

battle.'

'Pity no one told the other side that all-important nugget of information. Our Shimbans won't like that.'

Sure enough, their hosts, who had been oblivious to their altercation, were dismounting from their truck and walking briskly over to them.

'Would you like to go further up? The infidels have started early today!' shouted war Boss, his patch having switched to his right eye.

'Yes' called Golem, to the obvious and intended discomfort of his trembling assistant, 'let us proceed!'

* * *

The soldiers on both sides of the river looked to be in a shared state of unreadiness, surprised to have got down to the business that brought them there so quickly. And now that it had started, many looked like they were not entirely certain what was required of them, staring quizzically at their foe as though waiting for answers.

'If they don't get stuck in we'll never get across the water Sir.'

'Yeah, it's not exactly "A Bridge Too Far", I'll give you that.'

'A Luton-Wimbledon scoreless draw.'

Pagan had not seen it unravelling like this but should have, after losing Elder and their arriving late, there really was no excuse. Where Elder was, he could not guess, what state he might be in was also a mystery. What was clear was that they could not stay in this embarkation point for long.

'Mind your head, they're getting closer.'

Although people were shooting at one another not many of them were being killed. Very few even looked like they were taking aim, waving their rifles over their heads like periscopes and firing off rounds at make-believe angles. It reminded him of children using sticks and playing war in the park. Yet thousands of people had died in this conflict and here and there, mostly as a result of mortar or artillery fire, bodies were being knocked down and not getting back up.

'Relax; we're in the right place. They like to start their hostilities late here, gives them time to warm up.'

Hightower, who was pressed up against the makeshift parapet they were all taking cover behind guffawed loudly, 'that's a good one sir, warming up!'

Pagan felt sorry for him, there was something in the timbre of his laughter that revealed the precise limits of his intelligence. Nearly everything about him was young soldiery pretending to be old, the affectations of one too simple to see the dangers of acceptance in an institution that would regard him as less than unique. Better to be atomised and lonely, if such a state revealed anything worth discovering, which in Hightower's case it might not. Maybe the army knew the true worth of its raw material, that for every Einstein there were fifty longbow men who never did anything worth recounting, except die for their country at a time most advantageous for it.

'Hightower, you'll want to get your head down, if you want to keep it that is.'

Hightower appeared transfixed by the black current of the river, the foul smell of it almost physical in its intensity, 'you what Sir?'

A stray bullet, in this skirmish all bullets took on that hue, smacked against the parapet sending splinters in every direction. Kingston, who had wisely kept his head between his legs coughed as Hightower, red faced with embarrassment, pulled a fat wood chip out of the end of his nose, blood oozing out as jam from a doughnut.

'Oh Jesus, not me nose.'

'Take the hint, get down!'

'Could have been my head I suppose!'

If it had been, how would Pagan have summed up his life,

since if the army knew these boys were not individuals, The News at Ten and their parents did not. Once a man was dead, no matter how insignificant, humourless, thick or just plain unlucky he had been in life, he was transformed into a big-hearted hero who was the life and soul of the regiment. That had to be one of the advantages of being killed, to be acknowledged at last in all your singular separateness. At least the SAS did not go in for such platitudes because when it came down to it, telling the truth, which in this case meant that Pagan regarded Hightower and Kingston as alright if he regarded them at all, was not the glowing tribute their deaths required.

'The thing about starting an attack is that once the firing's over, you've got to start moving bodies along. This lot aren't budging.'

'Should we do something to get things going Sir?'

'Absolutely not, they're meant to be our diversion. Last thing we want to do is become the centrepiece exhibit.'

Sure enough, most of the government soldiers, with the exception of one or two officers who were standing bolt upright screaming at their men, were flat on their stomachs or shooting from kneeling positions safely ensconced in cover. No one looked in a hurry to go anywhere. Things were not much better on the Mahdi's side of the river where a couple of turbaned youths had been gunned down at the river's edge, discouraging their track suited brethren from making any further attempts to cross. Only an isolated figure in black combat fatigues was visible, exhorting the others to attack.

'What's that?' Hightower pointed to a moving commotion coming towards them over the bridge, 'looks like one of our Land Rovers, isn't it?'

It was. The Land Rover was swaying across the narrow bridge like a drunk on the run from the law, Elder behind the wheel, the blood splattered head of his driver flopped across his lap. Behind him two other jeeps were in fierce pursuit and behind them a column of screaming militia, the Land Rover's sudden appearance acting as a catalyst the battle needed to realise itself.

'How the hell did he get to that side of the river?' cried Pagan.

'If he lost his way they might have crossed up river without realising it, apparently it's little more than a stream the further up you go,' said Kingston. 'Well he knows which side to come to now.'

'Shouldn't he have stayed over there, that's the way we're meant to be going, right Sir?'

'I wouldn't bet that's at the forefront of his mind at the moment.'

'I thought this kind of thing didn't happen to the SAS' said Kingston with mournful sarcasm, 'our recruiting officers said you were "dark phantoms."

'No, it happens to everyone, we're just the best improvisers, looks like we're going to be our own decoy today. Covering Fire,' ordered Pagan, another domino effect of errors well under way.

* * *

It had been a bloody awful morning, one as bloody and as awful as any the SAS had subjected Elder to. Much as he tried to be someone on whom nothing was lost, it was a struggle to keep up with the sheer number of things that had gone wrong. The first shot from the rotating canon on the jeep they were pursued by had finished off their driver, which given his sense of direction was no bad thing. The second shot showed that the first was no fluke, or that they were exceptionally unlucky, blowing Corporal Walter's head in a south-westerly direction, so that it landed between the armrest and brake. Despite the inconvenience of having it there, Elder was loath to move it.

'Oops a daisy' muttered Beasley who, having smashed the back window was returning fire, 'could be in hot water now.'

'Hot water keeps you clean,' replied Francis to Beasley's

enormous delight, 'turn the car right round Captain, right here, we can turn round and go back the way we came, it'll surprise them. They expect us to run.'

'We never run from anyone Francis,' Elder stammered as he regained the wheel from the rest of Walter's corpse, pushing it unceremoniously through the door, 'it's not our way.' Truly he was grateful for the suggestion, as neither manipulating four-wheel drives nor thinking under fire was his forte. Pressure always separated the part of him that thought from the one that acted, and since reversing his father's Range Rover over a prize cockerel he had avoided heavy vehicles. Fortunately today he was deprived of any choice in the matter. Focusing purely on the road, he wheeled the metallic beast round, changing its direction like a sail catching the wind, and accelerated.

'Text book, text book,' roared Beasley, 'hell for leather, more like it!'

Francis was right; the ruse had worked, at least for the moment. Their pursuers, for all their persistence, suffered from delayed reactions and were all over the road in an attempt to cut off their prey. Veering onto what he hoped was a dirt track, but turned out to be a fork in the road, Elder shouted to the other two, 'it's imperative we catch up with the others. '

'They're not ahead of us Captain Elder? We're going backwards.'

'What, you think we should turn round again Francis? Please, I'm being serious.'

'No, this is right, we came too far to start with. It's why we're in Mahdi country. I can't think Captain Pagan will have made the same mistake.'

'But Captain Elder can, thanks very much Francis.'

'I didn't mean that Sir.'

'I still don't know how we did, it's never happened to me before.'

Beasley bared his teeth and said nothing.

'It's not our fault the driver your leader supplied us with didn't know where he was going.'

'He was not our usual man Captain, he…'

'Shit!' cried Elder glancing into the rear view mirror, 'this lot have watched Mad Max, look! They're on to us again.'

Far away, but not far enough, were the two Land Cruisers, firing wildly in their general direction and quickly gaining ground.

'How did they get on our case like that?'

'Probably by breaking the speed limit. Step on it Sir! These aren't called "off road" vehicles for nothing, get off the road!'

'Where?'

'Anywhere! They can cut bloody corners but so can we, into the bush!'

And so began a feverish half hour of relentless pursuit, a wacky race played for existential stakes, Beasley ranting and shooting, Elder driving and sweating and Francis directing them calmly on.

'What are those?'

'Slow down Captain, those are Militia vehicles the other side of those huts.'

'And a river, it's the Ongolo, must be, we've made it thank God!'

Beasley knowing better thrust another magazine into his pistol and pushed Francis's head down; 'if we've got the right river Sir then trust me, we're on the wrong side, it's just the nature of the beast, the way these things work…'

* * *

'If you move any further forward you'll end up getting your feet wet' shouted Artay from behind the rear wheel of the truck he was hiding under.

Golem could see his point, and since Artay was only

following the example of their Shimban hosts, he could not hold
him up for special criticism. The vehicle Artay had chosen was
shared with a wide spread of Shimban soldiery ranging from
General War Boss to various members of the African Taliban.
Admittedly none of them looked as frightened as Artay, but nor
did any of them seem ready to make the supreme sacrifice for
Allah. Golem remembered battles where staying still meant
death and others where movement guaranteed an on the spot
funeral, yet this skirmish fitted neither model. There was
something inconsequential about it, that its very existence was
unnecessary so that to die would not be anything the living
would thank you for. He pitied the turbaned youths lying dead
on the edge of the river; their misreading of the occasion as well
as their poor timing had let them down. Even the Government
soldiers, who were taking advantage of superior firepower so as
not to attack, had erred on the side of caution. But what were they
all afraid of? Mortar rounds and shells were landing in random
sequences that posed so little danger that Golem would have
considered it an accident if one actually hit him. This disregard
for the advantages of remaining alive, or natural curiosity as he
saw it, was winning him the admiration of his African hosts who
were whooping and clapping as Golem motioned them to join
him by the bank. Perhaps they would be less appreciative if they
knew he was well on his way to uncovering a suicidal streak that
habit and love for his family had thus far suppressed.

'Come on brothers' he shouted a little lamely, 'Allah favours
the brave,' and then with more conviction, 'who wants to live
forever?' It was a favourite line of his from the first Gulf War, its
roots attributable to a fat Englishman who dressed up as a Space
Hawk, and it usually worked.

The Mahdi's high command, having followed the example of
their followers in remaining static, grinned to one another, and
rose to their feet. As they ducked and weaved towards him they
collected child soldiers cowering behind rocks, picking some up

by their ears, and dragging others along by their arms. It was not the sort of heroic charge that would go down in the history of warfare, Golem decided, but at least he was leading it, and after years spent in safety, that was enough.

'Don't bunch up, spread out...' to be in command again made him light-headed, proof that all these colours and shapes really were life, 'save your fire for a target.'

At first he thought the Land Rover speeding across the bridge was part of his attack, the driving was certainly fast enough to be a Shimban. Addressing those gathered round the bridgehead he yelled, 'coordinate, hurry, follow the jeep!'

Despite a more concentrated line of fire greeting the attackers, the young men did as they were told, their sudden movement encouraging others so that in a matter of seconds, the bridge was full of screaming youths.

But the truck did not slow down; it sped up. And on the other side of the river, to his bemusement, there was another Land Rover pulling out from under some trees and moving towards it. Could a Land Rover duel be part of the Shimban art of war, their equivalent of two jousting Knights in a medieval tournament?

No one else had seemed to notice, and as the Government soldiers were now pouring across the water, it was reasonable to suppose there were more pressing concerns on their minds. However, the intelligence officer in Golem was on overdrive, and as his eyes followed the trajectory of the first Land Rover something strange happened. Instead of running down the first government soldiers rushing towards it, or slowing down for its own men to catch up, it spun round so it was blocking the bridge and turned over, deliberately he thought, on its side. At the same time the second Land Rover had driven in to the shallow part of the river, beyond the bridge, and stopped. Out of the first Land Rover came two white men in khaki, and a black man in a Mandela bush shirt who threw himself off the low-lying beam into the river. The taller of the two whites pulled a grenade out of his backpack and dropped it into the window of the upturned jeep, before virtually pushing his companion off and joining the black man in the water.

Just as the Land Rover blew apart two Land Cruisers charged on to the platform, scything down Militia and, unable to control their speed, drove straight into its burning shell. The rising flames reminded Golem of an ammunition dump hit in an air raid, blazing oil and hot metal scattering over the combatants who, perversely, appeared excited by the entropic mess that fell about them. Indeed, there was an element of carnival in the air, as the two sides hopped about, avoiding fiery splinters, in a parody of a war dance.

Golem was probably alone in watching the second Land Rover double as a lifeguard, waiting a little way down river and picking up the three floating survivors. He felt a hand on his shoulder, it was General Amnesty, 'a great victory my friend, look at the dogs run!' There was irony in his voice but conviction in his eyes, 'thank you for getting that started.'

As doubtful as the first sentence was there was no denying the second, the government soldiers had returned to their trucks and were in the process of vacating the scene as hurriedly as they could.

'Many battles end like this in Shimba,' sighed Amnesty realistically, 'it is often enough to show you are ready to fight for the enemy to be ready to run.'

Golem could feel the white glare of the sun darken his neck, and as he stood listening wondered briefly what white sunbathers thought of after they'd finished their cocktails and trashy airport novels.

'The important thing is not how you win, but winning. You agree?'

Golem nodded, another less reassuring thought beginning to take shape, that the British were here and it was not like them to come without a reason. He looked down into the water. The plot was not going to get any thinner and he did not want it to, the elements were coalescing just as they should. He trusted his God, who knew what he did not.

'I think it is time,' he said to Amnesty, 'to meet the Mahdi.'

CHAPTER FIVE

The Long and Winding Road

'It was odd. I noticed you didn't bribe anyone. What did you say to get us through?' asked Foy. Offering the wrong amount of money at the wrong time to the wrong person was a mistake Foy often fell into. Though she was not particularly interested in becoming a huckster she wanted to contribute something to the journey, and as the car was silent, the question did not feel completely spurious.

'You like your questions don't you?'

'I'm interested, anything other people are good at that I can't do myself is interesting, whether that's getting through roadblocks or playing drums in a punk band...' Foy checked her tone; through the natural desire to defend herself she was falling into being a smart arse. Haunted by the fear that she was little more than a pretty face, humoured for her shallow wish to do good, the chance to be bit objectionable was akin to character building. To get past her looks and their complementary mannerisms meant she had to be ready to take a stand, even if that meant treading on the occasional toe.

'Did you learn to speak Shimban on a course or have you picked it up as you go along? I'm absolutely rubbish with languages.'

'And?'

It was ridiculous, it wasn't as though she was really being offensive, 'I'm surprised you're so good at them as you told me earlier that you've never read a book and left school at sixteen. Not that there's anything wrong with that.'

'I need to stop for a piss' said Nelson ignoring her entirely. They had driven into green foliage and were now surrounded by creepers in near-jungle, 'at least you can find a tree to go behind,' offered Foy, and to her relief Tawny smiled.

'Think we should all get out, stretch our legs a bit,' yawned Mr Webster, 'you go mad if your feet don't touch the ground once in a while. That and cramp.'

'Do you really think it's safe to stop yet?'

'Sure, sure, you came here on holiday didn't you?'

'Not exactly.'

'My point my girl, take in some sights, enjoy the country a bit, look at all that, lovely eh? That's your proper Africa, not your disgusting cities.'

Foy's experience of Shimba had been largely restricted to towns and the dusty lowlands of the South. Here she could hear the agitated grunts of a baboon pack and the barking of what may have been a bird. This was more like the country she had anticipated. The trees were tall, high-trunked and looked very old. It would be nice to wander round and explore, she mused, picking up a branch and brandishing it like a riding crop. That part of her life, however, was coming to an end. None go so far as those who don't know where they are going, and she had gone far enough. Without the Websters' intervention she might already have been dead, which was too high a price for modest self-discovery and a chance to leave the Home Counties. Perhaps she had already learnt the lesson she sought, though she had to acknowledge it was a disappointing one. What mattered now was a passage home, and anything else, glimpses of jungle wildlife included, was a free gift she could live without.

'No sense in saying anything about it now...'

'She'll twig herself sooner or later. Best tell her before then.'

'What's the use in worrying her? Life as it is, life as it ought to be. There'll be time later.'

'If you don't want to tell her then I will.'

In spite of the large choice of trees, Nelson was urinating over the road and exchanging angry words with his sister. Both of them caught Foy wandering over, and their debate grew fiercer. It was hard to avoid the suspicion that their conversation alluded to her, that she was slowing them down or insufficiently streetwise. It was frustrating that her skills had no way of making themselves apparent in the middle of a jungle. The very idea of being able to speak French, not Shimbali, the polygot of Swahili Nelson seemed to have picked up, made her go red. Even her map reading would be inferior to theirs and as there was no call for a cook it was best to shut up and make herself small.

Kicking out at a pebble, Foy noticed that Mr Webster was staring at her and stroking his chin, making no effort to avert or disguise his gaze. Dispelling the ridiculous fear that he intended to rape her, she grinned imbecilically and, taking care to not sound nervous, asked him the time.

'What's it to you girly, we're making the decisions for you now.'

'I'm sorry?'

'It's only those in charge that need to know what time it is.'

'What do you mean by that?'

'Why nothing, only we're looking after all the boring stuff. Being responsible for you in a way.'

'That I appreciate, though I'm not a complete idiot you know. I did at least manage to get to Shimba on my own.'

'No one ever said you were girly...' at this Foy heard a laugh behind her. To her disconcertment Nelson was practically at her shoulder, shaking childishly. Just as oddly his sister, who had not appeared to share his sense of humour thus far, was also trying to stifle a giggle.

'I'm sorry, I don't get the joke, if there is one.'

'Well girly, the way I see it is that I keep telling small lies to keep in practice for the really big ones. To keep on my toes like.'

'I'm afraid I've no idea what you're talking about,' Foy's voice was tight, it was best to play dumber than she was, at least they might take pity on her.

'For a clever girl like you you're sure slow on the uptake.'

'I'm sorry. Have I said or done something to offend you?'

'Here's a good example; I said I worked on Golf Courses, not that you called it, well, that for one was a lie. That make it any clearer girly?'

'I *knew* that' announced Foy boldly, 'I know you and your son have spent some time in prison too, that's what all those tattoos mean isn't it? They give them to you in jail.'

'My son?' Mr Webster's jaw wobbled with spontaneous mirth, 'that bloody hooligan my son? Give over, my nephew; son, no thank you girly, not that ugly, oh no! Nephew is what he be, nephew and great ape! Love him though I do.'

The other two now joined him in open and scornful laughter. Foy felt her knees grow heavy and calves tremble. Nothing would have given her greater pleasure than witnessing a stereotype proved wrong but this was hopeless. She was entirely at the mercy of these hooligans and had been from the moment they first approached her. Her desperation and naivety had, taken together, proven lethal. On the bright side her Shimban adventure was far from over, and this intimation, and the humour it contained, stopped her from grovelling. She still had something about her, more in truth than she thought.

'We don't even know if *you're* really mine do we Tawny, because you look a little like that Wrestler what lived up the road, what was his name, Giant Pasty?'

'Give over Dad, she thinks we're chavs enough as it is.'

'Good that she's learning a lesson, that we're no simpletons.'

'Don't play with me. What do you want?'

'I don't want you trying to run away Miss Foy, because sooner or later you were goin' to notice we weren't takin' you anywhere near the sea,' the voice was nasty now, an instrument to cajole and control, its earlier warmth utterly illusionary.

'So we're not going to the sea then?'

'Very good, she's fast on the uptake, I like that.'

Foy glanced at the jungle track, Websters' eyes following hers as she did so. Nearby was a battered old sign and an overgrown road, a relic from an earlier empire and time.

'You'd better forget about that right now. Forget it I say. You may not like us but I swear you'll not like what's in there any better.'

Webster pulled off his floppy hat and wiped the sweat of his bald pate, 'that's why I was lookin' at your pretty long legs, good and strong for running with and we don't want any of that. You're to stay with us and not make a fuss. No harm will come. But you got to be good see, good.'

Foy experienced a spasm of hope flutter in her tummy. If they wanted her alive then they were not going to kill her, not yet. That meant there would be time to think. So long as she did not antagonise them unnecessarily, which might be hard if they kept laughing at her.

'I'm not going to run away but stop laughing, you've no right to. I'd rather be a mug like me than a liar like all of you.'

'Wohoo! Hear the little scrubber, got her goat we have' said Nelson, 'we may not be clever like you but we is smart, smart where it counts…'

Foy could tell he was the kind of thug who moved freely between fun and violence and then back again, so she replied softly, 'I don't doubt you're smart, I don't doubt that at all, just don't hurt me and don't make fun of me and I'll not run away, I promise.'

Tawny snorted, 'I say we just tie the hoity toity tart up, stuff a rag in her mouth and pound the living shit out of her till she leaks. Look at her, soft as cunt she is, soft as cunt…'

Mr Webster licked his lips, 'calm down for God's sake, you'll make us sound like a bunch of bloody savages. No, she'll be easier if we hold her to her promise; cooperation Tawny is the wheel that turns the trolley.'

Tawny scowled, a wart on her brow popping up like a

molehill, 'just so she knows what will happen to her if she don't.'

'Oh, she knows alright.'

Foy caught sight of her toe, the varnish peeling off, remembering that when she last noticed it life seemed a lot kinder. The other toe was still red, a good omen, it had to be.

'Just so she knows what happens if she don't keep that promise' Nelson repeated, and picking the stick Foy had dropped, broke it over his knee.

'And what happens if I do keep it, what will you do to me then, what do you want me for?'

The Websters looked at each other, not laughing anymore.

'We all get rich, even you my already rich one, even you.'

* * *

2 hours later

Elder knew that there was a kind of cheerfulness he adopted when everything went wrong that irritated people, so forcing a frown, he shook his head and said, 'shit. We ought to have made a better job of that.'

'All done with now Sir,' replied Beasley who enjoyed a good disaster, 'what's fucked is fucked. Best thing now is to let Francis here lead us to the Mahdi; he knows his way around. It was he who found the bridge, face facts.'

'Thank you Beasley, if I weren't a confident man you'd erode my instinct for command,' countered Elder. Beasley had the unfortunate knack of being on the right side of most operational decisions, and bringing attention to this before his superiors. He was certainly correct in his estimation of Francis, which left Elder with one last suggestion of his own, 'we should stick with our motor transports until we hit the jungle, that's where Francis says we'll find our man and any fool can do things the hard way. What do you think Sean?'

'Or swap our wheels altogether, they'll know what to look for now,' said Pagan collecting ammunition belts from the dead men they had just slaughtered. 'Look at this, an old American open top, they're either in these or if they're high-ups in Toyotas. We stick out like Christmas trees in the Land Rover, better to go native, eh Francis?'

'Yes Sir, then they won't know who we are until it's too late, like these poor fellows,' said Francis smiling, perhaps pleased to make new friends. Pagan felt good about that, and though he didn't subscribe to the school of killing for pleasure, he could admit that it was sometimes satisfying. After the mess of the past few hours, to run across two jeeps' worth of militia was a good way of re-establishing their bearings and purpose. Besides, it had been an unpleasant squash in one Land Rover.

'They didn't have time to put up much of a fight.'

'That is because they are not fighters,' said Francis, pointing to the blue overalls the dead men were wearing, 'they double as guards at the Shimbite mine, they are not warriors.'

Francis interested Pagan, which made it all the more important to put on a bit of a show, if only to demonstrate what double crossing them might achieve. For as long as they were carried by an external momentum, any desire to double cross them remained introspective, or with luck, retrospective, though once they met the Mahdi Francis might again wonder which side his bread was buttered. These corpses provided him with a pre-emptive answer.

'A good idea to look less conspicuous Kingston, get that officer's jacket, and throw some silk over your head. Go for the local look.'

'What about the rest of their stuff?' Kingston, though black and small, looked nothing like an African Militiaman, his T-shirt tucked neatly into his combat trousers, which still bore fastidious creases down their middle, 'man it stinks.'

'Use judgement and training for God's sake, what would you want if you were going on a jungle trek? And Francis, don't stand

72

there watching us, pick out a gun, you're going to be more use to us with one. Try this.' Pagan held out the assault rifle and slammed a magazine into its breach. 'Hightower, give Kingston a hand with those, it looks like he's scared he'll catch something.'

Clumsily Hightower pulled off the arm of a man Beasley had hit in the armpit with the Magnum he carried for such occasions. Recoiling, he made a gagging reflex, fought it and turned to face the others for a clean gasp of air. With his ruddy face straining for composure, he could have been a holidaymaker regretting that he chose a full English over the Continental option, Pagan's confidence in him slipping even further down a sliding scale.

Judging by his low groaning Beasley agreed, 'Leave that one, a few worms short of a proper corpse. Honestly you blokes, Kingston, you don't need to be so bloody respectful with that dead numpty's water bottle, it was life, no more than life and then it went. Remember? You bloody killed him.'

'It's bad luck taking a dead man's things.'

Beasley winked at Francis, 'take a leaf out of this lad's book Kingston, cool as air conditioning aren't you Francis, Africans are surrounded by it all the time...'

'By what?' asked Kingston.

'By death,' said Francis, imitating Beasley's intonation with faultless precision, 'death Mr Kingston, a massive thing of which there is very little to say.'

'Oh I like this boy, I like him very much, he's got talent, could go a long way with a bit of promoting!' Beasley clicked his tongue, 'here Francis, get out of those holiday togs and put some real soldier's clothes on, you look like a Honolulu night club owner in that get up, stand out worse than we do.'

Almost shyly Francis accepted the pea green jacket, buttoning it up over his decorative bush shirt. The figure he cut was still more tour guide than soldier, though the calmness of his movements did more to reassure than the rifle dangling over his shoulder, its barrel pointing the wrong way.

'You didn't do much actual fighting for the Mahdi, did you Francis?' Pagan more or less asserted.

'That's true Sir. I did some.'

'I'm surprised they didn't force you to be a bit more hands on.'

'They have respect for book men; I could read, The Bible, The Koran, Jeffery Archer, though the twists in his tales are all exactly the same.'

Pagan saw that Elder was grinning too and wondered whether they were all being played, 'what was your exact role then, apart from being the Mahdi's first follower and boyhood chum?'

'It's hard to explain, I don't know whether the English have them, or how you would say it in English.'

'Weren't you a sort of spiritual advisor, like one of our army chaplains?' offered Elder, 'that was my impression from what Hector told us. John the Baptist to his Jesus.'

'No Captain Elder, you are way too kind. More of a teacher, showing the younger ones how to read and write. And sometimes leading religious discussions, sharing what I knew.'

'Really? I had imagined something more dramatic than that.'

'It was a very practical role Mr Elder. I was like an elder brother, you understand, to many of our soldiers who were no more than girls and boys. Not like these others who have joined the Mahdi now, the Talibans from the religious schools who are, how would you put it, like your hardcore bible bashers, but worse. They preach suicide.'

'You're not ready to take one for the team for Allah eh?' asked Beasley, the question not rhetorical for once, 'thought that was the big difference between you lot and the Church of England. That you people took the great almighty a little more seriously than us.'

'That man should sacrifice his life for God was a belief I held right up to the time I began to really believe in him,' Francis snapped, quickly adding, 'the Islamic militias have made the Mahdi an imperialist in his own country, if not now then certainly in the time to come. I have no wish to be a subject of the Caliphate. I am a Shimban.'

'I can't imagine that's the kind of view that would have made you very popular with your old master Francis,' said Elder, regretting his use of the word master, 'after all, his followers believe he's the descendent of the Prophet, don't they?'

'The Mahdi is only the proper name for the collective activity of a section of the Shimban people, nothing more, I knew him when he was only Julius, a boy who played kiss chase with the girls like any other boy. The voices, the visions, they have been happening in our villages for centuries. Julius decided to put them to…a different use. To project a reality over a deeper, a more profound truth.'

He's not the only one guilty of that, you ever been to Soho House?'

'I'm sorry?'

'Don't worry, I'm just joking with you,' said Elder, 'just wanted to make the point that the Mahdi isn't the only one living in a bubble.'

'His reality is that he is the Mahdi, the deeper truth is that he is not.'

'Yet you believed once?' pressed Elder, 'enough to follow him into the jungle and help begin this crazy war.'

'I thought I did, yes.'

'And what do you believe now?'

'I am a holist Sir; I believe we are all God and that the human race is the moral improvement of God on a local level. I am against the big man theory that Julius Limbani and the ignorant ones who follow him espouse. Religion likes to do away with the real mystery of God.'

'Very interesting,' said Elder, meaning it.

'Bloody hell Francis, looks like you're all set to start a cult of your own!' laughed Beasley incredulously, 'you've got to hand it to the missionary schools, they did their work alright, some of you boys talk like you've been gargling dictionaries since you were three.'

Francis bowed his head sheepishly, his passion having caught him as well as his listeners off guard. Sensing that he would have continued, had his enthusiasm not been pointed out to him, Elder repeated, 'very interesting. You're a surprise I wasn't expecting Francis.'

'As he said, the Mahdi tolerated him because he was a reader' Pagan announced in a way he hoped would bring the discussion to some kind of conclusion. The mid afternoon flies were now as interested in the living as the dead and he could feel their purpose escaping them, 'but if you ask me, which I doubt any of you would, it all sounds like a nice set of ideas delivered to the wrong universe. If we've got everything, let's move out of here.'

Piling onto the two jeeps, Hightower driving one and the wiry Kingston taking the other, the men resumed their journey, their visions of God smaller than the Divinity they hoped watched over them all. The exception was Pagan, thoughts of God like those of marriage and sleep containing a finality he refused to be bound by, the space these ideas were stored in remaining firmly shut.

* * *

Foy was finding that the fear of not knowing what will happen next had created a certain consistency she could live with. And to her immense satisfaction, she was actually better at trekking, or plain walking with a heavy load, than the Websters. They still appeared to know where they were going, whereas she did not, but they were getting there very slowly. Her long agile limbs were virtually dancing over the fallen branches and anthills, as Mr Webster wheezed behind her, his daughter cursing and nephew tumbling headlong at her heels, 'slow down missy, what did we tell you about running away!'

Lifted by the knowledge that she was only giving thirty percent to what was a thirty percent job, Foy replied innocently, 'I can help you carry some of that if you want.'

Since leaving the car all three Websters had produced ugly looking firearms that appeared to have undergone some customisation. Unfortunately for them, none had discovered the easiest way of carrying them with the rest of their loads, and there was much arm changing and stopping to rearrange the balance of their packs.

'I don't need your bloody help,' Nelson spluttered.

Remembering that it was crucial for a hostage to retain her humanity in front of her captors, Foy persisted, 'look, I don't know what to think anymore, but if I can't offer help to someone then I know I'm lost in more ways than one...'

'Oh fuck off with that. That's all we need, you preaching to us.'

Foy held the red inside her cheeks, no one had ever told her to fuck off in anger before, not even her younger sister or best friend. Swearing was always something to joke with, never a formal utterance. Still, at least she had riled this evil looking Caliban, 'I was only trying to help.'

'Arse, you only help people you pity. We scare you, if you help us it's because you want us to end up carrying your bags. Re-establish your natural order, forget it.'

Nelson's natural pride and wish not to be seen as what he was, an utterly wicked person, surprised Foy who thought a criminal would be comfortable acknowledging himself as such, 'it's got nothing to do with wanting to put you down...'

'Help someone who needs it, and stop looking at me like that. Go on, trot on.'

'I thought you didn't want me to run away.'

Nelson strained to say something, but gave up, the weight of the pack and jungle humidity were too much, yesterday's booze running down his back and forearms.

His discomfort inspired Foy so with a look of mock concern, and wings under her buttocks, she bounded ahead, the others actually seeming to follow her three or four paces behind, panting as they went.

She was not sure how much time had passed when she heard Webster yell up at her, 'not that way girl, we've gone up as far as we need, want you to go down now.' He was pointing at a jutting plateau that dropped into a long open meadow, the grassy lush basin and wooded hilltops reminding her more of an iron age fort in Wiltshire than of wherever in Africa she actually was.

'And slow down a little, it isn't a race.'

'No? Then what is it?'

'You've got to stop talking to her Pa,' called Tawny 'we don't want to be makin' friends with her, not fair on her or us. She'll get the wrong idea.'

There's no danger of that, thought Foy, Tawny and Nelson playing a fast game of musical chairs for the title of least favourite Webster.

'Come now,' said Webster in a way that reminded Foy that this deranged Silverback was the evil genius behind the two front of house bullies, 'we might be the last real friends she has out here. So where's the danger in a little bit of honest to goodness cordiality eh, where's the danger in that?'

* * *

The way Artay had made friends with the contingent of African Taliban made Golem nervous. He preferred it when his companion was whining or showing that he was out of his depth. This new alliance had made the Shimban Generals uneasy too, demonstrating cracks in their fragile coalition of the unwilling. For the past hour Artay had happily lectured a truckload of apparently willing listeners on the differences between Shia and Shimban Islam, exalting one at the expense of the other without a murmur of protest from his audience. The fact that most of the occupants of the heavy goods vehicle they were travelling in were asleep helped, but the three bearded gunmen closest to Golem's deputy were, if not hanging on every word, humming in a way that expressed general assent.

'Crazies always flock together hah!' General War Boss dug a finger into Golem's side. The two men were sitting at the back of the truck, its canvas tarpaulin flapping wildly as they hurtled along the potholed road. Amnesty had dispensed with his eye patch altogether, revealing two perfectly normal eyes, his accessory of choice a pair of yellow sunglasses.

'I dislike these kind of conversations, they bore you know, they bore.'

'I could not agree more' said Golem.

If Artay had started to make an impression on a section of their hosts Golem was enjoying a head start with his own power base. War Boss, the immaculately dressed Amnesty and their fellow Generals, at least before they fell asleep to the rumble of the truck's hypnotic engine, were in thrall to Golem's war stories. The gas attacks, trench warfare and tank battles a world away from their haphazard skirmishing, had struck a chord with these enthusiasts that theology had not. Of course, the tales gained in the telling, Golem was sensible enough to play to the interests of his audience, emphasising military hardware and its uses over geo politics and ideology. Nor was he falsely modest, taking care to make every story concrete by illustrating his role in it. Like these veterans he discovered they shared the same distrust of politicians, awe of Western firepower and fear of religious leaders he had experienced in the trenches facing Saddam's Republican guard thirty years before. As Artay droned remorselessly on, Golem swapped anecdotes and something like genuine affection with these Generals barely out of their twenties, until one by one they nodded off leaving him with War Boss, their unacknowledged leader, sharing a beer.

'In your country as in ours the religious man has the power, the one who is in touch with spirits.'

'I wouldn't say that my young accomplice has the power, or is in touch with spirits. I don't think even he would say that, fool that he is.'

'Nonetheless my friend, he acts like he wants to be the boss man.'

Golem smirked, 'impossible not to notice, eh!'

War Boss nodded, glad that they had agreed on the funda-mentals, leading Golem to sense this was the prelude to some suggestion. He was right.

'The other Generals and I have not been blind. We know you hate this man.'

'Hate? That's a strong way of putting it, too strong...'

War Boss raised his hand, 'no, you are our friend and do not need to lie to us. You hate this man and would like to see his remains in a hyena's belly. We will kill him for you if you like.'

'I...'

'We have an old saying, "the sky can only hold one comet at a time". This man does not know his place, he shows you no respect and shows us no respect. He has not come here to learn from us but to brainwash us. Make him more like those fools,' War Boss tilted his head towards Artay's study group at the front of the truck. 'I have learnt that men like this must die. They cannot be trusted. Once we have killed the President they will have their time too.'

Poised between fulfilling a deeply held desire to see the back of Artay, but betray his country in the process and set a precedent he might later be the victim of, Golem took the less risky option. Adopting the face of one who could size up every option in a finger flick, he took the decision to risk alienating his new friend and said, 'all fools will find their proper punishment in hell. Allah is the master executioner and the settler of all accounts.'

For a worrying second War Boss looked puzzled, if not

downright cheated, before, to Golem's massive relief, he puckered his lips and nodded again, 'wise words my friend, wise words.' And that, Golem hoped, as War Boss closed his eyes and joined his friends in sleep, would be the end of the matter. Uneasily he tried to follow suit, thoughts of his wife and home occurring to him for the first time, as they always did when the going went from good to bad. They were two days from the Mahdi's camp and what then? Their instructions were an infuriating mix of the vague and exact, so much resting on subjective interpretation, which in turn called for confidence in one's judgement. To his great discomfort he realised that he did not have an opinion "on what to do", and had been making his plans up as he went along in the hope that the facts would lead him towards some kind of tentative conclusion. They had done nothing of the kind. It was clear that an inconclusive meeting with an exchange of platitudes and a photo or two of the Mahdi would not be enough to satisfy Tehran. But what else could he do, lead the revolution in a direction compatible with Iranian interests or ask the Mahdi to come back home with him and explain himself to Jafari? Or else terminate the man with extreme prejudice and face a field of angry Africans, though at least in this scenario the responsibility of living would be taken out of his hands, an increasingly attractive outcome, though he hated to admit it.

Like an amateur his excitement at leaving the prison house of Iran had blinded him to preparing even the simplest of plans, that and a hunch that the Mahdi, whatever his "fact finding" mission would uncover, was sincere. Which was not something Jafari wanted to hear, that much was obvious. Somehow, through this irresolvable fog, Golem drifted off and dreamt of his wife scolding him for leaving his used razor by her toothbrush, even the pettiest visions of home a welcome distraction for the troubled envoy.

CHAPTER SIX

Love and Marriage

'Who do you think lived here?'

'Judging by the look of the place, whites I'd say.'

'You would, Beasley.'

'Honestly Kingston, what sort of black would have wasted time building this? They'd have had more important things to do.'

Kingston squinted, unsure of which direction to tack in. Beasley was nothing if unpredictable, and when predictable ambiguous, in his politics, 'planters you think?'

'No,' Francis intervened, 'this was the home of retired people. No one worked here. Rich old men and women from Europe, they must have had happy memories of their Safaris and decided to come and live out their days where the sun is hot.'

'And the living easy and life cheap,' said Pagan, 'it can't have turned out the way they reckoned. Ought have gone somewhere safe like Skegness. Nearer the grandchildren.'

'No sympathy with these tax exile bastards anyway,' Beasley spat, 'never having done no good for anyone and then buggering off to read their International editions of The Mail on fucking Sunday. Good riddance.'

'They may not have been Mail readers,' Elder wondered aloud, picking up the arm of a wicker chair, smashed to pieces on what was once the veranda, 'they might have taken the Express, or the Telegraph. I guess they left in a hurry when the fighting started.'

'Or hung on and got killed, prepared for their retirement but not death, rock on England.'

'Oh come on Beasley' said Elder, 'they might have been Dutch or German. England isn't at the bottom of every disaster.'

'What, with this in the garden?' Beasley straightened the bent flagpole, a tatty Cross of St George at the end of it. 'Can't think of any other nation wanting one of these hung aloft in a World Cup year, can you?'

Evening was drawing in and it was noisy, the animals talking to each other, or perhaps just making meaningless noises for all Pagan cared. Crucially they had found shelter for the night, the building that stood before them far superior to anything he could have hoped to sleep in. Pagan wished he could stop thinking in blunt conclusions but the habit was too old, the pattern too strong, 'be careful now, empty places and nasty surprises.'

Standing on slats, the ranch was built in the shape of a Zulu fighting formation, the horns of the building protruding outwards to create a corral. Thick pillars of wood held up the high thatched ceilings in which birds had already started to nest, geckoes and other small lizards running across the supporting beams. Above, a sloping pyramid roof ran along the curved length of the building, like a bent arm pointing towards the far off snow capped mountains of the northeast. Looters had pulled out furniture, books and other ornaments, casting them over the unwatered brown lawn. Further down the sloping drive, torn photo albums, gold plated reading lamps and a mahogany chest of drawers lay strewn amidst broken glass, the odd bit of cutlery civilising the mess.

'They're like our burglars back home,' Beasley observed wryly, 'they go for the electrical goods first.'

'I just can't understand why people destroy things of beauty,' said Elder, wiping the sweat off the inside brim of his floppy hat. His expression was miserable, akin to a curator returning to a vandalised museum exhibit.

At their feet lay the remains of a large banqueting table, and as Elder carefully stepped over it, he visualised drunken expats eating their dinner on its once stable surface, the twinkling stars confirming, however briefly, their dreams of a great Continent.

'It's all so unnecessary. When in a pack they behave with the wild conformism of children. There's just no need.'

'The locals who turned this place over you mean?'

'Of course I mean them, the owners are hardly likely to have run wild in their own house. Bloody ungrateful bunch, those who can't create destroy my Mum used to say, and she was right.'

'Bollocks Sir, we're not inventing the wheel here. The reason they're lazy buggers who don't give a toss and tear up fancy mod cons is because the foreigners were living up here and they were living down there in the African Barrett complex,' Beasley pointed to the half finished concrete blocks that lay the other side of a barbed wire fence. 'No more complicated than that. It's their land.'

'That's very even-handed of you Beasley; far be it from me to repeat simple formulations, but I'm sure you've heard the one about how all there would be here is dust and heat if it weren't for the whites. Might it not have occurred to you that the reason they're at the bottom is because they deserve to be there? And that's where they'll remain now they've driven the wealth creators out. The underdog is not always right.'

'I'm not sticking up for anyone.'

'God forbid, you just need a world view with good guys and bad guys because without it you'd lose your vocation, grousing, and the bogus certainties that enable it.'

'It's not grousing, it's politics. Suffer long and hard enough and you'll be blamed for it so the well off can live with an easy conscience and think their good luck well deserved. Living with their guilt by rationalising it and blaming the victim, justifying their gain through merit, you follow me Sir, so that after a while sympathy for the victim turns to hatred for the victim?'

'Bolshevist horseshit, I'd have credited you with more sense Beasley.'

Pagan touched Elder's shoulder, 'I wouldn't discount everything he says Justin.'

'Why the hell not? I'm sick of us taking shit off this wind-up merchant.'

'There are depths and insights his prejudice against us Ruperts gives him access to, that enlightened thinking can't.'

'What's that supposed to mean, why are you taking his part?'

'Relax Sir,' said Beasley, 'it's all just noise, right?'

'Maybe to you.'

'Come on,' said Pagan, carefully stepping over a thick black column of ants, 'let's see what's inside.'

* * *

Kingston and Hightower had watched the debate dispassionately, each consumed with his own troubles. For Kingston Operation Wild Geese had turned out exactly as expected, which was no cause for celebration. A mixture of danger and vagueness was what he had come to fear from life in the service, the less exact and more interpretive a mission, the more to dread. The line between doing one's duty and overdoing it could always be blurred. This was especially so thousands of miles from home in a loose command structure, and though Kingston trusted Pagan on this score, Elder showed signs of lethal over-enthusiasm.

'Damn, look at that sky, it's way too big.'

'The bigger the land the bigger the sky.'

As the youngest of a family of thirteen, military service initially promised a way out of the dark green humidity of Belize. Basic training had not been too bad, the countryside outside Andover quite pretty, and Kingston's English girlfriends the fruit in the cake. Unlike his spotty, and sometimes mentally remedial comrades, recruited from the care homes of Liverpool and Glasgow, Kingston had rhythm and a global outlook, which combined with his tracking skills had got him to where he was and did not want to be. A good career ought not to entail the possibility of death or mutilation, and unfortunately, the more competent at soldiering he got, the closer he came to these twin devils. If only he had shown less aptitude he could have been preparing marinades for battery farm chickens in the catering corps, or perhaps skimming off a slice as a quartermaster back in England, but pride and a capacity for endurance had dealt him a bum rap, that of the hero.

Not so Hightower, nicknamed (by himself) "the happy warrior", who was exactly where he intended to be. Operation Wild Geese was as he had imagined it, but to his amazement, he found he was not really enjoying himself. No one had made more of a fuss of wishing to satisfy their warrior instincts, complained more at how every mission they were sent on was indistinguishable from ordinary infantry operations and, in frustration had ended in the guard house for drunken fist fighting with townies. Yet here he was, dejected and not a little scared by their evident isolation. The further in he looked the worse it got. Aside from his nose being a bleeding mess, far worse than any kicking he had ever received, his back ached like an old man, and having thrown his wet socks away, both feet were badly blistered. Just standing straight and still was agonising whilst the rush of fear experienced earlier in combat had not made him feel like he was living the dream. On the contrary, it seemed to render his safety unimportant, warning him life was superfluous and that his death would be unmourned. The sights and sensations were as anticipated, it was the feelings they caused that were so unexpected, running against the grain of his simple and convivial nature, leading him to conclude that for the first time in his life he might actually be mildly depressed. Death had never had anything to do with army life before, now he felt surrounded by it, its hold over him as intense as it was innocuous.

Both men caught each other out at the same time, 'you alright Kingston?'

'Yeah.'

'Alright.'

'A smoke?'

'Why not.'

'You think we're going to get this mad fucker?'

'I don't want to think. I'd had the idea, crazy I know, that we knew where he was.'

'Me too. This is a human safari, he could be anywhere.'

'Glad we're not relying on Justin Elder, that's all.'

'Ahh, he's a good bloke, cares about us more than the other hard bastard. You see how old Sean Pagan takes care of himself? Most of his gear is American stuff from the army surplus shop in Hereford, not the crap we're issued with.'

'Give me a hard selfish bastard over a good bloke with no sense of direction, you see where he ended up in his jeep.'

'That was the chalky driver's fault, no offence.'

'None taken. Our Justin is like one of those hearty public school boys from a hundred years ago, he should never be allowed on operations like this. And I tell you, nor should I.'

Hightower slapped at a mosquito, missing it and stinging his neck. 'Here, let's have one of those malaria pills. I feel like I'm coming down with something. I don't like this at all...I can't get on top of this bad feeling I keep getting. It's so powerful, coming from right in me...'

'Fuck that, you'll jinx us.'

The sun was going down behind a bank of clouds, distant figures silhouetted against a thorn fence walking across the horizon, whether towards or away from them the men could not tell.

'Guard duty, one of you in ten minutes,' said Beasley, poking them both in the back, 'and if you can't do better than the chat I just heard, then I suggest it's vows of silence all round. Tomorrow's going to be a big one and I don't want your bad karma wiped over my natural optimism, understand?'

'Sir.'

'Sir.'

A Hyena let out the first of a series of cries and an unpleasant wind, blowing over from an outhouse full of human compost, reached the men, who each carefully buried their noses in their sleeves, the urge to be sick coming over them all.

'Might be a good idea if we slept round the other side,' said Beasley eyeing the horizon warily, 'get a good solid wall between us and…all this.'

Once inside, the ranch stopped looking comfortable as it became obvious why the looters had chosen to smash and grab rather than simply occupy the building. The space belonged to its former inhabitants, photo collages of naked parties, stuffed antelope heads and imported furniture suggesting a no man's land that was neither Europe nor Africa.

'No self respecting follower of superstition would drop their anchor in this place.'

'Or of fashion, these are the sort of things Mobutu would have had in his palaces. Interesting overlap between two different kinds of African, white old money and black new. Doesn't say much for the taste, or morality, of either.'

'Both overlords if Beasley is to be believed.'

'You know Justin, you're a fucking fool to be drawn into his debates; notice he never has them if you're alone together, only when there's an audience to embarrass you in front of. It's not the Africans he cares about, it's making you huff and puff. The only war for him is the class war.'

'And those against our foreign friends.'

'We can take that one for granted.'

'Looks as though they didn't want anyone to get in there,' said Pagan, 'see, over there Justin, it's been blocked. Wonder why.'

A cabinet of riding trophies barred the way towards a door that had been double bolted from the outside.

'What do you think, something they might have wanted to

come back to?'

'Intriguing. Pull the wood out of the way. We'll bed down in there.'

Elder brought the cabinet down with force, guiltily enjoying the sound of its contents clattering over the floor, 'the doors locked, I'll shoot it off.'

'Very Wild West.'

The door swung open revealing a trolley with a torn plastic sheet piled over it. On the wall was a poster of the meridian lines that cover a human body, the writing beneath them in Chinese. A faded print of Buddha looked over the mess, less passive than accusatory.

Pagan picked up one of a pile of cards and snorted, 'would you believe it, "alternative medicines and acupuncture", this bloke, wait for it, "Archibald Logan St. Ledger", actually thought he could build up a practice here of all places.'

'I think that's quite noble of him.'

'Here? An acupuncturist in a land ravaged by Aids? A dose of crystals instead of a trip to the Witch Doctor, don't make me laugh!'

Elder took the thin cushion off the trolley, brushing the dust off it, 'so this is bed I suppose. I'm exhausted. We haven't done too badly have we?'

'Badly enough sunshine,' Pagan replied, 'two dead is never good is it? And for no return, that's bad, unless you're Delta Force or bedded in for a war of attrition.'

'I must admit, since having got here, our plans seem vaguer than they did back home, before we left.'

'That, Justin, is the nature of the beast. Remember the post war plans for Iraq? No? Well nor do I. Can't say vaguer than that, but I don't remember anyone complaining at the time, certainly not any of our higher-ups. Haven't you noticed that's the way, our plans are always vague, the politicians don't know what they're unleashing, our Generals do but pass the problem down to us, and we charge around like headless chickens saying it's not our fault when the media complain about our slotting the wrong house full of wedding guests. Or when some dickhead squaddie blows a looter away or when we just let a country go to shit. I could go on but why bother.'

'Look at the positives Sean, they must have had a lot of trust in us, in you and me, to sanction this...'

'You think that's what it is? We're expendable,' Pagan was laughing now, 'really we are. It's not all bad though, Francis having a brain on him has to be considered a plus. And we found this place, which is better than a night with the tics, snakes and midges.'

'Where there's sleep there's hope.'

'If there's a path to the Mahdi, Francis will be on to it. On our own it would have been speculative at best. We've maps of the routes of his march trails, old camps and so on but there's no telling he'd be there waiting for us to arrest him. He's never far from his troops, a lead of sorts I guess, but how easy would it be to nab him surrounded by whatever constitutes his elite. Francis gives us something extra.'

'The lot we came up against today were clowns.'

'What, even the ones who chased you to the bridge?'

Elder blushed, 'we weren't chased Sean, they just happened to be following us on our way back there. We fucked up completely with our driver.'

'I know that, what I'm saying is that it won't be the piece of piss. Our radio equipment was in the Land Rover and there isn't one of us who can even get a mobile signal.'

'You want to know how I'd get him?'

'All ears.'

'Look, there are only two main routes through the jungle if you're travelling in convoy,' said Elder running his finger along the dusty wall, 'which he almost certainly will be, the warlord at the front of an advancing army, you've said yourself he doesn't like to play it low key. That narrows things down pretty well don't you think?'

Pagan lit a cigarette, throwing one at Elder as he did so, 'that's *two* routes though. Pick the wrong one and we've fucked it. Completely. It's too risky, and once he's with his main army there's no way we can take him without calling in reinforcements. If we still had the other two I'd split us up and go into the jungle as planned, you going your way and me going mine, but with just three to a group...well, better to watch clearings and feel his collar when he comes out for air. Otherwise it's fifty-fifty, and frankly, I don't think our lives are worth the *national interest* in this case. The Mahdi will not be in Brighton for tea if we fail to nab or slot him. I don't mind going home empty handed if we have to.'

'I don't know' said Elder, 'the idea of sitting tight and waiting doesn't go well with me. Not really part of the regimental ethos eh?'

'No, nor with me Justin, but this is our last trip out...'

'Exactly.'

Pagan blew a line of smoke over his hand, looking at it as if for a clue, 'fuck it then, playing safe's usually as dangerous as shit or bust. We go for it, two groups, me with Beasley and Francis, you take the two young lads, we stake out the paths, pick out a meeting point and see what we find on the way. You keep the jeep and take the outside route, I'll go in.'

Elder nodded eagerly, pleased that mutual respect meant that in practice his friend was not his superior, as he was on designated operations like this, rather the joint commander of a shared enterprise. Few people knew it, but Pagan disliked the experience of being his own peer group.

'So you think we can trust Francis?' Elder asked.

'Not completely,' Pagan yawned, 'or else I'd let you take him as part of your group. It's hard to believe a man's telling the truth when you'd lie in his place.'

'"Don't equate me with your petty morals," is what he'd say if he heard you say that, he thinks a lot of himself that man.'

'Which is also his strength and value to us. And he's not incompetent, you saw that.'

'Yeah, I'm trying not to hold it against him too much. Too clever by half that bloke, that's what Beasley said; mind you, look who's talking eh? He's a barrack room lawyer if ever there was; the Regiment's always attracted a minority of articulate misfits who get their loyalty back to front, and Beasley, God I wish we had someone else with his experience so we didn't have to rely on him so much.'

'Yeah.'

'Still, cranky arsehole that he is, at least Beasley won't write one of those Bravo Two bullshit books like those arseholes Mc'knob and Cryin' Ryan. That's what I'd always be afraid of appearing in, like finding your photo on Facebook. Beasley's got too much pride for that. Of course, the worst is getting some spotty little hack to write your book for you, then putting your name on the cover to give it the big "I am a hero". Christ knows what the public think they're buying into but it sure as hell isn't authenticity. Well, 'night mate.'

Elder waited for a reply, but Pagan having finished what he had to say was already asleep.

Francis laid his mat out on the stone floor, a safe distance away from Beasley's snores. It had been like this for as long as he could remember, no matter whom he was with. The same holding back and fear of how much of himself to reveal to others, his intelligence hidden in case it cast him as a black Iago: the shifty African who can never be trusted. Forthrightness could lead to a firing squad for getting ideas above one's station, reticence taken for servility or worse. Even in the village it had been difficult telling the difference between rebels who would shoot you for knowing how to read, or take you to their leader and spare your life for the same skill. The whites had distrusted a worker with too much education when the work provided did not require it, and so on to the endless Kangaroo courts in which he would be accused of cheating them, stealing, siphoning off fuel, as though intelligence in a certain kind of person, a native one, could only find its proper home in criminality. To become a guerrilla, to hone his native skills to his advantage was the only honourable choice, and yet even here he had encountered suspicion, so once again he learnt to hold back, reveal less than what he knew and hide in a self- constructed enigma. Until now, where among these strange, almost comical men, who argued amongst themselves with no consequence, and encouraged him to speak with no penalty and without coercion, he had finally let his guard down and opened up. For a man used to knowing his own mind by virtue of concealment, the act of saying more than he thought and discovering what he thought by saying it, was as great a surprise as being given something he had wanted but never asked for.

Smiling at this, Francis said his prayers, taking care to lay special emphasis on his own safety, and that of his new friends, before rolling onto his side and dreaming of new beginnings.

* * *

Others were not finding sleep so easy. Foy was having erotic nightmares, stripped naked to her waist wiping the chlorine off schoolboys in their swimming trunks. Occasionally one of them would lead her into a shower for lively sex, before returning her to the changing room to help the other boys on with their suits and ties. This confusing ritual was broken up with trying to fit into the same swimming costume as her brother-in-law, who looked like Roger Moore, the "Bond" she loathed herself for loving. Coming to and badly needing to urinate, the reality she woke in was considerably worse than her predicament in either dream. The thick trees had blotted out the sun long before it had gone down, rendering the clearing they were camped in coal black. Only a thin lick of flame, burning on a candle the Websters had stuck into their "perimeter", shed any light on their surroundings. On one side there were sharp sticks of bamboo covering the forest floor like spears and on the other a swamp. Foy peered into the damp foliage, clumps of moss and the bugs that lived in it bouncing off her bare arms with the force of coins. Armies of insects were swarming over the furthest candle, the light from which revealed thousands more lying dead below. Foy disliked insects of any stripe, especially flying ones. Normally this alone would have been enough to excite her fears, but now there were bigger pests to consider. The wetness of their surroundings was why the Websters had rejected the idea of building a fire, their readiness to give up surprising Foy as much as her own offer to build one had surprised them.

'You won't find anything to burn Missy, and things to burn is what makes a fire. Ain't goin' to do nothin' with moist wood 'less you're packin' a flame thrower or you got some of that napalm.'

'What you trying to prove anyway, you ain't the Girl Guides honey bunch.'

'She'll give up and go to bed before she lights the first twig!'

And they were right, except that now she was awake again, and though she could hear the low groaning of two snoring Websters in tandem, she wasn't going to hold in a piss just because they might think she was running away.

Carefully, so as not to arouse suspicion or disturb any passing snakes, Foy drew her legs out of her sleeping bag and groped round for her trainers. She had not so much as slipped her foot in to one, when the burning candle that a second ago had been on the ground was thrust in her face. Unable to control her balance she fell clumsily on to her bag, shielding her eyes protectively from the flame that followed her down.

'I've been watching you Flamingo, waiting to see when you

lifted the first of those legs out and tried to make a run for it!'

'What are you talking about, I needed a piss, do you really think I'd try and run away now, at night? I'd be safer here with you.'

Nelson lowered the torch slightly, impressed with the strength of her logic, a disappointed tone entering his voice, 'you're not wrong there, this jungle is piggin' lethal.'

Foy really ought to have left it at that, yet the temptation to punish Nelson, now that he was on the back foot, took over, 'you would have to be a deaf, dumb and blind moron to think someone would even consider escape in a place like this, it's the best guard you've got over me. Save your paranoia up for when we hit civilisation, because the only thing I want to do tonight is empty my bloody bladder. I may not like the hole I'm in, but it's a lot better than being eaten by whatever's out there.'

Nelson grinned evilly, an idea slowly forming, 'a piss you say, you say you want a piss?'

'Bingo, spot on.'

'Well go on then, take one.'

'What did you think I was trying to do?'

'No, take one, take one here, right here, over all your sleeping stuff so I can see you.'

'Are you mad…you must be fucking joking. That's disgusting, vile.'

'You wish I was, don't you?' Nelson pulled Foy to her feet with a single tug of his arm and, holding the candle to her face with one hand, pulled at the elastic of her shorts with the other, 'now as I say, I want to see you pee, watch all that water come forth and if it don't I'll be right up there to fetch it…'

Foy closed her eyes but the blow she was expecting landed on one who was not expecting it.

Nelson went down so quickly that Foy did not even realise that the warm mass of flesh at her feet, groaning forgiveness, or maybe only groaning, was her tormentor.

'Hard to know which of you to blame more' said Mr Webster, lowering an ugly looking club, before raising it again and bringing it to bear on the point of Nelson's back with tremendous force.

'One stupid bastard and a dizzy bint, don't get me wrong my girl, in normal times I wouldn't give a peanut addled shit if that prat fiddled with you. Fiddled with you all he liked, but these are no normal times. I need you as clean as a whistle.'

'For your ransom?' Foy was determined not to cry and to keep the words coming out in a sane and rational flow, no matter how far behind them she actually lurked, 'it's all about money isn't it? For you.'

Mr Webster chuckled, 'you impress me my girl, no doubt about it, you've been going up in my estimations, thought you were just a pretty face to start with, which was your downfall when you come to think of it. Money, yes, but ransom, well truthfully I hadn't even thought of that, not my place to, 'cos you see, it won't be up to me.'

The urge to go to the lavatory had given way to an overwhelming desire to know where she stood. 'Tell me, once and for all, what do you want from me?' Foy cried, 'why are you leading me into this...hell, what for? Why are you doing this to me?' As she said these words Foy noticed something; she had grown, in valour if not morally, though not in a way that was one hundred percent advisable.

'Hmmm,' Webster gazed thoughtfully at Nelson, who was unsuccessfully trying to haul himself up off the broken bamboo patch he had landed on, 'what you think Tawny, what do we lose by telling now?'

Tawny rubbed her eyes irritably, 'just tell, not anythin' she can do about it anyway, we're too far for her to run back, we're all she has, you heard her, the jungle's death. She's in for the long haul whether she likes it or not. And fuck me, will she not like it!'

'Sit down,' said Webster, 'this'll take some believing, though it'll all be true. No, first take that piss, no sense in you doing it in your smalls when you hear what I've got to tell you...'

Despite the humidity, that made her want to faint, Foy folded her arms defiantly, digging the toe of her trainer into the space that separated her from the Websters. Making sure they were watching, she proceeded to drag it back and forth in a way she hoped would show aggressive intent, 'how can I believe anything you tell me? I've asked you so many questions and as far as I know there hasn't been a single thing you haven't lied about.' The fear of losing everything was having a liberating affect on her loquaciousness, all her old fears of appearing a snob, an idiot, or plain boring seeming so petty to her now.

'I said I figured you for brains,' said Mr Webster, 'but you've a way to go.'

'Wouldn't lecture Pa, she's too up herself to learn anyhow.'

'Oh no, please continue, I've so much to learn.'

Mr Webster chuckled again; 'sarcastic bitch 'aintcha? If you'd kept your mouth shut you'd have had our measure. But you couldn't stop feeding us cues, all your stupid questions inspired us, you might say, to sell you the whole bull-farm.'

'I like giving people the benefit of the doubt, so kill me.'

'Nah, you enjoy projectin'. And look at the good it's done you. I'll tell you what we are, we're Mercenaries darlin', not Pikies on the African leg of a world tour! Mercenaries, Dogs of War!'

At this all three Websters exploded with laughter, Tawny slapping her father's bottom, 'she thought she were joining the Chav's African adventure! Bunch of bloody holidaymakers she could patronise, look at her face, priceless!'

'What? What are you talking about, *mercenaries*?'

'We're no Scotch-swilling Etonians, that I grant you. Or Bruce Willis or that Van Damme prick either. You're looking at the real deal honey, mercenaries, those who kill for money and turn people to paint.'

'You're lying.'

'I never lie when I'm tired.'

Foy bit her finger, 'prove it then!'

'We just have!' Nelson practically screamed, on his feet again, 'we fuckin' kidnapped you didn't we? We carry guns and we're in the middle of the bloody jungle! What more you expect?'

'John Rambo jumping out of a plane on his way to slaughter a division of gooks!' beamed Webster, drawing out an ugly looking knife, 'see this my girl, my Pa first used it in National Service in Malaya, gave it to me, and I blooded it in the ribs of a filthy Mick, Belfast, about the time you were born. And it's sort of gone on from there, I like it abroad, you do what you want. None of these fuckin' rules they throw at you all the time back home, can't smoke here, can't say that, can't drive after a jar, fuck all that you know? Fuck all that.'

Foy took a step back from the line she had drawn in the ground; it did not feel very protective. Once more she found herself believing Webster; the difference was that this time it was a physical belief, one that adumbrated in her sweating and vulnerable extremities.

'So, whether you believe us or not matters not one fuckin' wit, facts are facts, however you tweak their titties. We are what we are; however over the top we may look to you, we're real, see?'

'What about those two,' Foy pointed at Nelson and Tawny, 'so they're real but they can't be mercenaries...they're too young, aren't they?'

'What would you know of it,' shouted Tawny, 'don't know your front pocket from your back, you!'

'God,' said Foy, 'would it be too much to expect anything nice from you?'

'You don't know the first thing about me,' shouted Tawny, 'you only know me in one capacity is all, why would I bother opening up to someone I don't respect, she didn't even have the brains to figure us out did she Pa?'

'Easy girl,' Webster drew Tawny over to him and pulled up her hooded top, her bare chest revealing a network of scars and nicks. 'See here, courtesy of the Hutu militia we were meant to be training up, after they'd taken turns with her mind. No, we're what you might call a family enterprise, me daughter, nephew and me. Lost the boy Luke in Columbia back in '96 and their Uncle up in Myanmar year before last, but we keep on keepin' on because the world is what it is. An honest to goodness shit hole.'

'So you're mercenaries, great, good for you, I should have realised shouldn't I? And Tawny, so sorry to have underestimated you, I really won't stoop to gender stereotyping again, I promise, never ever...because of course, the world really needs people like you. Ha ha!'

Webster slapped Foy in the face. 'You're in shock girl, hardly surprising with what we've put you through, though I don't have time to indulge.'

Foy felt her cut lip; there was a speck of blood on her finger. Slowly she licked it off and faced her tormentors. 'Okay' she announced proudly, 'where do I fit in to your weird and wonderful world?'

'Ever heard of the Mahdi?' Nelson asked.

'Hard not to have here.'

'I don't mean the news reports, you really know anythin' 'bout him?'

'Only what most people know. That he's mad, bad and dangerous. And that if it weren't for him I probably wouldn't be in this mess. Is that enough for you?'

Tawny snorted as the skinhead continued self-importantly, 'thing is we work for him...'

'Oh come on!'

'Hear him out' grinned Webster, 'you're in a world where the tall tales are the only ones you can trust.'

'We're what you might call his special snatch squad.'

'I beg your pardon?'

'We do the jobs his African brethren don't have the qualifications for.'

'And what might they be?'

'Kidnap white girls.'

'Here,' Webster pushed Nelson out of the way, 'was a bit optimistic hoping old useless here could explain this right.'

'How the hell did the Mahdi end up choosing you lot for anything, you come from Norwich, or wherever it is, for fuck's sake, how would he have even heard of you! Stop pissing about with me!'

'Now, now, don't be rude about Norwich, and I thought I'd told you 'bout stupid questions, it's enough for you to know we're tellin' the truth, that's all that's relevant. Now Nelson, do you want to go on goin' sideways or would you like me to take over so we finish this year?'

Nelson shrugged sulkily, 'whatever.'

'Don't use Americanisms boy, they's for secretaries, they don't suit you. So Miss Foy, our employer the Mahdi, and you'd better believe it is him, is of a different religious persuasion from us C of E loving devotees.'

'He's a Muslim of course, what does that have to do with anything...'

'It has everythin' to with why you're here!' laughed Tawny, 'go on, tell her Pa, can't wait to see her face.'

'Yes, go on Pa, tell me,' said Foy raising her chin defiantly, 'what other little surprises have you in store?'

'Not a little surprise, a big one girl! As I was saying, he's a Muslim, and as a Muslim, well, his Allah, their God, allows him a bit more on the side than our one does us. Wives is what I'm getting at. Your normal Muslim is allowed five, but this Mahdi's in the market for twelve. That's the number he claims his great, great granddad their Prophet had, and he thinks it only fair that he has the same number, you follow me?'

'Oh absolutely, and perhaps you'd like to tell me what his

favourite colour is or where he buys his socks?'

'You keep it up, you'll see. Because our Mahdi wants to go one better than his hero, or his grandfather or whatever you want to believe is the truth about the bloke, and take advantage of the benefits of Air Travel in a way they couldn't when they went wife hunting in the days of old...you must see it coming now my girl!'

Foy could not and frowned.

'He wants a white woman, doesn't he? A European.'

Foy saw it now and opened her mouth in the shape of a letter O. She may have screamed, she did not know, only that she came to in the uncomforting arms of Webster and heard him say, 'You're going to be his wife darling, his thirteenth, you're going to marry the Mahdi and make us all Maharajas!'

* * *

Golem had wanted to talk to Artay before they turned in, remind him that they were on the same side and perhaps even pray together. His assistant had snubbed him, feigning exaggerated tiredness in front of his new African friends who had formed a mini-camp round their teacher. Condemning himself was a way for Golem to restore perspective after a perceived insult, yet this was something he found hard to do with Artay. It worried him how Artay was in the wrong over every disagreement, even those he had not instigated. Being trapped within one's individual perspective might have been normal for most people but for Golem it meant he could not do his job. An agent unable to see the world as others did was worse than useless. Curiously he found that in spite of their antagonism he cared what his assistant thought of him and resented Artay's obvious lack of respect for his achievements, none of which registered with the young fanatic. The source of Artay's confident belligerence was a mystery to him, especially as Jafari had instructed him to obey

Golem's word as he would his father's, leading him to wonder why this untested youth had been chosen as his assistant. All of which brought him to the verge of an unpleasant conclusion. Artay was not on trial; he was.

He yawned. It was not possible to think about Artay for very long without irritation giving way to indifference. The boy would condemn himself and be humiliated in front of his new disciples, or, God willing, tread on a mine or serpent. There were other, less specific things keeping him awake.

Golem stared into the black night, sleeping bodies scattered round him like fallen leaves, a melancholic reminder of his Autumn in England. Only the mosquitoes and chatter of small insects kept him in Africa, his mind was continents away. It had been a policy of his never to project too far in to the future, far less look back. Sadly this was no longer the case. The excitement of being in the field again had worn off at the point he wondered *what* he was in the field for. Instead he visualised the pleasure of opening a bottle of Black Label, Fleetwood Mac on his stereo and the wife and child he loved (without being particularly interested in either) safely asleep. The present moment, far from being seized, was there to be endured and sluiced through; a half-realised memory of the past keeping him going towards a future he had no confidence in. It was in the air, even here in Africa. The wolves were out for him, he had been sent to Africa either because he was expendable or as a test of his loyalty, neither option reassured. The important men would follow later, once it was safe to. How long had this unhappy situation been in the offing, or had it always been thus, the mask of ideology blinding him to his unimportance? Dutifully he got down on to his knees to ask God, confident that he would be given strength, if not an answer.

* * *

Pagan was the first up. In the field he did not go through his usual ritual of lying motionless, pretty much at the mercy of his memory, until disappointment finally drove him out of bed. Instead he was on his feet, wiping his grimy body down with an old towel he found, the water coming from one of the many Volvic bottles hoarded in an airing cupboard with a pile of old slimming magazines. The night had not quite let go, and as strange birds with long beaks paraded round their jeep, Pagan stepped onto the veranda and rehydrated, finishing the water in deep slugs, not for him the stereotypical black coffee and contemplative cigarette, not since turning thirty. Although he did not like to show it, he was not without physical vanity, and as the creases in his face showed no signs of softening, he took them for the harbingers of old age they were, an article about mineral water controlling wrinkles influencing his choice of beverage.

He had doubts about his eyesight too, despite regular check ups and not having drunk for over a week. Objects seemed to shimmer and glow instead of standing fast in the absolute clarity they once had. Perhaps this was why he was unsure whether the figure on the horizon, three figures to be exact, were men or ostriches, or maybe one camel, it was embarrassing but he could not tell. Instinctively he reached into the jeep and pulled out his rifle, staring down the telescopic lens to locate a target. Pagan was in luck: three men, walking away from him, almost certainly ignorant of the SAS presence in the ranch. From their dress there was no doubting they were with the Mahdi, turbaned heads, veiled faces, white smocks worn in a near-parody of fundamentalist fervour. Three perfect targets to kick-start the day with. It never ceased to amaze Pagan how a single reflex, command, or mistake, could make the difference between breathing and not being able to breathe at all. There was certainly something ostrich-like about the largest of the three, fat even, and the two smaller ones, much smaller in fact, looked no bigger than children. There was also a clean looking quality to them all, in spite of the distance, they appeared to have put their best robes on for the occasion of their deaths. Pagan got it. This was their first morning on their way to the war, to answer the Mahdi's call, Fatty was the father, the two smaller ones sons or nephews, it reminded him of discovering a nest full of wood pigeons, the mother feeding the babies, two generations of Jihadis wiped out in three bullets, goodnight Vienna. Pagan tensed his firing eye and watched them walk for a while, walk right over the horizon, until they were well out of range.

'Captain Pagan,' it was Francis holding a large apple, 'I thought you might like one of your "five a day".'

Warily Pagan lowered his rifle and swapped it with Francis for the apple, Francis taking the gun off him like a bearer on safari.

'Inconsistent Sir, they live to fight another day.'

Pagan could not tell whether this was humour or a reproach, but taking a guess that this man's idea of the darkly comic was not so different from his own, he retorted, 'yeah, they'll probably be the three that kill us. And eat our entrails for desert.'

Francis frowned, taking this in and giving the scenario its fair due, then replying with a smile, 'it's these little breakdowns in logic that make us human Sir.'

The first blast of sunlight broke over the scrub a moment later, long enough for Francis not to notice, Pagan hoped, how moved he was by this remark.

'Not to worry, they'll die soon, and die well, these fanatics lack the imagination to take their lives seriously,' Pagan said, conscious of the forced dissonance in his voice, 'and then off to their paradise they'll go.'

'Not our paradise too Sir?'

'Well, I can't speak for you Francis but not mine, mine is the sort of heaven they don't allow mad cunts into. Or maybe the kind they *only* let mad cunts into, I dunno'. Now do me a favour and wake Elder up, he'll need the fuel from our jeep. You, Beasley and I are going on, on foot from here.'

'Very good Sir,' said Francis, and gave a mock salute, the sort of a thing a waiter pretending to be a sailor would do for a customer after a generous tip, thought Pagan, happier to notice poignancy than be stuck on the profound.

INTERLUDE

Qom, Iran

Jafari quickly replaced the first éclair, jammed in his mouth, with a second, the speed and seamlessness of the operation as rare and pure as a dream come true. It helped to not be too aware of what he was doing or else risk the wish that confectionery should carry fewer calories, and its corollary, that he should eat less. Cakes were one thing, his dog, "Hamas", an English Jack Russell, another. The animal may have been no more than a benign energy locked to a weak soul, yet he and his family had come to love the pet in spite of the regime's ban on them. The subject was raised, if not actually thrown in his face, every time a colleague sought to contradict or disagree with him. It was unfair that the things he loved were, considered through the light of politics, liabilities, though none so serious as Golem's drinking and liberal tendencies. At least he was free of these contaminations, dog or no dog.

Jafari fanned himself like a peacock; the broken air conditioning had turned his chamber into a furnace. One by one his chins were beginning to stick together, disagreeable granules of sugar caught in their folds. From the tannoy he could hear the call to prayer, immediate and thrilling like a favourite record coming on at a party, or so Golem had once unadvisedly said. In fact, it was hard to think of Golem without remembering the vast mass of calculated insults wrapped up as tactless blunders (or was it the other way round, Jafari could never be sure) the Intelligence Chief sprinkled round, barely concealed by the good humour which hid an incondign and disobedient heart. For all that Jafari liked him, it was hard not to when there were so few people who could make him laugh. This warmth persisted even when Golem explained that the problem with Jafari, indeed with all ayatollahs, was that they had lost their healthy appreciation for eternity, confusing the idea for an institution, and becoming metaphysical bureaucrats in the process. If it were not for his cunning at second guessing the moves of his western counterparts and popularity amongst veterans in high places, Jafari included, Golem would have been fed to the theocrats long ago. Jafari was not sure that now Golem had the chance to save himself he would take it, hence the regrettable necessity of saddling him with Artay, to make sure that when the time came, Golem's instincts would not desert him. Jafari uncrossed his legs and toyed with the prospect of another bun. Espionage reminded him of a novel in which the writer knew what was coming and so did the reader, the pleasure lay in watching the characters be taken by surprise.

Jafari made a move towards his plate but a fly, having taken personally an earlier attempt to swat it, landed on the chosen morsel before his hand could, spoiling the cleric's sense of propriety. Ever since the worms on a dead goat moved from his father's yard to his mother's kitchen, Jafari had insisted on absolute fastidiousness in guarding his food from other animals, a matter not helped by the bluebottle squadron that gathered at his lodgings every mealtime.

Still, it could not be much better in the jungle for the Mahdi, surrounded by serpents, bats and leeches, he mused, a sensual life of banal suffering would be the least of that man's troubles. One bad turn deserved another, and the Mahdi was proving an ungrateful recipient of Iranian aid. His last proclamation, released a day earlier, had widened his attack from the usual suspects, America, the Zionists and the Shimban government, to include those co-religionist hypocrites who acted in the name of Allah for base interest. Though Jafari would like to think the

Mahdi meant the Saudi's, or perhaps Al Qaeda at a stretch, it was perfectly obvious that it was only a matter of time before the Iranian Revolution was denounced as another false God. That was always the way with ideologues, never content with only one set of enemies, they saw it as their purpose to cultivate an entire raft of them, the more potentially sympathetic to their cause the better. *Potentially sympathetic* was the key phrase here, as what Jafari knew of the Mahdi had not exactly made him want to rush to the jungle and declare his allegiance to the messenger. Was not one prophet enough and did not Islam already have a perfectly serviceable one? Religious truth had never been something contingent to every day events, far less unplanned ones that were still in the process of unravelling. Service to Allah, as he understood it, depended on obedience to an unchanging past, set in scripture, fixed meaning and an agreed-upon set of interpretations. No doubt this was why the upstart accused East and West alike of turning their backs on true faith. It had not escaped Jafari's notice that a historical process had played out in Iran, in which the regime's insistence on "textual fidelity" had the effect of explaining the need for religious revelation away, which was doubtless Allah's intention, even if it did make him somewhat unnecessary. The trouble was that the Godless metaphysicians in the West had done something structurally similar, first claiming that the Divinity was not needed as a first cause, then as a meaning giver, before removing him from public life altogether. Was manipulating his word in the service of realpolitick so very different...Jafari recoiled from an idea that might have had him instigate an Islamic renaissance, tearing, instead, into another bun. Heresies like this would herald the carnival of their decline, and no government in the world least of all his, needed help with that. Golem would do the right thing and if he did not, Artay would, and if he did not...Jafari smiled, well there was always Allah.

SOUTHERN BRITAIN

The Headmaster brushed the dust off an old photograph of him standing next to a man he had married the widow of, he was sure he would understand, and two others left to die on a hilltop in a botched helicopter rescue. What they thought of that, he would never know, though he hoped they would be most understanding too. That was the thing with the best photographs; the people in them were still looking at you, and would always do so. So long as one could remain in touching distance of oneself and not go mad it was worth having a few reminders of the past up, though not too many, an office was not a museum. With due care to not spill any ash, the Headmaster lowered his Rothman's on to an engraved steel plate, poured himself a quarter pint of Glenmorangie and tried to remember, word for word, what the Foreign Minister had said to him.

"It is the order of things, the will of everyone, but no one man." Incredible, the grovelling little bastard had actually had the brass balls to quote Tolstoy and pass it off as his own. The Minister had even mentioned God, which was embarrassing enough, as he no more believed in him than the policies he had been elected on.

'Must take me for a cunt,' snorted the Headmaster. The trouble was the Minister did, and not only him, but his predecessor and the minister before that. Whereas it had once been implied, then whispered, it was now screamingly obvious. The politicians could not have any less respect for him if he came out as a Libyan double agent with a phallic ring and lilac rinse.

The Headmaster turned on his chair, what was he if not an eagle led by pigeons? A shy conceit he would not have shared with the pigeons. Double talk, obfuscation, getting others to carry the can and outright lying were not new constructs, yet in the hands of the current government, they blazed with the force of true originality. Not only did the new breed have a knack for the dark arts, they were masters at masking their intentions, forcing him to follow their trail and run the last ten yards solo. Even now he struggled to decipher the true meaning of his conversation with the Minister, the space between "hello" and "goodbye" filled by a larval flow of semantic dross.

Army life had trained him to obey orders, not understand inferences. How exactly to take the legend, "well you could do that if you don't mind making the Americans unhappy…" So what if he did make them unhappy? It might be a desirable state of affairs, from the point of view of previous Labour administrations, however much the Vicar had wanted his Party to love the Cowboy. Still, he was not naïve. Without American support everything went to shit, that was the timeless law of diplomacy bequeathed by Suez, taught at Staff College and tacitly obeyed whenever a new operation was touted. So far, so realistic. What the Headmaster found staggering was his being asked to withdraw his men, so a Delta Force team could perform the same operation, transplanting American interests for British ones. If, of course, that really was what he was being asked. What he knew for sure was a major British Shimbite concern had become an Anglo-American one a week before and was now in the last stages of becoming an all-American one, "changing priorities on the ground", the Minister had said.

The Minister was clear on only two things: he wanted the team on the ground to know he was thinking of them and that he was losing sleep over their predicament. Well which way did he want it, insomnia or Alzheimer's, were they going to be hung out to dry or just quietly forgotten?

The Headmaster pulled open the drawer where the Glenmorangie lived and eyed it like an old friend who has seen the worst of one's dark corners. His life was an exercise in delaying doing the wrong thing. Today's mistakes led to tomorrow's inevitabilities, or, the Headmaster calculated, the wrong choice now meant that those who followed would have no choice when it came to their turn. They would simply have to bite the bullet and succumb to a fate already determined for them. As a conservative anarchist he knew that with anarchy came great responsibility, for oneself and for future conservative anarchists. Making the wrong call and then blaming someone else was not in his make-up, as a child he had even enjoyed owning up to things he had not done. His being forced to wash his hands of a mission he felt a rare passion for was an abomination too far.

The British Ambassador to Shimba was a man after his own heart. The diplomat was sacked earlier that day for having shared his conscience with the Guardian letters page and the Today Programme, accusing the African state of being a bog standard Kleptocracy, held together by state terror and Western aid. In other words ripe for Islamic (or was that Corporate?) takeover. The chap had not been too thrilled about an SAS team operating on his turf, especially as he had only found out through an intelligence leak. That was this morning, since then the information was public knowledge, the whole success of the operation compromised and the Americans presented with the perfect excuse to take over. Which is where he came in, to take the blame and bring the boys back home.

Picking up the bottle, the Headmaster slowly unscrewed the cap and poured a larger measure than before. It would only be a matter of time before the voices kicked in, errant thoughts confused for independent entities, memories and conjecture uniting in a boozy ball of confusion. So what? The Headmaster felt he had every right to be sad and untranquil in moments like this, his volition caught amidst currents of doubt and speculative hypotheses. Unlike the mad Mahdi he had no God to turn to for advice, life was simply for living and those that required transcendental guidance must find the living lacking. The Headmaster pulled up his blind and stared across the deserted parade ground. Looking carefully, he tried to detect signs of God but saw only a parade ground. He had no need of him, ideology or any of those other foreign imports, just another glass or two of the brown lady and bed. And in the morning he'd tell the Minister to go and fuck himself.

SHIMBA

'The Lord our God is one Lord; they who serve other gods, God shall judge.' It was one of the few holy lines he had committed to memory, most of the time he preferred to go where the word led him. One could only learn from journeys one did not know the end of; too much memory meant neat repetition, a sin against a world in flux. The Mahdi picked a bit of coconut out of his tooth and looked down, wondering how his lonely silhouette must look to those by the fire and makeshift shelters of the camp. The Lord of all he saw and commanded, is what he wanted them to see, though this was not the sole explanation as to why he clung to his lofty perch. Nightfall was precious and he had to get away from humans to understand it properly, to search the strips of blackening cloud for clues as to why he was chosen and others were not. Impatience was the essence of this particular night, the crack in the world was growing larger and in days his men would be in the capital. In weeks Tanzania, then Kenya, Africa, other Continents, the culmination of a journey through his life into all life, lay ahead, his enemies reduced to consenting bewilderment. The thought roared through his heart, first in stages, then all at once. This is how he had taught himself to think and how he wanted others to see him. His own thoughts, those that reflected mere life, and not the whole of reality, were of no concern. It was better to remain a puzzle to oneself and therefore a true instrument of God.

So instead of sleep he meditated over his destiny, a lingering fear that to live forever might be like insomnia weighing against his desire for everlasting consciousness. Immortality would bring him face to face with his slain foes; their unlived lives were his lived, their potentialities the soft dusks he was alive to appreciate, on earth and later in heaven. With a regal wave he released another prayer for their lame and base souls, limited by perspective and humanity. He would have to overcome both to be worthy of his destiny, one achieved through deeds, not prayer. The interception of a purely selfish prayer was one of the devil's best weapons, a trap for the unwary who confused having been created by Allah with favoured status.

The Mahdi laughed into the blending shades of purple that were gradually enveloping him. At the best of times his was not a face that could be seen at once, the various faces it consisted of did not look like they belonged to the same man or were the product of a single intelligence. It could inspire trust and its opposite at the same moment but what was never in question was its ability to inspire. If God were a sculptor the Mahdi was one of his more accomplished creations, generous enough to recognise his inventor's hand, though autonomous to the point of self-creation, a fact he was most uncomfortable with. For not even the Mahdi knew whether he was a fraud or prophet, a liar or being lied to. These evening hours were essential to refine the balance between insanity and divine guidance. If his destiny was a true one, he was none the wiser, for he was in it, and it was already taking place. There was no point outside fate that he could judge its truth from. All he could do was act. And as long as he acted, he believed; some ruled the world, others were the world. Whether his Iranian backers believed in him or not was a matter of the most delicious indifference. Hell would be full of the devout, Iranian or Shimban, men who believed in God without succeeding in pleasing him the way he had. And to think his enemies called him the mad one. The Mahdi laughed again, louder this time, the sound echoing back to him as the voice of his illustrious forbear:

Exalted is he who holds all control in his hands; who has power over all things; who created death; who created life to test you and reveal which of you performs best.

The Mahdi knew the answer to that one. Raising his head jubilantly, he lifted his rifle to the night sky, pointed at the evening star, and began his descent...in to more of his dreams.

'Can you hear me? Do you see my finger?'

The Doctor, a harassed-looking man kidnapped from a village clinic took his pulse, 'he is still alive?' asked General Strike, the sweat pouring down his knees and into his wellingtons.

'Yes, just feverish, he would not be muttering to himself if he were dead.'

'He is dreaming, he is experiencing more visions...it is Allah talking to him, that is what you hear,' said Strike hopefully.

'Maybe, or maybe delirious gibberish, I can only make out talk of sunsets and victories, I would not make too much of it if I were you.'

'His visions often come to him in a state of delirium...'

'I know all that. He has not moved from this bed in two days, that is the paramount fact so far as I'm concerned. And unless you allow me to take blood tests I cannot tell you what is wrong with him.'

'Impossible! He is the Mahdi, the messenger of Allah...'

'Yes, yes, I know all that too, but to me he is a very sick man, a patient who has been reduced to immobility, my guess is that he may be suffering from malaria, maybe even cholera, after the time he's spent in the jungle it could be either or both or something else, maybe even the first stages of a cancer, Aids...'

'Enough' Strike raised his hand in imitation of his master, bearing a greater resemblance to a lollipop lady than the great, great grandson of Muhammad. Ever since the Mahdi had been taken ill he had been charged with disguising his absence through a range of ever more ingenuous excuses and the widespread use of body doubles, one of whom was coming off the rock that overlooked the camp as he had done the past two nights. It was crucial that the army did not find out that their leader's latest round of fits, or visions of divinity to give them their proper name, had ended up in a severe vomiting session followed by a mild coma. For the moment the doubles were keeping up a successful pretence, but Strike knew it was only a matter of time before big mouths and prying eyes found him out and he would be forced to explain himself before the fractious coalition.

'The Mahdi cannot be operated on, or tested like a laboratory mouse. It is forbidden.'

'By whom?'

'You do not operate on a Prophet.' In truth, Strike, the meekest and also most loyal of the Mahdi's devotees, did not know who had first made up this prohibition, defying as it did common sense and the immediate facts. What he was positive of, or at least, hoped he was positive of, was that the Mahdi took this view himself, or would have if he were in possession of his senses. A year earlier, when on the run from Government troops, the Mahdi's party had come to a river, in open country, that they had to wade through. With the process underway the small group had come under sustained fire, taking heavy casualties. A bullet had scratched the Mahdi, hitting his earlobe and causing a globule of blood to burst forth. When safely across the other side an orderly had offered to dress the wound and the Mahdi had firmly rebuffed the man, telling him that a prophet relied on Allah for protection and not modern medicine. Strike was much taken by this, though it was worth considering that the scratch had not been very serious whereas this...this whatever it was, had every appearance of being life-threatening. And in the absences of War Boss and Amnesty, Strike was next in the chain of command, a thought that terrified him, as he knew no one would follow *him* into battle and the Army would surely fragment. He had, therefore, every interest in the Mahdi waking from his troubled and dreaming slumber, and regaining command of a void no one else was big enough to fill.

'The decision is yours, I am only a prisoner here.'

'He will get better,' replied Strike.

'Let me tell you this, and mark my words, if he is left in his own sweat to rant and rave without medical intervention he will die and it will be on your head, not mine, you understand me?'

Strike was about to let loose with some half-remembered invective worthy of his master when he noticed a slight stirring on the bed; the Mahdi had opened an eye and was beckoning. With his shaking hand, he bade his devoted servant to come to him. Strike leapt with joy, deliberately killing the urge to click his heels together and howl in a most irreligious way.

'Mahdi, Mahdi, what have you seen, what visions...'

The Mahdi put a feeble finger to his lips, drawing his disciple in closer, and held the back of his head next to his quivering mouth.

'What is it, what is it...'

'An aspirin you fool, my head is like a crocodile.'

The Doctor smiled in a way that might mean anything, and drew the confused Strike away from his patient.

'Go back to the army, I can take over here.'

Weakly Strike nodded his consent and watched his Master turn over on his side, ready to fall into the comforting embrace of another deep and eventful vision.

PART TWO

THE LIGHT POURS OUT OF ME

'The leaders of a revolution are usually those who have been able to profit from the cultural advantages of the system they are attacking.'
C.L.R James

CHAPTER SEVEN

Of hearts and minds

Elder could enjoy life again. He felt better without Beasley around. Not an appropriate response to a man who had saved his life more than once, one might think, certainly not a feeling he could justify in public, but true nonetheless. His grounds for relaxing in the man's absence reflected poorly on him, yet there was no doubt that his wit, walk, and sense of direction were all more assured without Beasley there. He made life too easy for Beasley by being emasculated by his criticisms, especially as his tendency to make mistakes in his company invited them. What he wanted the others to realise was that these errors occurred only when Beasley was on the scene, casting his Sergeant in the role of a heroic rescuer correcting the blunders of a chinless wonder.

'I think this is the crossroads Sir.'

'So it is.'

Of course, Elder could make mistakes on his own too, the kind everyone did, the kind that could be got away with or buried under a handful or two of bullshit. Not the kind he seemed to in front of Beasley, which would keep everyone talking until he was finally dishonourably discharged with no pension.

'Which way Sir?'

'Take the left fork. We want to stick to the tracks round the forest, not get into it yet.'

Elder scratched the loose skin off his sunburnt nose. The priority was to not bring attention to the type of officer he was afraid of becoming, one who had to *work* at it and not one who simply *knew* like Pagan. What struck him as pitiful was his ingratitude, would it really be better to rush into danger, or be saved from it by a wiseacre who sometimes got on his nerves? 'Better dead than saved by a smart arse' did not make for a good motto, yet in practice this is what Elder embraced. Beasley wanted to help so that he could show him up, or more subversively, have his job by showing the others he was incapable of doing it properly.

'Locals Sir, want me to try some small talk?'

Elder hated this way of thinking and recognised its absurdity, the entire paranoiac rationale constructed upon a partial truth, amplified by insecurities, kept alive by ineptitude.

'Sir?'

'Oh, I beg your pardon,' Elder blinked, 'you think they'll understand you?'

'Might pretend not to but they should be Swahili speakers,' replied Kingston, 'if not that, Shimbali.'

'Ask them which tribe they're in. Then say we're lost, separated from the aid agency and want to get away from the Mahdi's army. Say we want to go in the opposite direction from wherever they're coming. Make a pretence of being scared.'

'That won't require any acting,' chortled Hightower as Kingston got out of the jeep and took a few tentative steps towards the three men who had stopped collecting wood and were staring at Elder. At first their stare seemed like the curious outrage all Africans had once they had grown too old to smile and wave at cars. On closer inspection Elder saw something else, the kind of stare he got off workmen on rainy days back in England, one that said, 'how would you like to be me, doing what I do?'

Kingston, pulling his shawl down to accentuate his blackness repeated his questions in a way that might, were he not carrying a gun, pass for friendly, and waited. The men looked at each other, one of them nodded, and without further ado, all three ran into the undergrowth.

'Hearts and Minds' muttered Elder, 'hearts and bloody

minds.'

Kingston let his gun arm flop to his side, 'sorry Sir, I guess they didn't know what we fitted into and got scared.'

'No,' replied Elder, 'they knew very well. And unfortunately for us, so will everyone they tell.'

* * *

Golem was already wishing he had not joined Artay's early morning sermon. Even his new disciples had left their small circle as soon as it could be deemed polite, and aside from himself, only one other, a flat eyed boy muttering prayers to his gun, remained. It had been a long time since Golem had spent a night engaged in prayer, and he had found the experience edifying if inconclusive. Morning had brought the urge to seek out fellow believers, and in doing so, he was at once reminded why organised religion, or even being around anyone religious, had left his adolescent self cold. It was the middle part of his life, the *main* part, that he was having trouble understanding the point of.

'We are the last religion,' Artay solemnly intoned, 'the one that came to correct all others…'

'Oh come on' interrupted Golem, 'you're not even praying, you're not even *trying*. Any half-enlightened goatherd could repeat these platitudes.'

'You deny it?' In spite of his tiredness Artay's eyes blazed up, 'you have the nerve to question something so obvious?'

And in spite of *his* tiredness, and the injunction against talking to fools, Golem snapped back 'all the religions could only guess at the true identity of the Divinity and His commandments, from the pagans to ourselves. We thought we corrected Christianity, which thought it corrected Judaism, and we were all an improvement on the calf worshippers. And now science says it has corrected us. Put a time line on it, like you have, and a priest from the future will tell us we have all guessed incorrectly and what has yet to be revealed is larger than anything we think we know.'

'Are you mad? What are you talking about, this has nothing to do with religion, any religion, you are talking heresy, apostasy, not even an infidel, a maniac!'

'Think about what I'm saying and cool off in the river.'

'Stop!' Artay got to his feet and stamped them petulantly.

Golem did stop and though he did not feel in the slightest bit mad, had to admit that he was not exactly espousing orthodox religious cant either. Balancing theological duties with political ones was expected of every leading functionary, but this was not theology, more the kind of thinking aloud that led to a jail cell.

'Do you even understand what you're saying? It's atheist idle talk, I have a duty to report it,' Golem snarled, as though demonstrating how offended he was might give him the orthodox high ground.

'There is no defence!'

'I...what I'm showing you...' he was in double time again, the space between what he knew he should say and what he could actually hear his mind think, the point at which he was talking to himself whilst speaking to someone else, 'is a *point of view*, maybe you're too young to remember a time when that wasn't outrageous.'

'I tell you you're mad. Do you know what could happen to you if I report back?'

Artay had a point. Golem was not paying attention to the important dichotomy between the inside and outside, allowing what was inside his head out into a place where it could be observed and condemned. Bluffly, he rubbed his chin and tutted.

'They would laugh at you. Of course I don't believe in decadent secularist speculation, but if we fail to understand why people do, then we give our enemy the advantage over us...'

'What advantage?'

'The most deceptively simple thing in life, to see the world from behind the eyes of another. A feat well beyond you. It's what keeps us ahead of those who would destroy us.'

'I don't believe you.'

'Believe what you like, I have nothing to prove to you.'

Artay's ardour dimmed slightly. Continuing in the reassuring but disappointing state of being in one's right mind, Golem added, 'if you can't perform the simplest thought exercises you'll never be any use to the Republic, not unless the height of your ambition is rehashing banalities.'

'You confuse me, one minute you say one thing and then you say another.'

'Try and keep up.'

'So you don't deny that Allah is the one true God and Muhammad his messenger?' A puzzled look was developing round Artay's quivering mouth, and Golem took heart from it.

'Of course not, I want to help you and allow you to learn from me. They call it tough love.' Golem could see that part of the problem was that the sly intelligence he attributed to Artay did not exist. This was a boy he could manipulate in his sleep; his error was in treating him with too much respect.

Artay rubbed his eyes, this new information draining the life out of his voice, 'I, I didn't know what you were talking about...'

'Hey hey!' bowling towards them was General War Boss, virtually panting with excitement, 'our scouts have news, locals, a mile or two away, have seen a jeep with white men, soldiers!'

'Your people?'

'Government mercenaries, foreigners! They heard them speak English!'

'English, maybe American,' Golem turned to Artay, 'so we're not the only ones interested in Shimba.'

Clutching Golem by the shoulder War Boss took hold of his hand and thrust his automatic pistol into it, 'we must attack them, we have allies in the forest who are following them as I speak but you will lead the attack again, it will be your honour!'

'What does this have to do with our mission?' asked Artay worriedly, 'this is a distraction, surely.'

'It could have everything to do with our mission; if these men are who I think they are, we need them alive for questioning. If the Americans or their allies are here the importance of this country rises tenfold.'

Turning to War Boss who was shaking with impatience, Golem asked, 'how quickly can we move out?'

War Boss pointed to the column of gunmen rapidly forming around their one armoured car, 'now my friend, the morning rides behind us!'

Two miles away

They were two miles into the jungle when Francis, noticing a Vulture picking clean a human skull, threw a rock at it. Until then the route had been a mixture of the scenic and mildly unnerving. Crossing over a stream on a raft of rolling logs, doubling as a kind of pole-bridge, into lush trees that had once been a National Park, endowed their journey with a misleading tranquillity. This air of a jolly day out was checked almost immediately by the abandoned grass huts they encountered in the first of the small clearings, rotting donkeys and hastily flattened fires suggesting the war had got there before them.

'Refugees, they go further and further into the jungle to escape the fighting,' explained Francis uneasily, 'normally it would only be pygmies and animals living in the forest.'

'Look at the way the vultures can get in between the trees' said Beasley pointing to a pack that had collected over a carcass, 'I've never seen so many.'

Francis picked up a second rock to throw at the birds and paused. The shock was like a needle perforating an eardrum; he dropped the rock. It was a human skull, picked off a tidy pile gathered by his feet. The jungle floor was covered with them.

'My God.'

Beasley grasped his shoulder, steadying him.

'Relax, take a deep breath and relax mate.'

'You see?'

'Ssssh. Steady.'

'Thank you.'

The vultures carried on with their meal. A minute or two passed.

'By these marks I'd say this lot have been killed by hand, heads staved in by shovels...'

'They're everywhere.'

Like stars in the night sky, the more they looked the more they saw, the brush slowly converting into an irregular pattern of bones, shoes and faded strips of clothing.

'This place has been deliberately cornered off,' called Pagan from the far side of the clearing, his body trembling despite his best attempts to control it. 'Fuck.' He was standing over a cord of human intestines tied between two tree stumps, or at least, that was what the roll of gloopy translucence was when it had been part of a human body. Holding his nose he continued, 'this site has been used more than once. It's no spontaneously constructed village, this is where they bring people to massacre them, look, some of it is fresh.'

A man, still in uniform and for the most part in possession of his flesh, was tied to a post, a sick caricature of a May Pole, his nose and ears cut off and a deep gash in his arms which were tied behind his back. He had been left to bleed there, the rope long enough for him to dance round the pole to pass the time or to entertain an audience, for there were beer bottles and cans littered among the human remains.

'Something else you'd never see on safari' growled Beasley, his voice falsely monotone in his effort to control it, 'reminds you of how much your average undeclared murderer has to gain from war throwing out the rule book.'

Pagan had trained for this, prepared himself for what he would feel when he found it. For Pagan all dead bodies were dead and always had been, but for the other two humans, less rehearsed, there was still the memory of life and the once living in the contorted array of death they were surrounded by.

Beasley covered his mouth, 'don't want to swallow a fly here,' he mumbled, looking like that would at least give him the excuse he needed to pass out, 'what are those, kids?'

'No' replied Francis brushing the flies from his face, 'Pygmies. They must kill a few to guarantee the loyalty of the rest.'

'I wonder how close they are, the ones who did it all' said Pagan unlocking his rifle and walking round the perimeter. In the silence the clearing had become an unfinished graveyard in which the bodies had arrived before the headstones. 'I thought the tribes in this corner of the forest were famously peaceful, never heard of war.' He stopped to spit, with his handkerchief over his nose he sounded like Donald Duck, 'aren't your countrymen meant to respect their ancestral neutrality? This lot are mostly civilians.'

'Before the war this was a reserve, these people had no sides,' said Francis sanguinely. Despite the many mutilations, in their stillness the bodies did not look fully dead to him, only asleep, and his voice kept low as though he were afraid of waking them.

'Neutrality, another myth like the big pricks and perfect white teeth' said Beasley, taking care not to step on a corpse, its genitals noticeably absent, 'another one who's left the world of long term plans.'

'The teeth is the fault of sulphur, there is too much in the water, it sends the people's teeth brown, the "pricks" is not this man's fault, someone has taken his, or made a snack out of it.'

Beasley nearly smirked. Discovering that Francis's literalism was quietly subversive was not, however, enough to lighten their surroundings. The route out was narrow and cramped, bushy heads burnt into little black clumps, legs piled in spiral heaps, the odd arm poking out from behind a leaf, a gross assortment of the completely disembowelled and only half there. Nothing except the farm tools used to perform this operation maintained any semblance of regularity, the soiled implements piled neatly in a pyramid opposite the May Pole.

'Context Francis' said Pagan, wary of being angry with the only African present to be angry with, the long-term causes for this carnage a feeble abstraction so close to so much blood, 'give me some context. These people were killed by your government, a dose of tribal torture and the modern kind serving as an example to those who help the Mahdi, is that it? Or killed by the Mahdi to teach the old forest gods a lesson, that his deity is king now? Then again, it might be neither of the above, is there someone else we need to watch out for...that banner, hung in the tree, what's it say?'

Francis pulled the cloth off the hanging body it was wrapped round without much fuss: unlike the Europeans he was determined now to keep his feelings to himself.

'What does it say?'

"Our lives end in the light", it is an evangelical slogan used in the missionary schools, since I was little.'

'You think the Mahdi's men instigated a religious massacre here, against Christians? I thought these unfortunates were forest pagans?'

"Our lives end in the light", snorted Beasley, 'that's cute, all life ends in failure and it ends in failure because you die, die, you don't even have to get killed like these poor bastards. And their children, there's no need.'

'Over here, these two, they're moving.'

Under the tree were an unclothed boy and girl, lying on their backs and holding hands. Though their bodies appeared dead, their eyes were still seeing, a drifting consciousness having outlasted their wounds and however many nights of exposure. Both faces mirrored the reality of a make-believe game gone wrong, each wishing to be reassured it was all pretend, that it was time to stop and go back to real life. Pagan could not have agreed more. The game had got out of hand and exceeded its limits or, for the first time, revealed its true nature, that it was not a game at all.

'Shit, shit. What to do for these two.'

The corners of Francis's mouth turned downwards. Pagan could not tell whether he was going to cry or was just disappointed that outsiders should see this, Shimba and secularism let down by barbarism. Beasley had reached the kinder conclusion and putting his arm on Francis's shoulder said, 'you shouldn't mind mate; it's not your fault. But I don't think we can do much here. Bless them, it was probably their keeping each other company that got them this far. Her leg's all gone, and his other hand, look at it for fuck's sake. Or don't.'

Recognising himself as the subject of their conversation, the boy opened his mouth and emitted an airless whisper. Silently gurgling, he closed his eyes, the effort of dying too much for him.

'Nothing we can do except ring the imaginary helicopter to take them to the imaginary hospital where the imaginary doctors will love him back to life. Or leave him as he is for the jackals to rip apart,' said Pagan. 'The first sip of water would probably kill them, they're covered in holes.'

Beasley and Francis turned the other way. The violence in the clearing had touched the surrounding trees, their overground roots twisted, as if they too had wanted to turn their backs. 'Devastation's all part of nature. Look at the jungle, a bloody mess long before we turned up. You've your work cut out civilising this place.'

'The "civilisation" will come,' said Francis softly, 'with the money. Your countries will change ours, capitalism is the organised face of the state of nature, our President's words. If you believe it.'

'Good for you if you can't,' said Beasley, 'good for you...look at what happened to us.' A shot rang out followed by another, the pause long enough for Beasley to wonder what went through Pagan's mind in the narrow gap before he fired the second, 'boom and busts, we've just had another one, only consolation was that though the rich were dragging us down, they'd at least feel our pain for a change, instead we've been asked to feel theirs. It's a fucker of a world.' Behind him he could sense Pagan's impatience with words, the way in which they could soothe and smooth the raw horror of what was. Beasley knew his commander was a man of hard-earned and passionate hatreds, feigning cynical misanthropy as it was easier than hating; hating being too much like caring. There were times when this had been true of Beasley too. Killing people provided the perfect excuse for angst; no one at home knowing how what they were going through dignified their exclusion, and exposure to death freed them from the requirement to be happy. The task of Special Forces was to serve the dim-witted, well-adjusted and easily-pleased, those who did not believe suffering existed unless they saw it, and often not even then. Beasley did not mind getting between the civilians and the dark matter reality actually consisted of. That was why there were only wavering moments in which he wobbled and why, unlike Pagan, he still cared.

'We off then Sir?'

Pagan had turned a dull grey, his back bent and hands resting on his knees like a geriatric gardener. Beasley hoped he was not about to throw up, 'looks like you've swallowed one of those flies Sir. What say we leave the unhappy land of "this never happened" and continue on our way?'

'You know Beasley,' Pagan intoned glassily, 'and don't even think of rolling your eyes,' he added, 'everyone I've killed has, in a way, killed me too.'

'I can accept that Sir. In fact, a pleasant surprise to hear it I might say.'

'Alright' Pagan nodded, 'that's your fabulous fact for the

fucking day, let's go.'

Hesitantly the three men headed on, a rumble of thunder ahead providing a welcome distraction from all they did not wish to look back on.

Three miles further in jungle

Nelson regarded the world as little better than his own worst failings. Trust, or letting one's guard down, was a death sentence, particularly in regard to females. He did not believe anything any of them said, which was no great hardship as they had little to say to him: little that was nice anyway. Men were hardly better, though in their case, having never wanted to trust one, their hostility came as no loss. Dimly Nelson guessed that if he were to enjoy the benefits of a willing female, trust, even if it were just the belief that he would not be laughed at, was necessary. More imperatively, some measure of trust was required just to get to know a female, to talk, and to not scare or repel her through a mere greeting. And there was the crux. He did not know any females, had never really *known* any, meaning there had never been anyone to safely try "trust" out on. All attempts at sociability usually floundered with the defensive posture women adopted when he came close and tried to make their acquaintance. At moments like this he did not know what came over him, frustration at the very least. Matters would quickly graduate from introducing himself to a drink being thrown over his face and, on one occasion, the use of pepper spray. From there on in it was a case of running down back alleys to avoid the rough intervention of chivalrous bystanders, all thoughts of a little romance torpedoed hellwards.

It did not help that there was no one to talk to about relationships, the curse he carried for being the morning star of a trustless universe. Nor was there the consolation of prostitutes or Internet pornography. One bad experience with an elderly streetwalker had left him impotent in all future encounters, an affliction he had taken out in a spate of stabbings on pimps in the Ipswich area. As for the World Wide Web, he did not know how to use computers, his cousin taking care of the technical aspects of their operation. Admittedly he could have asked her to help him, though experience had taught him to be wary. Tawny, who admittedly did not count as a female, not even by her own lights, laughed if he expressed sentiments that fell on the tender side of severity, especially inquiries pertaining to females. On the one occasion in which she heard him out, she narrowed her eyes and blew a raspberry,

'Where do you get off boy? You've got the whole of bleedin' Africa and God knows where else to score, a gun and a war chest of TNT, experiences your ordinary beer boys would swap theirs for, so where you get off? You get off on complaining! All 'cos the gal at the bus stop back home won't take your dick out and call it Percy! And I'm not bloody surprised she don't. Losers the world over would die for your breaks, live like you. Trouble is, you don't get it. You want to be loved for yourself, who you really are, don't you diddums? Well I can tell you what you are, you're an ugly evil-looking bastard, and even I wouldn't do you. So why the fuck would Sharon Davies or Sue Barker? No one's ever going to want to fuck you and no one ever will! Not unless you made 'em. Deal with it.'

Nelson had been so upset that he threw pride aside and pleaded, encouraging Tawny to dig her heels in even further, 'not even if you won the lottery boy, not even then!'

That summed up his cousin and as for his Uncle, well, Nelson shuddered, if he breathed word of such concerns to him, he would in all probability have his neck broken on the spot. There would be no help; Nelson was on his own and had always known himself to be. He may have admired their resourcefulness and pluck, but when it came to love, his family played out their parts with the tenderness of a pack of bull sharks.

He yawned, tired but not sleepy, there was no place small

enough for him to curl up and vanish. Loosening the larger, perhaps cancerous, of his testicles from his thigh, Nelson rolled over on to his aching back and opened a bloodshot eye. The others had yet to wake and aside from his uncle, who was breaking wind like a torn dingy, the jungle was quiet, the morning light bleeding into an emergent bird song, distinct, polytonal and widening.

Even now memories would not stop talking, the type that those who sleep never hear. Except that this time the repetitious ticking over was forcing a breakthrough of a kind, what he believed others referred to as progress. Whatever acts of ordinary kindness he experimented with had always been interpreted as the creepy overtures of one who intended harm, and in that sat the clue. For if he was honest, he did mean harm, in a manner. It was not enough (how could it be for anyone?) to simply meet a female, then allow her to go free, to bugger off and leave it to her whether she came back or not. What if she chose not to, thought better of it or more likely, never thought of him again? In a world predicated on distrust it was an insane risk to take, particularly when one fell beneath and before a female's contempt. In a roundabout way he had to admit that he was not blameless, that there *was* something unwholesome about his fantasies, more often involving wenches chained and caged in his cellar, than holding hands and kissing on a romantic walk. Were they wrong, then, to conclude contact with him was charged with risk?

None of which put him in a strong position with Foy, who though captured, was far from captivated. It had been he who had first spotted her in the café, neither Tawny or his father had the first idea of what kind of girl a raging Warlord with the horn would go for, pointing to measly specimens guaranteed to disappoint the Mahdi on delivery. The trouble was the "Tatler" crowd did not take their holidays in Shimba, preferring to sun their legs in St Tropez. In the circumstances Foy was a gift from the Gods.

Since the abduction he had not stopped thinking about her, which was not difficult, as he had not stopped looking at her, a realistic attitude to take towards a prisoner he reasoned. At that moment he could make out the outline of her bottom, barely a foot away, wrapped up in her bag, her beautiful femaleness tantalisingly close to his need...

Realism was part of the problem here, for Nelson had encountered too much of it to believe he could take Foy willingly, even in his dreams he could not enter her without falling out, her screwed up face screaming for help. So even in fantasy he had to face facts and admit the necessity of coercion, opting out of the ordinary rules, and rape. The rules were okay for good-looking blokes who could get what they wanted simply by asking, the ones females enjoyed being harassed and hassled by. For Nelson though, obedience to a moral code meant he would never make Foy Fox-Harris his in the only way that mattered. There would never be a better opening. The Mahdi had not specified wanting a virgin, which he was certain Foy was not in any case, but he would have to do it right. Since for reasons he could not assent to, his uncle had decided that there should not be any "fiddling with the goods" after what happened to the first girl they had nabbed...

Perhaps Nelson would have derived some grudging satisfaction in knowing Foy was very much awake too, her thoughts no less urgent than his. From the time of her capture sleep, normally a state she could rely upon after half past ten at night, was elusive. Her favoured trick for nodding off, on those rare occasions when she could not, was to turn her thoughts inwards, toward warm places and heartfelt memories. The total denial of her immediate environment this now entailed struck her as dangerously escapist. So her musings were redirected outwards to her situation, and what ruthlessly practical solution could resolve it. The novelty of having to think in this way was unexpectedly invigorating, the thought of escape literally electric, her toes springing to attention and breasts hardening in anticipation of doing something dangerous. To remain passive and let events unravel of their own accord was the same as allowing oneself to drown, that she was certain of. Foy licked her lips, she did not know how far away from the Mahdi they were, no more than another morning's walk, which left her with scant time. Shimba was not the Congo, no journey need take more than four days and they had already been walking for two. This meant that if she headed in the right direction getting back was distinctly possible. Of course, there was no guarantee of a friendly welcome, but what could be worse than the Websters, and the fate they had in store for her? Life was offering her the chance try out a new personality, the daring escapee, the question was how to do it, what, in this position of apparent helplessness, was her great strength? And here the darkness set in because it was perfectly clear to her that she possessed only one advantage, her physical attractiveness to Nelson, who had yet to take his eyes off her, and Tawny, not that the latter was as aware of it as Foy. Both these monsters were susceptible to being led off to one side, sexually distracted, and punished for it, as neither thought Foy capable of violent action. Nor had Foy until she felt her life at stake. With no hope of ever sleeping in her own bed again, she would try anything, even bounding down a jungle path on her own without so much as a compass. Bitterly she smiled; she had fooled them by keeping something in reserve she did not know she had. The question was which of the two Websters to select, without the other knowing. Or to put it more crudely, would she rather bite off Nelson's cock or Tawny's tongue, because there was no way she was going to get away from them with her innocence intact.

The choice was mercifully made for her right there and then and not in a way she was expecting.

Nelson had entered that trip zone where effect overtakes cause, actions appear to precede the decision to take them, and a degenerate can find himself in the middle of doing something he did not know he had begun. Nelson was no longer in his sleeping bag but walking, walking towards Foy as well as his erection would allow him to. If he could do it before he knew it was happening it would be okay, if he could do it before *she* knew it was happening it would be okay, these were the mental spurs for this first, highly unconventional, date.

'You're coming with me', he hissed, brusquely lifting her by the arm and stuffing a (remarkably clean) sock in her mouth, 'can't, can't take it', and then, more strangely, 'we need to be together. Can't go on like this. You know it.'

Foy knew that he did not refer to the circumstances of her captivity, knew by the semi bulge in his trousers as he held her to him, lost in the reverie of having got this close to her at last, that this was it. It hung for her by a hair. The brute was not going to do anything here, he needed to get her as far from his family as she secretly wished him to go, all she had to do was to let him make the running. This she surmised in a second, her detachment and calm calculation coming as a surprise.

Roughly Nelson pushed her through the undergrowth, stopping a couple of times to consider a place, recognising that no part of the jungle floor doubled as a bed on close inspection,

'Fuck it, bend over that there' Nelson pointed to an uprooted old tree, 'quickly' he muttered tearing at his zip, 'you just be nice, you hear?'

'It's not very private...'

'Shut it, bend.'

If it went wrong she was twice the loser, violated by this detestable skinhead and still a prisoner of the Websters. *Act, Foy, act, look back one day and wretch but act...*

Turning against his grip she touched his cheek, 'you know a boy like you doesn't have to do it this way.'

'You what?' Nelson appeared stung, her soft reproach taken as a blow.

'You're too handsome, too good for this. We can do better than this…' she dropped to her knees, level with his crotch, which even from the safe side of his fatigues, was soaking.

Nelson suddenly looked embarrassed, his head darting back and forth as if to make sure they weren't being spied on.

'What you doing?'

'Sssh silly…'

Boldly Foy pulled down his shorts and took it all in. There was no need to act the seductress now she was in charge, only to overcome the urge to be squeamish, a denouement that would hand the initiative back to her attacker. Matter of factly she got at his penis and put it in her mouth; it was cold and hard and fast disappearing. Taken with his testicles Nelson's genitals resembled a shrunken bag of plaster cast lumps, the smell no worse than his breath on her neck.

'What you doing…' he repeated dumbly, incomprehension a mask to disguise his shame. A consensual blowjob was not a sex act he was accustomed to, or to his growing horror, aroused by.

For Foy too the trouble was there was nothing to get between her teeth, or from Nelson's point of view nothing of him to suck, her willingness to take the bull by the horns a greater shock to the predator than prey. Glancing up she saw his reddening face poised between trying harder and giving up altogether. If he went with the latter, she guessed, he would beat her to death by way of compensation. Her guardian angel, sounding a little like a cheering parent at a Lacrosse match, was demanding that she be audacious.

'Get out of it'. Nelson grabbed a handful of hair, hard, 'you doin' it all wrong.'

She held the thunder, now to scatter the bolts. Taking the whole loathsome package, balls scrotum and all, Foy bit down, jerking her head down like a tigress tearing at a carcass, not letting go until she was sure her mouthful of him was unattached.

And then she sprang up and ran, into the jungle and away from the memory, Nelson's dying screams, starting before she did or so she felt, following close behind her bare calloused heels.

'What in the name of hell is that?' yawned Webster, 'I'm tellin' you, I'm getting too old for this lark, feelin' all blisters and bruises...God, say it ain't so...'

Tawny turned to him grimly; her rifle already slung over her back, 'ain't no dying ostrich, that'll be Nelson's hollerin'. Our bird's flown.'

'Flown and damn certain unplucked, damn!' Websters face had coarsened into a burning brick wall, his jowls swelling dangerously, 'let's be getting her back girl, back an' in shackles.'

All Nelson could think of was what a mistake it was to have trusted the bitch, he'd have cursed life too, but the pain was so bad that dying might be a merciful release and he expected that God had little use for ungrateful bastards in heaven. Spinning on the balls of his feet he hopped a few paces and then fell, his legs kicking ludicrously at the ground, the hurting too great to do anything about.

'Nelson, Nelson you div, which way did she take off?'

It was his cousin, towering over him like a crane and wrecking ball, 'which way? Point if you can't speak.'

Not only could he not speak, he could not point, this in spite of every part of his body wobbling every which way, involuntary jerkings better than lying still and pretending nothing was happening.

'Naaah,' he heard his uncle's voice, 'he's gone, a fuckin' embarrassment.' And there it was, his soul either sucked towards the light, or rapidly rolling downhill towards the darkness, fast, much too fast, for him to tell.

CHAPTER EIGHT

Picture this

Elder did not know if he was reacting to a situation or responsible for it. What was beyond any doubt was his responsibility for thirty more men than he left Pagan with, extra numbers a more ruthless officer may have done something drastic to reduce. Not Justin Elder: he had allowed the men to join him, sensing a rare opportunity to turn disaster to his advantage. Out of nowhere, or so it seemed, three Government tanks had rolled out of the forest, blocking the drove-way his small group were proceeding along. To their embarrassment, even allowing for the terrible clanking these machines made, the SAS men were unprepared for their arrival. Elder guessed that if the newcomers had been with the Mahdi, it was not at all certain who would be dead. With red faces they watched the old Russian T-62's limber forward from the one good road leading out of the jungle, Islamic militia-men tied to the bows and gun carriages to protect the crews from surprise attack. Behind them poured a pack of stragglers, alarmed looking and glancing behind their backs for marauding ghosts or worse. The obvious answer to this intrusion was to accelerate away, but Elder paused long enough for the leading tank commander to interpret the situation creatively. To these hunted men, the lone jeep was a sign of better things to come. Excitedly the commander, in giant aviator shades and a tweed cap, leapt from his turret, sweat steaming off his shoulders in wet puffs.

'Thank God you've come.'

Elder, who wished he had not been listening so carefully to Kingston and Hightower's debate on the merits of digital versus vinyl, hoped the man could not sense his tension. With no mobile or radio contact, all lost in the jeep on the bridge, they were as good as naked.

'I beg your pardon?'

'You have arrived!'

'So we have.' At least the character was friendly, or ready to pretend to be, if somewhat spooked.

'You have no idea what we have gone through to get here. I am glad we found you, the President said help would come, and you have come.'

As a rule Elder enjoyed making people happy, sometimes indulging in a white lie to do it; this would not do today, 'I think you're making a mistake, we're not the UN you know.'

'It doesn't matter' said the man gripping his arm, 'the Mahdi, the jungle is full of his men, they are coming after us, you have to help.'

'I'm afraid we have business of our own here.'

'We have his nephew with us' said the tank commander, ignoring Elder's protest, 'there' he pointed to a youth strapped to the front of his tank, 'he has kept us alive but he is also the reason the Mahdi is coming, with many men. How many more are there with you?'

'I've already told you...' Elder stopped, an idea rising from this farcical mess, providing he could turn the chaos to his advantage.

'You say he's after you, your column, scouting and tracking you, yes?'

'Yes! Yes I tell you, for two days now, we've had to abandon our jungle fort at Simba Simba and run for our lives, there were thousands attacking us, we'd have died if we stayed. They kill everyone who won't join them. Our orders were to abandon the post if we were attacked, I tell you, it's the truth. Many were slaughtered.'

Elder looked at the sunglasses, slipping down the man's

perspiring nose, in to the contracting eyes. It was a novel experience, believing an African, something he had not been able to do whilst listening to the Chief of Police brief them on terrorist statistics, or the urchin who offered him a "fair price" for an air conditioning unit. He was not so self-righteous as to dismiss his own role in this failure of trust, ready to blame his residual racism if need be. It was this prejudice that told him this man was no decoy, double agent or deserter, rather, in fear for his life and in earnest.

'Where were you heading for?'

'Anywhere! To get away.'

'Look, we can help you, but not yet, you have to bear with us, trust me.'

The man let go of Elder's arm and nodded gratefully. 'We must go at once though, right now!'

It was sad that at the very moment Elder acknowledged the man's sincerity it fell to him to become the liar, 'the thing is, we're rendezvousing with the rest of our special response team, we're British as you may have guessed. They won't get here for another hour or so and we've said we'd meet them at this actual spot…so we have to stay here, just for a short while, until they get here.'

'We can't, haven't you heard me right, I told you, the Militia are following us, they could be here any time, we must go.'

'I know, I realise that, though you see, from our point of view, we have a plan and we have to stick with it, we can't go tearing off because of what's happened to you, with due respect.'

The Tank Commander, still visibly scared, looked round at the jungle he had come from with difficulty, and, holding his nerve, muttered, 'so as soon as your men get here we go?'

'Of course, to the nearest town to regroup and take stock, there'll be plenty of water there, supplies, new clothes, all that, the charities are leaving everything behind. So really the best thing to do now is proceed to that hillock there,' Elder pointed to a small bump off the drove-way, 'and form a defensive corral we can hold in case of attack. But all things being equal, I don't think it will come to that, our friends won't take long and as you know, the British are never late.'

'Nor is the Mahdi,' said the commander, clearly unhappy with the situation yet ready to accept any compromise short of going on alone, 'you say your friends will come with helicopters? I have nearly run out of fuel. Our tanks have only a mile or two left in them before they stop.'

'Yes' said Elder, knowing perfectly well that he had not mentioned helicopters and that Pagan would not arrive in one even if he had, 'bound to. We've an entire strike force actually.' Whoever showed up, the bluff was worth it, what surer way could there be to bring the Mahdi to them than by dangling bait?

The Commander, satisfied he was not being humoured, stepped off the jeep and ran back to his tank, his driver daring to poke his head out of the cockpit and offer the SAS men a tentative thumbs up.

'Let's hope the Mahdi shows up before the cavalry don't,' said Kingston returning the greeting.

Hightower cleared his throat and tapped Elder's leg with a respectful wink, 'unconventional Sir, but a black cat's as good as white one if it catches the same mouse.'

'Quite,' Elder replied, 'now let's get ready to face the music.'

Far from scoffing at the cliché, Hightower adopted a stern martial expression, as though he knew what was expected of him, 'me and Kingston will fix a perimeter; judging by the look of this lot it's hard to know where they end and the Mahdi's gang will start.'

It was true, Elder observed, there did not seem to be any cut off point in the people coming out of the jungle. A steady trickle of life was still issuing forth, men and women nervously checking the open country, in two minds as to whether it was safer than the jungle they were fleeing, breaking in small groups. Their urgency was further proof that what lay behind them was nothing a sane person would hang around for. It had been a long time since Elder had thought of himself as one of those, and vicariously, he enjoyed the way a perverse calm took hold of him in obverse proportion to the panic he was surrounded by.

'Here' it was the Tank Commander again, a half dressed unfortunate dragged behind him, 'take this, the one the Mahdi wants, his nephew Samuel, I'll get my men to tie him to your bonnet. We will all need a little insurance if we have to run again, helicopters or no helicopters.'

The hastily-formed band of brothers had not got far with their defensive corral before they were attacked. Unlike most of the attacks they were used to this one did not start with tracer fire, smoke grenades or noise of any kind at all. It was so subtle that Kingston and Hightower responded to an attack that had not happened, and were slow to recognise the actual one when it had. Elder also, was deep in conversation with his new friends, imploring them not to bind the ropes that bound the Mahdi's nephew to his jeep too tightly. To refuse their offer outright struck him as rude, whilst accepting it was absurd. With the boy screaming that the metal bonnet was burning his bare back, Elder had no time to notice the Commander hanging in suspended animation off his turret, a tiny dart lodged in his neck.

'The only black people I've seen as miserable as this,' said Kingston, 'were catching a bus from Basingstoke to Aldershot.' The trickle of people fleeing the forest had become a stream and was now, once again, slowing to a trickle.

'Not a cheerful bunch, that's for sure, here' Hightower pulled a bottle of water out of his pack and threw it at a sullen-looking boy hiding behind a tree, 'take it' he said, his encouragement sounding horribly like an order. The boy looked at the bottle lying at his feet, looked back at Hightower and disappeared into the jungle.

'Hey, you're going the wrong way stupid,' shouted Hightower, a note of hurt in his voice, 'don't know what the matter with this lot is, in Iraq you only had to throw one of these off a lorry to start a fight, guaranteed, broke up many a dull journey.'

'Well done for helping us lose another war Hightower. Hey!' Kingston fired a shot into a bush, 'in there, a gunman!'

Not waiting for the Mahdi and his militia to descend for certainty's sake, Hightower flung a grenade in the direction Kingston had pointed, a sharp explosion and scream revealing nothing more dangerous than an elderly man, his arm hanging off a small bag of belongings, the rest of him shredded over the grass.

'Fuck...how did he get there?'

'Probably hiding.'

'So are they attacking?'

'Who's they?'

'Whichever of this lot wants to do us.'

'I can't tell the bottom from the top.'

'There's no point hanging on here, it's indefensible. Won't be us doing the creeping up, it'll be them. Let's get back to the jeep, box ourselves in so we can see what's coming.'

Hightower nodded, too benumbed to blame Kingston for his mistake.

'Wait.'

'What?'

'Did you hear that?'

'No...yes, shit, yes...'

One kind of noise, the retreating and scrambled chatter of the refugees and Government men, had switched to another kind, deeper, deliberate and incoming, like a weapon.

'Fuck me, it's a kind of chant, chanting. Isn't it?'

'Prayers' said Kingston, 'they're reciting prayers.' There was no one running out of the jungle now, the people had vanished leaving a new presence decidedly more unnerving for not being seen.

'I hate hearing, just listening. It's the arsehole. Don't,' Kingston held Hightower's arm, 'no point firing or throwing anything else in there. Fact is, they can see us and there's no point looking any more scared than we are, oh man.'

Straining their eyes to look at the jungle, neither noticed that the Government soldiers behind them were falling faster than they could run, darts flying out of the jungle, over their heads and into the backs of their fleeing allies.

Kingston did not see the one that killed him. Elder did, and who was responsible for it. Stepping out from the base of an enormous canopy tree, a small figure reloaded his pipe and aimed again, this time at Hightower.

'Joseph bloody Conrad this,' said Elder, struggling to believe the reality of what he saw. The jungle had been transformed into a single catapult; volley after volley of poisoned darts landing with silent thwacks against military hardware designed to repel bullets, the only noise the abrupt groan of uncomprehending victims. The pre-battle prayer had stopped and, though the attack was proceeding quietly, Elder could hear orders being barked in a way that at least established their foe as sentient. Well, there was no point in waiting for them to surrender. Releasing the safety catch, he raised his rifle at the squatting figure, held his breath, and shot the man down.

'I've just saved your life Hightower,' he muttered, and repeated the action aiming and ending the life of another figure in a scarlet shawl (of all things) that had taken the first one's place. The top of the trees appeared to be moving and what looked to be falling coconuts were landing on the soldiers still at the forest edge. In them Elder saw more danger and, contrary to his deeply held belief that fruit was not dangerous, turned his fire at the next one he saw drop. To his amazement the bundle opened on impact with his bullet and, on hitting the ground, metamorphosed into a dead man, albeit a short one.

'Killer Pigmies?' Elder nearly laughed, but did not have time to, the Mahdi's cousin had loosened a wrist free from the bonnet and was making a play for his leg in an attempt to unbalance him. Elder brought his rifle down against the boy's shoulder joint, a satisfying crack bringing the immediate threat to a halt. Turning the gun the correct way round Elder began to fire indiscriminately at everything in front of him; the odds were appallingly uneven, how the hell could he even have thought he could have spotted, far less captured the Mahdi in the centre of this? It was a mistake to think of what he should have done, with events happening so fast, a mistake to think at all, he was still alive, if he kept adapting, kept ahead, something would turn up…

Hightower, reluctantly leaving Kingston for dead, was in the process of snapping the neck of the midget who had landed on his back like an unwanted pterodactyl dropping, the ordinary rules of engagement left elsewhere. Tiring of the small one's scratches and bites, Hightower finished his attacker with a violent tug of the head and threw the still sweating body off his legs. What he saw next did not look like much of an improvement; in fact, he registered it as more of a let-down. From all sides raging forest pygmies, dressed in baggy Shalwar Kameezes, presumably a gift from kind extremist donors, were charging out of the undergrowth with harmful intent in mind. The circus aspect of the experience was matched by its lethality, the Government crews panicking and throwing the prisoners off their tanks, crushing them in their spinning tracks as they reversed in circles.

Elder felt exposed from top to bottom. Hightower had disappeared under a swarm of tiny bodies leaving him as the last man standing. The hillock he had intended to defend was not even comparatively safe and he guessed that if he were not already surrounded he soon would be. There was not even a wall to make his last stand against or comrade to fight back to back with. Scores of men lay dead on the ground, so many more than seemed alive moments earlier. A burning arrow struck his buttock, sticking out ludicrously at an angle, just beyond easy reach. Maybe the reinforcements would come after all, how could he be sure he lied about them? A second arrow scraped the top of his ear, his flesh naked under the cut. Everyone who was not killed or being killed seemed to be attacking him, and with his command reduced to Hightower, who was lost underneath a pile of machete-wielding bodies, Elder decided it was time to get out.

There was, of course, nowhere to go now, Elder's last volley into the advancing natives making no discernable difference to their numbers or ferocity. Admittedly there was no time to count, and with one hand firing wildly, Elder snapped the burning arrow off his bottom, the humiliation of literally having his arse burnt checked for the moment. No sooner had he disposed of the arrow, than another one bounced off his dashboard and a third hit his calf, stopped by his boot. At last a feeling close to fear, not blind and uncontrollable, though close and near to it, set in, and his hands started to shake. Nothing is inevitable until it has happened, Elder repeated like a mantra, the voice in his head accelerating to a hysterical speed. An empty clicking signalled his magazine needed replacing and like a penalty he could see scored, before taking the kick, Elder found he was losing hope. The supposedly peace-loving pygmies, herded up by their militia handlers, had nothing else to do except come for him, he was the only one left. The key to the jeep was still in the ignition, it was not impossible to try and drive through them. No, he would be pulled out and hacked to death. There was still his pistol, a bullet with his own name on it? No, that would not do, Elder would rather be tortured to death or face the shame of becoming a hostage, suicide was out of the question. And what of the Mahdi's nephew, lying unconscious on the bonnet? If he was to blow the lad's head off the pygmies would definitely kill him, he did not have the guts for it, capture was fast becoming the light at the end of the tunnel, alive he was worth something to them, damn the reputation of the Regiment and HMG.

Instinctively he flung the rifle over his shoulder and held his hands in the air, the first time he had done so in his military career. They were all around him; he was safe, safe in a perfectly calm, blind terror. He closed his eyes and saw himself driving straight into a clean white wall and experiencing the most beautiful impact, the worst over, and the best too.

He did not feel the rope slung round his throat, or hear the jeers, as hand after small hand grabbed his clothing, tearing at his lips and eyes and hair until a voice in Persian asked them to stop.

* * *

Had the animistic spirits of the forest spied Foy's spirited charge away from the dying Nelson, they may have thought she was one of them, a white gazelle with two legs burning through the moisture. Foy was in the zone, ready to run until she decided to stop. Considerations of tiredness, sore feet and contracting lungs were an irrelevance. Sprinting was always her way of working off depressions at school, and the shrieks of the Websters were fast replaced by the disciplined thump of her heart. She was aware that she was not running in a straight line, unintentionally criss-crossing onto paths that were already cleared, therefore increasing the chances of being found, but the exhilaration of being free again overruled any thought of tactics. Besides, the second worst thing to captivity was being lost and at least she could now see signs of humanity, a put-out fire and stacks of kindling bunched between the Wattle trees. The deceptively pretty creepers of a water hyacinth suggested a river, boats and other means of escape. The chances were the locals would be curious if not friendly, and as there was no way she could sprint back to Surrey on her own, there was no point in delaying the moment of contact.

Entering the edges of the temporary habitation, Foy stumbled straight into Artay who had loosened his trousers and begun a much-needed urination. Of the two he was easily the more surprised, Foy having inured herself to the unforeseen by now. Her first thought, as the startled Iranian moved to cover his crinkling member, was that she had run into Nelson again, albeit a reincarnated and brown version of the original. Almost at once she felt ashamed to have made the link. Artay's expression of sophomoric shock had given way to one of protective (or was that corrective?) propriety. It made Foy wonder what, after biting a man's penis off and running bare foot through the jungle, a girl must look like, intimidating she hoped, and a bit ghastly too. Trying almost too hard to avert his eyes, with exaggerated courtesy or dismay, Foy was not sure, Artay hauled off his black smock, which looked far too heavy to be wearing, and offered it to Foy like a giant handkerchief. Hurriedly, not wishing to offend her new benefactor, Foy accepted it, a pleasant mix of incense and fried food rising off its lining as she wrapped it round her shoulders. It was by far the warmest thing she had worn since coming to Africa, her parents had warned her to pack a pullover or top, whereas she insisted on travelling light and only taking what she was sure to need. In her dishevelled state, Artay's gift lent her the air of a sackcloth and ashes martyr, Saint Joan or the adulteress Christ saved from stoning. It would be a miracle if anyone from her former life would recognise her and, not for the first time, Foy became conscious of how much she had changed. It was a shift in essence, experienced over her skin and under it too, pertaining to every part of her, inside then out. Ceremoniously, and without touching her, Artay beckoned Foy to follow him, his dark eyebrows so far up his head they were practically touching his hairline, a sign, Foy felt, that her appearance was not an event he would soon forget.

What she had mistaken for a settlement was in fact a camp and Artay, far from being a native of the forest, resembled an Arab of some sort, the fragmented greenery as alien for him as her. Could he be a Bedouin slaver, which in the circumstances struck Foy as funny, as there could only be so many potential kidnappers in a single country? If events carried on in the same vein she half expected to be abducted by Tarzan next, or cannibals who would have her head shrunk into a wastepaper basket…and into it would go her memories, one night stands, old pairs of Converse…catching her toe on a vine jolted Foy upright, she had practically fallen asleep on Artay's shoulder and with mixed feelings, she observed they were not alone.

Pushing a large hanging branch to one side, Artay led Foy over a little stream, and up on to a bank where a row of sullen pygmies were sat in what looked like oversized pyjamas, that is, until they saw Foy, whereupon they exploded into excited speculations.

Again, Artay looked more put out than Foy, and began to gesture at a huddle of uniformed men of normal height who appeared to be in command of the diminutive ones, urging them to keep their charges in check. Shouting, finger pointing and an exchange of exasperated faces followed, then a short pause as Foy did something she could not help. Whether it was exhaustion or plain mischievousness was a matter for Artay to judge, but lifting her freckled arm, Foy waved regally at the midgets and had to stop herself from actually blowing a kiss. She was feeling light headed to the point of being drugged, free now from fear, having been exposed to so much of it, consciousness was where life was at, everything else a bonus.

'Hi there! Hi there little ones!' she waved.

Thirty two stab wounds and a severed head would not have stopped her from positively skipping over to the pot of boiling coffee and performing a little dance for her new audience, so it was left to Artay to roughly grab her wrist and shake her back to her senses.

'Are you crazy?' he asked in heavily accented English, his worst fears about the decadent West and their women coming horribly true, 'these men are animals, they will kill you.'

Unfortunately for his argument, the nearest of the pygmies was busy proving it untrue. Approaching Foy with the gift of banana leaf and rice, another carrying a cup of water and a piratical looking officer, War Boss, bringing up the rear with a pineapple held out like a trophy, the threat they posed was one of which gift to accept first.

Foy tried to speak only to find herself laughing instead, 'they think I'm a Roman Princess' she gasped, somewhat hysterically, 'their Jungle Queen!'

In her euphoria she did not notice the SAS man, manfully attempting to gain her attention from the tree he was tied to, his mouth gagged and arms bound tightly to its spiky trunk. Or the war-like attire of her hosts, the odour of blood on their breath, the scared civilians hiding behind the cola trees or the ringlets of men's ears, the pygmies were trading for food.

In fact, Foy would have been free to airily trapeze round her jungle paradise for as long as she liked, until reality stepped out of the turbid jungle gloom and said, in a Suffolk accent, 'there's the prick tease that did for my boy's salami and all.'

After which she did what she had expected to do all along, she pulled her side parting down over her left eye, smiled generously and, leaning into thin air, fainted.

CHAPTER NINE

Round up the Usual Suspects

Elder's last stand had been a largely quiet affair, marked by the firing of a single tank shell in to the hightowering trunk of a Kapok Tree. Pagan heard it, or at least heard the animal uproar that followed, spreading like a Mexican wave from the scene of the battle to the path he was cutting with Beasley less than a mile away.

'Hear that?'

'Can't not.'

'Sounds like bad news for someone.'

'What you want to do about it Sir?'

'Listen.'

There was a rattle of gunfire, followed by an ordered succession of bullets, one man trying to shoot his way out of trouble, Pagan guessed, the short pause between each crack facilitating a masochistic pleasure he was unable to completely suppress. Gunfire had this effect on him, standing as it did in close relation to death, both as fast as each other, honest, and causally connected.

'Ahhh, I think the good Captain has made contact with the enemy.'

'Maybe not Beasley, we're not the only ones waging war in this country.

'True Sir, but we both know I'm right.'

'Trouble is, this place doesn't look dangerous until it does.' Pagan turned to Francis, 'which direction, exactly, is the shooting coming from, sounds to me like it's echoing everywhere at once?'

Francis wiped a thin line of perspiration from his moustache, 'from where the track runs in to the jungle, parallel to the way we came. From where Captain Elder would have got to now, in his jeep.'

'Couldn't call it unexpected.'

'I didn't expect them to find us first.'

'No' said Beasley archly. Pagan knew to what he referred. Elder was sweet natured enough to grab the short straw with both hands, believing he had bagged the prize turkey. In this case it meant volunteering to be the decoy, the hunted and not hunter, since a jeep in the open would be easier for the enemy to locate than the jungle route Pagan had opted to take. Of course, this was not how he sold the choice, or Elder understood it, more the way Pagan's preferences had a way of creating reality in their own image as a fait accompli.

'Reckon the brave and curious are going to be following that racket like flies to shizer.'

'Without radio or a mobile we won't know. If Justin isn't a prisoner he'll have accounted for a few of them. I credit him with wit enough to not be dead, not here at the hands of this lot.'

'That I agree with Sir, can't say I blame you for letting him volunteer, he's by far the keener of you two. Feel sorry for Hightower and Kingston though. We check it out then, get close but not too close?'

'Close but not too close, Francis, after you.'

Francis was already moving in the direction of the gunfire. He had always known he could make a better job of leading his fellow men than any Shimban in power, the novelty of these Europeans relying on him was a far more refined pleasure however, one he intended to make the most of.

'I don't know where the SAS, Shimba division would be without me,' he called.

'No' laughed Beasley, somewhat taken by surprise, 'no nor do we Francis, nor do we.'

* * *

When Foy came to, it was plain to see that her position in the camp had undergone a radical downgrading since she was last conscious. For a start, she was tied, rather too tightly, to the same trunk as Elder, who was doing his heroic best to convert his grimace into a reassuring smile. Artay and Webster were shouting at one another with War Boss One acting as a kind of intermediary, cheerfully turning his ear toward whichever man cursed last. Tawny, sharpening her knife showily, looked horribly at home amongst the pygmies, gunmen and now, though Foy hoped her eyes deceived her, hateful-looking boys with Bin Laden beards, scowling so hard she was afraid they would lose their balance.

'Wait till she wakes,' said Tawny, addressing no one in particular, 'just wait till she wakes.'

This scene in the camp represented normality. Each monster was going about its business in a way that could be construed as everyday. Foy remembered reading about the banality of evil, that dirty deeds were the work of ordinary and humdrum minds. She watched a pygmy empty a sack she supposed was full of rice, its contents not so wholesome on closer inspection, severed penises or handless fingers; whichever, the proper place for human anatomy was on a body, not a bag. How disappointing, these were the same sweet saviours who were offering her gifts of banana leaf, another illusion experience was not going to let her get away with. To believe in the banality of evil was to be taken in by appearances, if evil appeared boring and pedestrian it was only because nothing, not even negativity, could be at the top of its game all the time.

Noticing that Foy was watching the pygmy pretended to eat a finger, sniffing it with the air of a connoisseur inspecting a chipolata.

Foy closed her eyes. It was necessary to retain an idea of

herself as separate from all this, *simply the thing I am, shall make me live.*

'Her for him?' Webster yelled pointing at the tree she and Elder were tied to, 'she was ours to begin with! You must be havin' a laugh!'

Touchingly Artay seemed to be arguing her corner, his hands outstretched in an appeal. Elder was groaning good-naturedly, the gag in his mouth preventing him from doing any more, and realising she was free to speak, Foy whispered, 'it's alright, I'm okay, don't worry about me.' It was quite sweet, she noted, that even here good manners prevailed. Elder grunted and tried to wink, both eyes closing instead of only one. He had been badly beaten and Foy could sense that even at the best of times, he was probably not the most coordinated of men.

'How did that other bastard get here?'

'He is our prisoner. We will interrogate him.'

'But what's he doing here, in this country, get me? You understand; I'm English and so is he! Get me? I know what I'm doin' here, but what about him? What's *he* doin' here, what are you doin' with him?'

Webster caught Foy's eye, saw that she was watching him and snarled, more exasperated than furious, 'I need to know about him, see, he and I, we are Englishmen, come from the same country...'

What was it she felt? Optimism! Webster was scared, interested not only in her, not even primarily in her, but in the soldier trussed up at her side. Maybe the poor man was part of a rescue team, Britain always looked after her own, that was what Webster was frightened of! There were probably photos of him and his family on the ten o clock news, next to cute ones of her as a girl, beauty and the beast, the woman who would save Africa captured by a carrot crunching Untermensch...a country in outcry, the biggest news story since 25 Cromwell Street...she had felt so alone, overlooking the fact that there were people who cared about her, forgotten that they would not forget, they were coming for her, of course they were, they had to be...

To Webster's amazement Foy stuck her tongue out and raised her chin provocatively, every inch the defiant alley kitten, 'Webster you dick, you've blown it! Busted!'

Beneath his cuts Elder blushed, it was hard to be in control of a situation with a bloody great rope cutting the sides of his mouth, but it would be an improvement if he could just understand what was going on. The first thing he would say, if he could, was to warn this spunky lass that for the helpless, discretion was the better part of valour. How she was mixed up in this mattered less than her making a very unpleasant-looking man very angry.

'My, my, girl, that mouth of yours is good for more than biting, eh?' Webster looked approvingly at a dead body, Hightower's, wedged atop of a pile of corpses the pygmies had dragged off the battlefield. 'Got to hand it to you, got to keep handing it to you, you carry on like that Duracell bunny, if I knew the trouble you were goin' to be I'd have bled you way back when.'

'I have told you, she is not your prisoner...'

'You keep out of it,' Webster snapped at Artay, 'you ask any of your African friends who I am, they'll tell you, tell you not to mess with the one they call "Big Pink", I'm in with their leader see?'

'I'm not scared of you anymore, not of any of you' yelled Foy, addressing the wider group, who, for the time being, Tawny and Artay excepted, appeared to have had enough of her, 'you've overplayed your hand Webster, you're thick, really thick, I don't know what world you live in but you can't go kidnapping British nationals and think you can get away with it.' Foy was speaking to Artay, the tied-up soldier, to anyone who could understand English, it was imperative that they all knew *exactly* what had happened. For all she knew Webster might have pretended she was *his* wife, or some hysterical charge put in his care. 'They're coming for you Webster, you know it, it's you who needs to watch out now.'

Though upset and humiliated at the turn of events, Foy noticed that Webster was having difficulty looking at her, his attention wandering towards Elder the moment she stopped talking.

'Un-gag him, I'll deal with you later girly.'

Worryingly the African did as he was told, suggesting that the man from Suffolk held some authority with her captors. Craning her neck, Foy said to Elder, 'be sure of it, I can take care of myself, just let that wanker know what kind of trouble he's in, that you're on to him.'

Elder winked, this time successfully, he had no idea what she was talking about, though after the shame of capture it was time for redemption, the Regiment and this remarkable girl demanded it. Often in moments that required displays of courage, Elder would imagine he was being watched by a floating panel of beauties, women he had unsuccessfully tried to impress in civilian life, models he wished to marry, weather girls with a twinkle in their eye, and here one was, sitting there ready to appreciate him at his bravest. What was he waiting for?

Exhaling, inhaling, and regaining as much composure as he could, led to a rather muted opening sally, 'name rank and number is all you'll get.'

'You what boy?'

Elder could have kicked himself, name, rank and number were far more than he needed to give, in fact, the very things he wished to conceal.

'What you say?'

'Nothing.'

'Well that's no good is it?'

Swiftly recovering from his pratfall, Elder decided to go on the attack, 'you still have time to try and rectify this.'

That worked; at least Webster stuck his thumb into the gap

between his front teeth, looking lost for words.

'This is your only chance; there's still a way for you to make good. You must release us at once, if you want any hope of a fair trial in England. Persist in holding us prisoner and I'll have no choice but to hand you over to our African allies who, believe me, will dispense their own kind of justice, that is not ours.'

'You must be havin' a laugh,' said Tawny, coming to her father's aid, 'who you think you are, Henry V?'

'The same terms apply to you too,' said Elder noticing the female Webster, and wishing he hadn't, 'I give you my word.' The red faced farmer was one thing, this alleged woman, whose proper place would be behind the counter of a provincial Co-Op, quite another. What were these people doing in the middle of an African jungle?

'Your word?'

'Yes, my word. We don't know one another, but I'm hazarding a guess that you're out of your depth and still digging. Allow me and this woman to go free, whatever little racket you're playing, forget it, just let us go, it's the only way you can save yourselves. If you have any influence over these people use it now. Ask them to set us free.'

'Hold your horses boy, I ain't put it down for you to pick it up. I'm in the results business myself and I'm the one who'll be doin' the interrogatin'.'

'Why don't you just listen to him dickhead, he's offering you a way out,' said Foy, ignoring, or unaware of Elder's recurring blushes, 'don't you see, you're not in charge now?'

'Really? That's not the way it looks to me, not by a long one. You, Shakespeare, I don't see any regimental markings on you, I'm Royal British Legion myself, but you, no badge, insignia, truth is, only reason I'm takin' you for a soldier in the first place is because I don't reckon our African buddies would be startin' on a Safari, that, and that you sure don't talk like any mercenary I know. Don't know any who would be so damn foolish for a start, thinkin' they can dictate terms when they're trussed up like a turkey for Christmas.'

'Then why do you look like the one trying to talk his way out of a hanging party?' asked Elder. It was true, that of the two men, it was Webster who was more overcome with sweat, his hands barely capable of staying still. This was what brought Foy down to earth again; she had been around him long enough to guess that Webster had an ugly way of reacting to nervousness.

There were no such worries for Elder who had, unwisely, decided to approach Webster, much as security might a tipsy budget airline passenger, 'the question you should be asking isn't who I am, it's who you are, who are you to make threats when you may very well find yourself at the mercy of Her Majesty's consulate, once you wake up to your predicament that is. This isn't Brighton.'

'No, I dare say it isn't...'

'And another thing, if you persist in your offensive posture, I'll remind you that treason is still punishable by death in our country.'

Webster paled.

Elder taking false encouragement, finished with a flourish, 'untie us and we can decide where we go from here. And perhaps we can ask your Persian friend, if I'm not mistaken, what *he's* doing here. Though that depends which side you want to be on, really.' If they were expecting Stan Laurel they had got David Niven, Elder doing his best to feign cool diffidence, inwardly ablaze at his own performance and a shoo in for Foy's approval, so he reasoned.

The white in Webster's face had become steadily pinker, finally realising its destiny as a streak of burning scarlet most commonly associated with food allergies or cheap make up. 'You're china at the end of a shelf,' he said with great control.

'What?'

'I'm goin' to try and take it easy now, no sense havin' a heart attack, rather give you one. Tawny, give me that.'

With rather too much relish for Foy to dare to watch, Tawny handed her Father the knife she had been sharpening, a large Bowie aimed at the kind of collector who would never take it out of its sheath. For a second both Websters looked at each other, a hint of another life, spent in front of the television or shopping together for milk, passing before them.

'I'm goin' to show you what happens when one of these falls into the hands of one who knows how to use one,' said Webster grabbing Elder's hand, 'England never gave me anythin' boy, never had no love for her, and you remind me of most of what I don't love. I'm goin' to show you what I can do first, then ask questions.'

Elder only realised later that Webster had cut two fingers, and not one off at the first try, for at the time it was as if the cold blade had made contact with some part of his stimuli that normally remained covered, unpleasant certainly, but not irrevocable. The second cut, which took the third finger, affected his stomach and, lurching slightly, he vomited over Webster who barely seemed to notice, the sick splattering over his face like sea spray.

Muggily Elder struggled to keep his eyes open, his head dropping against Webster's shoulder, 'I...'

'You don't look like you have a mouth that's screamed out in terror before, so what you say you tell me who you are and what you're fuckin' doin' here, before I separate you from your lips?'

It wasn't the pain that made Elder faint, or the sound of Foy screaming, only that it took all the energy he had been saving to say, 'SAS,' before passing out. Artay pounced between the two men, smothering Elder's bleeding hand to stem the flow of blood, while Webster, looking as uncomfortable as he had intended his victim to be, rammed the knife into the tree and shouted 'untie her, we're off!'

Which would have been what happened had three figures not stepped out of the jungle, Pagan and Beasley with hands held aloft and behind them Francis, his gun pointed at their backs.

'I don't know whether this is gettin' better or worse' said Webster, dropping Elders freshly sliced finger underfoot, 'you, Persian, go easy on the antiseptic, and Tawny, with me now, good things come in three's they say...'

* * *

They were moving fast, their impatient momentum feeding itself, none of them knowing quite what they were charging into, though all eager for "contact", a chance to decide matters one way or another. Beasley, leading the way now, loath to relinquish his role as target man to Francis, enjoyed the jungle; Francis did not seem to notice it while Pagan tolerated it, just. How could anyone relax in such a place? The spiky caterpillar that flew back off the branch into his face, the tiny leaches that leapt onto his puttees looking for a warm lace hole to bed down in, and the filthy humidity were a formidable conspiracy against ease. Most soldiers would have stopped there; Pagan, with his concern for hygiene, found it hard to. Meaning that in addition to the enemy and beasties, he was aware of the damp shirt reeking off his back, the underpants stuck to his groin and the way the biscuit he tried to scoff turned into mush in his hands, so wet were they with perspiration. In fact, it was this aspect, beyond long periods away from home, physical danger or bad pay, that upset him most, a hidden meticulousness and desire for cleanliness (never comfort). The only psychiatrist to cross his path, one the army had forced him to see, toyed with the idea of obsessive compulsion, a need to be in control of men, the weather, his body and dirt. For Pagan it was more elemental than that, he had a very strong sense of smell and an unclean body was more likely to make him gag than a fresh dismembered one.

'I could use a pint,' lied Beasley. It was water he wanted. The perspiration was flowing, but there was no slowing down, like dogs programmed to chase a particular type of animal they had to continue until they bit. Voices were carrying over from a clearing, Beasley held a finger to his lips, a glow deeper than the one hastened by breathlessness spreading over his cheeks. For a soldier success is war, the event that gives a soldier the confidence he joined the army for, and Pagan could tell his NCO was on the verge of making just such a discovery, again.

'Look.'

'The body they're carrying?'

'The very one.'

'The Uniform. It's Kingston by the look of him, must be. The poor bastard.'

'Yeah. And the tree, next to…a girl I think.'

'Justin, shit, they've got Justin. The bloke standing over him, interrogator, what is he, an Afrikaner?'

'Fuck knows, but he's going for the Captain with something in his hand…'

'We've got to do something now.'

'Agreed.'

'I love it when a plan comes to together…Francis, here, we're your prisoners, get us to where we can grab the Captain, you're following me? Take my rifle, we're you're prisoners, that's who we are, so take us in and look happy about it.'

* * *

Golem had found the pygmies squabbling over the dead bodies extremely distasteful. He knew he ought to be grateful that they had listened to his instructions to clear the battlefield, though the manner in which they chose to do so revealed their own reasons for obeying him. Body parts were coming off wherever he looked; stored in purses, the larger parts pooled in communal sacks, the whole process executed with a buoyant rigour that was unnerving. Killing as a way of life seemed less humane than killing as a consequence of religious fervour, or nationalistic sentiment, however hypocritical it might be to admit it.

'Relax' General Amnesty said, 'you can't expect men, even these small men, to fight for nothing. Everyone has their price, no?'

'Not for Allah?'

General Amnesty slapped his stomach in an attempt to keep the laughter in, 'there is no Allah in their cosmos my friend. I tell you again, Shimba is not Iran! No missionary, Muslim or Christian, goes far with these people, not further than the surface.'

'They're cannibals as well then, is that what you are implying?'

'Some of them, yes, some of the time. But mostly, no.' In his light tailored jacket, grey patches spread over his hair, and desert boots, Amnesty had the air of a vicar on holiday. 'Cannibalism for them is a last resort, or a special treat, but not pretty standard practice. Not in this day and age.'

'No?'

'These are trophies, for sale or for spells...and for their religion, they use a hand as a symbol, a finger for a curse and so forth. They worship the one God when it comes to big matters, for personal issues still the old ones.'

Golem closed his eyes and tried to imagine how this deranged cosmology could be accepted as part of life, no different from a man doing a job he did not like, regrettable and natural. It was no use. This exercise in empathy was too much of a stretch, his training had taught him to be judgemental and suppress mixed feelings and besides, he was interrupted by more gunfire. This time he had no hesitation in firing over the heads of the offenders, two track suited idiots attempting to shoot an okapi, or maybe a zebra, since the Grand Ayatollah banned the Discovery Channel it was hard to tell at this distance, 'hold your fire you fools. For the love of Allah can't we show some mercy?'

'Boys will have their fun.'

'Enough, tell those two drunks and all the other...'

'Holy warriors,' laughed General Amnesty.

Golem tutted, 'whatever they are, tell them we're finished, I want to interrogate the European prisoner before Artay lets one of your midgets eat him.'

By the time Golem returned the interrogation was over and a bloody skirmish was comfortably under way, a slight consolation being that his prisoner was not yet among the dead. The catalyst for the mayhem was neither the pygmies nor Webster's over zealous interview technique. Francis had got things rolling on discovering he still had more friends in the Mahdi's army than he supposed.

'Francis, you must have a very big present for the Mahdi to dare come back after you left him. You hurt his feelings brother, you were family,' said War Boss, 'you are an intelligent man, so please tell me you know what you are doing.'

Thankfully Francis was nothing like as fazed by this introduction to the enemy camp as his prisoners were, 'Jerome...'

'Please Francis, I am General War Boss One now, just as you were "Hannibal Rex", the Mahdi had to find someone of talent to replace you.'

'And of modesty. These are SAS men, British, come to train Government men. I thought you would like them.'

'Let me see old friend, let me see them.'

'You know this fellow?' asked Webster, his piggy eyes narrowing sceptically.

'Yes, yes, Francis and I are old friends,' said War Boss.

Pagan did not know whether this was a good development or not, mainly because he had no idea how good a liar Francis was. If he had time to brief him on his role, he would probably have said that the thing about being in the SAS is that it's good idea to not let people know you are, especially when they're in a position to kill you. At least the black warlord was showing signs of accepting the gift, whereas the sunburnt blob in the floppy hat looked ready to do for them there and then. Lowering his head, Pagan took care to avoid his stare.

'Listen, listen to me, there's no pissin' round with these people, you get 'em you kill 'em, because you might not get the chance again,' said Webster, his mind firmly made up. 'Whatever they're doin' here you can be sure they're up to no good.'

'These are my prisoners, not yours Webster.'

'Your Mahdi hired me as an advisor, and that's what I'm doin', advisin' you.'

'He hired you as his pimp. You have got him his woman. Shut up.'

'Think of them Bond films, you've seen 'em, you know what happens, they have the bastard at their mercy and then talk their chance away just as we're doin' now!'

He was right about that, thought Pagan. They were still moving towards the tree and all it needed was a few more steps and he'd be within reaching distance of the captives. Elder was in a bad way, his hand covered in a handkerchief black with blood, which may or may not have still been pumping out. A tender sympathy and resolve to do something for his friend were experienced in the same instant. Their captors were filth who deserved to die, the difference between that judgement and his resolve to obey it infinitesimal. The girl next to Elder, for despite the grime and filth it was a girl who caught Pagan's eye imploringly, would have to be his second priority. By the tired lolling of her eyes, it was clear that this wasn't the first time she had expected to be rescued and, in a sudden upsurge of unforeseen sexuality, Pagan decided that in a parallel life he would have tried very hard to screw her.

'You're getting carried away, you ain't no General, me, I know what I'm talkin' about, get out of the way and let me pop 'em boy.'

'I am not your boy Webster.'

'You' said Francis addressing Pagan and pointing to the tree, 'go over there.'

Pagan, doing his best to impersonate a broken man, nodded obediently. The gist was obvious, there was no time to wait for a plan, better to hope that the other two would know what to do if he did something first.

'Bitch' Pagan said to Tawny who was standing over the captives, 'give me that gun.'

'What?' said Tawny looking down at the weapon loosely slung at her waist, 'you...'

Pagan's boot caught the fat of her second chin, knocking her backwards like a sofa dropped down a staircase.

'Justin! Look up!'

Cutting the rope that bound Elder to Foy, Pagan grabbed his unconscious friend, dropping him as the full force of Webster crashed into his rear.

That was enough to wake Elder, who opened a swollen eye as he fell face to face with the felled Tawny. A little to his left Foy obeyed a sensible impulse and scrambled behind the tree, Artay shouting at an excitable pygmy to hold his fire, whilst Beasley produced a pistol and shot the midget nearest to him in the leg. At which point Golem stepped into the breach.

A machine gun round forced him to fall flat on his chest; Francis was firing into the air in what appeared to be an intelligent attempt to slow down the situation. From his place on the ground, Golem unlocked his rifle, and lying on his side, fired at the tree the gatecrashers had coalesced around. The bullets ricocheted off the trunk, safely missing Elder who was trying to ignore the pain in his unusable right hand. Tawny had got up, jumped over to where the corpses from the earlier fire fight were piled, stuck her hand into the mangled chest of one, and was coming toward Elder with something bloody in her hand. The African guards were returning fire pinning Foy and Beasley down with Francis at the far side of the tree, leaving only Pagan, who had Webster round his neck, to protect him.

Elder tried to catch Pagan's attention by aiming a sliding kick at Webster's head, but he was too weak to move, and instead faced the unpalatable fact that there was nothing to stop Tawny mounting him.

'Sean' he gasped, 'Sean, help me.'

In a second she was sat astride his chest, 'you know what this is' she said brandishing a livery lump in her hand, 'the blacks call it "the main machine", a fuckin' heart to you or me.'

With all his remaining strength Elder brought his knee up, barely raising it an inch, Tawny's concrete frame too heavy for him to dislodge by force.

'You're goin' to eat it.'

If he had food enough in his stomach Elder would have wretched. Holding his nose with one hand, Tawny slammed the lumpy mess into Elder's unwilling mouth. He could smell the taste before it reached his tongue, an awful memory of Maltese goat's cheese, or dog food, wobbling round his senses, as Tawny punched the noxious substance further down his throat.

'Don't worry, it's Halal,' she breathed over his face.

Elder vainly tried to raise an arm, then tip his body over and imbalance her, both to no avail. The beating he had taken was too thorough, leaving no part of him operational.

'Eat.'

'Justin!'

It was Sean Pagan, his best friend, his rock: the cavalry that would rescue him.

'Justin, bite her fucking hand off!'

Elder knew that he could not do that, knew that if Sean had suggested it then he was otherwise disposed, that the cavalry were not going to make it in time for the end of the film.

'Bite Justin, bite!'

The desperation in Sean's voice said it all, Elder knew only too well what that meant. The detestable banshee was going to suffocate him to death. Elder never thought it would happen to him, that there would come a moment when he would realise that this was it, it was his turn to die. Thankfully, knowing that it was made it easier, partly because there wouldn't be any time later to think about it, or wonder how he could have got out of the unseemly mess. Hindsight was what made mistakes what they were, something to look back at and brood upon and regret. Not this time. In fact he was quite free to forget about his present situation and think about whatever he liked, which happened to be, unsurprisingly, England. His England. Just hearing that word said in an English accent, or even in an English accent in his head, was enough to make him cry, the cold feeling of Albion collecting her own and depositing his soul with those of his ancestors under Bournemouth pier...sweet sea air and joy...England, what do they know of England, only England knows.

'Result' said Tawny, 'not so famous SAS now.'

Tawny had less time to contemplate her end. Sitting triumphantly on Elder's shuddering chest she presented, once he became aware of her, a sitting target for Beasley who shot her straight through the head, killing her at once. Pagan's problems were not so close to being solved. Webster was wrapped too closely round him to get a punch in, tucked in tight in a wrestler's grapple. As a big man Pagan assumed Webster must run out of breath eventually, all that exertion would use up precious energy, which the slob could not have much of. The trouble was he did, or at least, sheer rage had allowed him to access a strategic reserve, for despite his wheezing and panting, Webster's grip was only tightening. Attacking his breathing was the key though, and prising his elbow free, Pagan launched it at the point of Websters Adam's apple. The result was instantaneous, Webster keeled to one side in an intense choking fit, losing the bear hug he held Pagan in. Following through with an almighty head-butt, Pagan kept his forehead pressed to the mush that was Websters face, and holding the back of Websters head with one hand, used the other to tear his left ear off. At that he felt he was getting somewhere. Propping the completely disorientated bigger man up as a bullet stopper, Pagan crawled sideways to the tree, dragging Webster beside him, the dull thuds hitting his mattress-like stomach illustrating the wisdom of using his enemy as a human shield. Pagan's little manoeuvre was coming off better than he could have hoped right up until he tried to stand up. He felt a sharp punch to his solar plexus and, as he sank to his knees, a gun draw level to his head.

'Please put down your weapons or I will kill this man' said Golem loudly in English, 'you have five seconds to comply, four, three, two....'

CHAPTER TEN

Under the Gun

They could hear Artay and Golem in animated discussion with Generals War Boss and Amnesty on their future status as living persons. The day was bruised, a thick melancholic fug in the air emphasising the likelihood of death. Foy looked to the skies, the sun firmly trapped behind a belt of clouds, and emitted a low whistle, 'well thanks for trying. Do you think they'll kill us?'

'Can't blame them for wanting to, isn't as though we've brought sunshine and joy in our wake,' Beasley was tied back to back with Francis, his countenance inexplicably cheerful, 'then again, I'm in no rush to join the poor old Captain...damn the bastards.'

'God rest his soul' said Francis.

Elder's head had been hacked off his shoulders and thrust on to a stake inches away from the captives. Its forlorn look had the serenity of a Saint in death; the others too close to the same state to properly mourn the dead man. All except Pagan, who had never once taken his eyes off the body as the pygmies slit the stomach open, and laid the innards which had not made the pot, out on the grass in front of him. What struck him most forcefully, and absurdly, was remembering all those times he was with Elder, and Elder did not know he was going to die. Times spent queuing, listening, laughing even when he did not understand a joke, sticking up for him and being Pagan's best friend. Elder had gone through all of that not knowing that one day his head would be placed on a stake in the middle some foreign shithole that wasn't worth the life of a single African, far less a man of England born...Pagan stopped himself, he was thinking bullshit, going mad with sentimentality and rage. Think of something, anything else, just a thought that promised a future and with it, life. Foy. Pagan watched her emotionlessly, with the level of calculation a human being needs for survival. If he could get out of here, buy her dinner and fuck her, all this would not have been in vain.

Foy was quiet, more hope leaving her body in the seconds it took to ask, 'you weren't here to rescue me, were you?'

'You don't want to know darling.'

'But you weren't...?'

'Afraid not. Who are you?' asked Beasley.

'Foy Fox-Harris, I'm an aid worker, I was kidnapped by the man and woman you killed over there. It was horrible, a horrible experience, they wanted to hand me over to the rebels, as a kind of, a kind...a slave basically. Thank you so much for getting me out of that.'

'Enough said. And I'd hold back on the thanks, I mean look around, we're not exactly out of the woods are we? Still...Foy, that's a nice name, isn't it Francis?'

'Yes, nice, I've never heard it before, it sounds very English.'

Pagan would have liked to say something, but for reasons he didn't understand, perhaps a back-handed compliment to his warrior tendencies, he had been gagged as well as bound hand by foot.

'What's your name?' Foy asked Francis.

'Francis' he replied.

'That sounds very English too, or a bit French, we're all a bit of a mix in Northern Europe. Are you all African?'

'All. They may torture me, and then kill me,' said Francis glumly, 'as far as they are concerned I am a traitor. I'm surprised I'm still alive.'

'That's a rare moment of candour for you Francis,' chuckled Beasley. 'Relax, they say tough times don't last but tough people do. Anyway, I thought a religious chap like you would be expecting some divine help any time now.'

'I think not Mr Beasley.'

'This is all there is then?'

'Even the religious have to accept, for the sake of argument, that as you say, "this is all there is". That way if we are wrong, and there is no God, we lose nothing. You don't have to believe in him for all this to mean something.'

'Wasn't quite what I was getting at Francis, I'm able to enjoy life without God's help no problem, its just a set of pretty pictures isn't it? It's in the near-death situations that I like the big man to declare his hand...this sort of situation really. A nice burning bush, then some thunderclap and lightning, the sea parts, and the big man gets us the fuck out of here.'

'Believe me Mr Beasley, you'll be ready to take the credit yourself if any of that happens.' Francis grinned to himself. It was true, he was surprised he had not been shot out of hand, but such mercies encouraged one of the more dangerous of his beliefs. That all men are spared for a purpose and only dispensed with when God no longer has a use for them, even his secular and non interventionist God. If he was still alive then it was for some *precise purpose.* The question was, would he be able to see what it was before it was too late?

'Maybe I will Francis, maybe I will. I certainly wouldn't mind sitting in the comfort of my armchair, a glass of Calvados in one hand and a cigar in the other, discussing this with you, and saying the part we enjoyed most was when we turned the tables on 'em when they least expected it! Christ, that would be a memory.'

'Let's not get carried away Mr Beasley, we need to turn the tables first!'

The two were laughing, the circle of absurdity complete.

'It's true what they say Francis, the last thing that will survive of us is our sense of humour, that and our incredible ability to talk shit.'

Despite his limited contribution to the conversation, which

she was full of admiration for, Foy knew Pagan was dying to say something, Beasley and Francis the funny men to his straight act. Ever since falling into the Websters' clutches, she had only been able to think of survival, her moments of general reflection involuntary and quickly over. Yet here were two men blithely discussing religious belief as a third sat raising his eyebrows as though he had heard it all before, not in some pub, but in front of their dismembered friend's head, all of them seconds away from a possible death. What surprised her the most was the degree to which Pagan had caught her attention, and she wondered whether the same would have been true if she were wandering down the high street back home, or whether this was a uniquely African, "near-death" kind of attraction. Because attraction it was, in spite of Pagan being different from her usual type, tall scruffy public school boys, not scowlers of medium height with murderous frowns.

'Course, the thing we need now is someone God would listen to, so my guess is you're our best bet Francis...'

At least she was not responsible for their friend dying, now that she realised they weren't here for her she could stop feeling guilty about that. Foy blushed, remembering her misplaced sense of self-importance. Whether the British Government cared about her or not, her best chance of survival still lay with these men. Pagan seemed to be moving his head from side to side in an attempt to communicate with her, as the others were talking she had been looking only at him, acknowledging a connection rather than seeking to make it. Following the direction of his eyes that were turned to his right Foy saw Golem, standing there listening to Beasley and Francis, hearing their every word.

'Very good' he interrupted, 'I admire soldiers who can look beyond their immediate fate and talk of other things.'

'Good of you to care' said Beasley, unable to bend his head round because of his proximity to Francis's back, 'that's very good English you have, makes me feel closer to civilisation; learn it at a Madrasah did you?'

'Civilisation? There was nothing very civilised about your fellow countryman and woman that you killed.'

'Tell our cold mutilated friend and this girl about it, the dead scum are with your lot, not us.'

'I'm sorry for your friend's tortures, like you, I am only a guest in this country and there is a limit to my influence,' Golem clapped his hands and two pygmies marched into the group and pulled Foy to her feet.

'Where are you taking her?' yelled Beasley, feeling this question preferable to the alternative, which would probably have been the rather prissy, and equally ineffectual, "unhand her".

'Keep calm' said Golem, 'there will be no raping. She looks like she was brought up by wolves, filthy, she needs to be washed in the river and then plenty of insect repellent, the mosquitoes will feast on a completely clean body, and lice on a dirty one. The rest of you can gather jungle muck, this girl is not used to it.'

'And once she's had her bath? You know why those animals kidnapped her, what will happen once you finish their delivery for them?'

'I'm afraid that is beyond my influence.'

'Bullshit. You're looking to give your African pals a sweetener, set them up for whatever you want in return.'

'I am going to ask you not to say anything else.'

Beasley curled his lip up in an Elvis sneer, careful, though, to do as he was told. Golem's manner was gregarious yet programmatically efficient, and Beasley had learned to listen to such voices.

Walking up to Pagan, Golem signalled to a nearby Pygmy to remove his gag and unbind his hands.

'You are all alive for now, I don't care about you killing English mercenaries, or you wasting my time and slowing down my journey, it's been an interesting diversion.'

'We're good like that' said Pagan rubbing the sides of his mouth, 'ready to put on a show even after the animals you call allies decapitated my friend.'

'Yes, the Pygmies are angry, three may have to have their legs amputated after you people shot them.'

'That'll give them something else to eat.'

'Beautiful, not a word too long, a typical British reply. The officer and enlisted man just the same.'

'If you know we're British then you'll know that this could be enough to take our two countries to war; you're a Persian, aren't you?'

'War? I don't think so!'

Pagan glared, knowing that his opponent had a point.

'You are not the same nation as the one of Churchill or Nelson. We humiliated British sailors and your papers called them heroes, you flee Iraq and have the Americans come to your aid in Afghanistan because you are a confused nation. No, I think this incident will remain extremely unnoticed by your Government.'

'Then why are we even talking, shoot us and leave our bodies in the jungle.'

'Because I man want to know what the British are doing in Shimba. Or maybe just doing in general. We don't have the time to interrogate you now, but when we do you will tell me and then we will leave you with our hosts, who will enjoy parading their prize before the eyes of the world, and when you and your Government have been humiliated enough, and have paid enough, you will be returned to your own country and who knows, maybe like your sailors you will be welcomed as heroes. Of course, you could choose to remain silent. In which case we will, as you say, kill you and leave you in the jungle, but why bother? You have no honour left to lose, as to whatever your mission was designed for, it has ended in failure.'

Pagan cleared his throat and swallowed, a dull flat feeling

moving towards his guts. Failure had found its place in his physiology. One day, if there were to be other days, he would look back and see none of this as his fault, that the mission had been an ill-thought-out farce from start to finish and that the real blame lay in a basic plan that never had any hope of success. How many times had this happened, how many people had he slaughtered when a helicopter landed on the wrong building and the terrorists turned out to be a family at breakfast? All this ennui was still to come, for the moment there was no consolation, only the angry knowledge that he was getting a little too good at being the one always to put on a brave face. If there was any karma in the universe then it was some other mug's turn, perhaps one of the ones that had left them in this place, used them, and abandoned them to their foes.

'Think about this before we talk again' said Golem, mistaking Pagan for a man for whom too much had gone wrong to care about a trifle like captivity and death. Mistaken because at that moment, not a moment later but then, Pagan would have spoken and sold out his mission from the very bitterness of his soul. Bitterness, though, was a luxury he could only afford at moments of success. Within seconds of his being left, Pagan's self-pity had turned into revulsion which in turn was transformed into the hardy resolve to escape at the first possible opportunity, his personality reinstalling discipline over his all too-human lapse. But all that was still seconds away, for as Golem spoke Pagan spat into the earth and said, 'ask away.'

'Typical British irony' said Golem admiringly, and walked off.

* * *

One Day Later

The journey had become one that could only be completed on foot. The line of marching prisoners resembled a benign slave gang, Golem's warning that if any one of them escaped, the rest would be shot, having the intended effect. Without any shackles to bind her, Foy could almost fool herself into thinking she was free, or at least as free as she had been for days. With the Websters safely dispatched to hell, she could observe the jungle in all its holiday green beauty, rather than suffer it as an oppressive backdrop to her enslavement. Though they had barely exchanged more than a few words, the way he had said them made Foy feel like the bond she experienced with Pagan was not wholly imagined. His quiet voice, gentle even when indignant, inspired a weightless confidence in her, uplifting in its apartness from their surroundings. Of course, after what she had been through, it was possible to confuse the first sign of kindness for a profound linkage between souls, or underestimate the power of a gainly female, any female, over a man in the back end of nowhere. Still, Pagan's guarded way of smiling, as though his mouth had to go through a lot to produce such an effect, gave her the confidence to believe that her affection was not a projection, and the protective way he smacked leeches off her bare leg was enough to make her shiver and tingle. Foy accepted that it was ridiculous to think like this, ridiculous and wonderful, for the silent flirtation created a tension preferable to the existing one, one she could enjoy, partake in and above all, exercise some control over.

'Thanks' she said as Pagan put a supportive hand under her bottom, allowing her to scramble up a small bank that she could have leapt over without difficulty. 'I wonder where they're taking us?' It was the first time since her wash that she had explicitly addressed their situation, almost feeling it bad luck to mention it directly, hoping that now the professionals were here they would have a plan of their own.

'Further into the jungle, to meet the Mahdi I'd guess. Try not to talk, we'll get you out of this...I promise.' Pagan paused, did he just say "I"? What was going through his head? Women never failed to inspire him to new feats of stupidity, especially ones whose seamless buttock to thigh movement were making him hypnotically giddy. Quickly correcting himself he said, 'we, we're used to this kind of scene. Trust us.' If a man's ridiculousness could be measured by how hard he tried, how many principles he trampled on or rules of his own he broke, to get sex, then Pagan was on the threshold that separated a fool from something worse. First there was the botched rescue to contend with, then the moral collapse in front of his Persian interrogator and finally his playing Sly Stallone to this lanky beauty's Brigit Neilson. It was pitiful. If he didn't get a grip quickly he could forget about making any commitments to the future.

'I do' said Foy, 'trust you. I haven't heard anyone call you by your name yet.'

'It's Sean.'

'Scottish?'

'Not Scotland, I'm as English as I sound.'

'Whereabouts?'

'Everywhere, from a services background. But if people ask me which football team I support I say Forest. I spent the most time in the Midlands; when my parents separated I stayed with my Dad. It probably shows.'

'Football again.'

'Sorry?'

'Nothing. Just something from earlier. I don't even know what to say about your friend Justin. It was horrible what they did to him.'

'Yes. I still don't believe it myself.'

'I'm sorry.'

'So am I. He was a great guy, an odd man Justin, but…well my friend. I don't want to think about him properly, not until we're out of here. Anyway, as the song goes, we'll meet again, he and I, probably.'

Foy felt the trail smooth under her feet, 'that's the way I think of it too, nothing else makes any sense.'

'It doesn't. You must have had a hard time of it too.'

'I did, I had already escaped once, before you found me.'

'How did you get away?'

Foy paused, 'I had to hurt someone pretty badly. I'm pretty sure I actually killed him.' Murdering Nelson in insalubrious circumstances had seemed so necessary, that Foy had not even thought of it as killing before, 'it's not a feeling I think I can share.' Glancing at Pagan's unmoved, though thoroughly understanding face, she could see that she just had. 'It will be one to tell the girls about when I get back home,' she joked feebly, and to her surprise he laughed, making his face younger, friendlier.

'Oi, Sir,' it was Beasley, catching up with them, 'have a butchers at Francis, he's really having a go!'

Francis, who was lagging some steps behind with War Boss and Amnesty, appeared to be in the middle of a fierce argument, goading the two captors in Shimbali.

'What an enigma that man of mystery is, first I have him down as serenity itself, now he's snapping at those two evil looking villains like a Staffordshire, and look at them, they're taking it.'

'You're right, he seems cross, what do you think they're saying?'

'Let's ask, Oi Francis, care to allow us into your debate?'

Francis raised his head, the faintest suggestion of annoyance on his face. This was nothing compared to the look of embarrassment and anger on the faces of War Boss and Amnesty.

'You should have kept your mouth shut Beasley.'

'Relax Sir, this'll be all to the good. Francis, want to translate for us?'

Francis hesitated, but seeing both his guards lower their heads, a touch shamefully, spoke up, 'I was asking these two men, old friends of mine from the same tribe as the Mahdi, I asked them why they follow this man who fights for the entity called Caliphate, an International Muslim state, and not their own country, Shimba.'

'Bloody good question mate, the dastardly turncoats, and what do you gents have to say to that?'

War Boss looked down at his watch and dropped back a foot or two, Amnesty doing likewise. For an instant Beasley expected them to unloosen their machine guns and mow him down, yet instead, they seemed intent on keeping a respectful distance.

'Blimey Francis, what was that I was saying about a sense of humour? You've put the tail between their legs, you sure that's all you were saying?'

Francis hesitated, 'I was explaining to them that the Caliphate is not a meaningful entity, and that when an entity makes no sense it falls apart. Nations too, the English stopped being British when your Union devolved, a Flemish man does not think of himself as Belgian, no one thought of themselves as Yugoslav but anyone can become an American. The entity must mean something for men to want to belong to it. These men are no more members of a Caliphate than they would be English if they turned up at your Dover asking for asylum. A tribe has to cohere and be comprehensible to become real, the Mahdi's isn't, it is a deranged phantasm he has convinced himself and weak-minded fools of, but it will not last its first serious test, which would be his death. I've told them they're following a false god with bad logic.'

Beasley clicked his tongue admiringly, 'you're quite a guy, most impressive Francis, war pursued by other means; you're a propaganda chief in the making, a king of spin.'

'These aren't what you would call thinking men, yet they are suspicious, they will follow a madman into battle but not a fraud. The Mahdi has told them the world is corrupt and unless the Caliphate is established life on earth will end. Deep down they can sense this is bullshit. The behaviour of a country is only comparable to the behaviour of another country, not some idealised point of view that has never existed, and never can, except as a way of criticising what *is*. The Caliphate is the creation of a man who can not live with reality, it exists in his mind's eye; once I realised this I was done with the man, they asked me why I deserted him and this is what I tell them. I am a pragmatic idealist, not a fantasist.'

'Can't say fairer than that,' said Beasley.

'It is important to put the seed of doubt in their minds Mr Beasley. You never know, it could be something as small as this that saves our life.' Francis winked knowingly, a habit he had copied off Beasley, but as he did this he realised he was lying. The reason he was delivering these speeches was not tactical, it was because he could not help it, no more help it than his old friend the Mahdi could help it whenever Allah spoke to him. So who was speaking through him when he lectured War Boss and Amnesty? Could it be that he was actually speaking through himself?

'Margins, all to do with the margins, perhaps you could subliminally introduce the idea of letting us go free in the next one of your debates.'

Francis smiled wanly but was stopped from saying anything else by the hovering presence of Artay who had stopped on the pretext of looking at a map, in spite of his eyes being firmly fixed on Foy's bare knees.

Seeing what he was looking at Beasley quipped, 'relax friend, frisky as you may feel today, our souls have no gender when we die.'

Artay turned red and drew his hand back to slap Beasley, a sudden commotion rippling down the line, diverting his attention for a second, long enough for Golem to take him by the arm and say, 'listen, this is news...'

Whoops of joy and exclamations followed by extravagant high fives were working their way towards the foreigners, pygmies embracing bearded warriors and General Murder marching down to meet them with a large cigar between his teeth.

'Gentlemen, big, big headlines! Our radios are working again...'

'That's the news?' asked Artay.

'And the messages they bring are music, music to our ears, the President is dead!'

'The President, how though? He's miles behind their lines, your armies cannot have possibly reached him so quickly...'

'Ha!'

'And his protection, bodyguards and so on. How did you get to him?'

'We did not have to, he did not die by our hand, his own guards killed him, paid off by Lebanese gangsters for welshing on a Shimbite deal!'

'Christ, if that's true all bets really are off,' said Beasley.

Golem frowned, 'I don't know what you have to be so blasé about, this is the worst news you and your country could be burdened with, a corrupt puppet dictator brought down like a common gangster.'

'Nothing of the sort, we thrive on unpredictability,' said Beasley smugly, 'and we're adaptable. Three weeks after we reopen diplomatic channels, we'll have their Mahdi as corrupt as the old boy was, and twice as nice, stops things from going stale.'

'And what do you say?' Golem asked Pagan.

'I don't.'

Golem smarted, angry at Pagan's snub and his failure to draw him out, 'if I were you I would not be so blunt,' he said, 'I did not get my job by hand holding alone...'

Ignoring him, Pagan caught sight of Foy's arse, objectified it instantly, took heart and continued on his way, Golem having no choice than to follow him up the path, blurring the definition between captive and captor, follower and leader.

Artay pulled at Golem's sleeve, 'wait a minute.'

'What is it?'

'Shouldn't we just kill the two men and keep the girl. And leave the African to the Africans? They might be our prisoners but I do not feel comfortable with them around, around or alive, it feels like they still have initiative, they are not broken men. '

'Are you mad? Two SAS men, Britain's elite, and you talk of killing them because you "don't feel comfortable"! They are gold dust, gold dust to us and our hosts. We'd be mad to throw them away on your hunch. They are worth a hundred rounds of ammunition to an African trying to make his name.'

'They are too dangerous to leave alive, I have thought about it.'

'Evidently too much or not enough. They stay alive.'

'What do you think they're doing here?'

'Training up whatever hired butchers the old regime were trying to knock into an army. I don't need to interrogate them about that. Britain sends these men out to all her old colonies, ever the benevolent teacher instructing her old pupils. These two were military advisors most likely.'

Artay appeared satisfied, not terribly committed to his idea of executing them in the first place, 'you don't think they'll make trouble for us, complicate our mission...'

'The only complicated thing about our mission is how vague it is. I've spent hours reading between the lines and still don't like the degree to which this journey rests on interpretation. My interpretation and therefore my responsibility. In my view the Mahdi will regard these men as free gifts from Allah, we should take advantage of that...it'll put us in a stronger position as an ally. That is what I think Jafari wants us to be to these people, for the moment.'

Wincing at Allah's name being taken in vain, Artay interrupted, 'so we won't take them back to Iran? You and I do not seem to agree on the basic issue regarding this mission, we are meant to be the ones in charge doing the judging, not the Shimbans.'

'I'm tired of what you think we should be doing in this mission, leave that to one side and let us deal with the matter in hand.'

'So we aren't to take our captives back with us when the time comes?'

'No, that would cause true complications; no, what we do is empty them like husks for whatever they know, take the intelligence we need and leave them here for ransom. If we need to interrogate them at all that is, perhaps they know no more than what they read in the papers, I doubt that they are very important men.'

'And the girl too?'

'The girl too.'

'Can you trust them with her, the Africans?'

'What are you talking about? She's a civilian and wholly not our concern, why bring her into it?'

'We can't leave her here with these animals...'

'Are you mad, we aren't knights of chivalry, we are intelligence operatives, have you gone soft on this woman or soft in the head?'

'You've seen how they are, how can you...'

'All those years in which you've ignored your natural inclinations have resulted in an unfortunate emission in the place where your judgment ought to be. Forget about this woman, trust those bearded holy warriors you've befriended to protect her virtue, if they don't behead her first, which might, when the dust settles, be the best thing she can hope for.'

'You are a Muslim! We have rules for the treatment of female captives.'

'There are no rules for the enemies of Allah, and no rules for the enemies of our state. They can be sodomised and fed shit for all he cares, and he will still love you, even if you enjoy doing it to them, because they are his enemies. Hasn't the regime taught you anything, or have the gloves they've treated you with dazzled you into premature blindness? This is a job for men...'

'I know that...'

'No, real men, ones who can beat a boy on the soles of his shackled feet, have his mother watch and throw acid over his sister's genitals to disguise what's been done to her in questioning. If you want to light a candle for your enemy instead of sticking one up his arse, I suggest you join the brats in the Green Movement, because intelligence work is not for you, and never will be. I think you have got me all wrong Artay, misunderstood me in some way, and perhaps that's my fault, I can strike some as eccentric, soft even. But I am not a nice man, and in a way, nor are you. So let's have no more talk of rules for female captives, are we clear?'

Artay was open mouthed, shocked and favourably struck by his superior's ruthlessness. How deeply held Golem's ruthlessness was, or whether it ought to be taken at face value was questionable. For Golem the worst of it was true, he had been a torturer; all he had lied about was an ongoing belief in its justification. It was not unusual to reinterpret past experience in the light of present revelations, no memory was guaranteed, Golem's difficulty was that his past was a raft of flimsy excuses that grew shabbier with age and overuse, their very sound enough to damn him. Were it not for Artay's piety and priggish humbuggery, he would not have been angered into saying far more than he meant. Of course he would raise the issue of ransoming the girl with the Generals. They were all reasonable and greedy enough to arrange for her to disappear before the handover to their master, for although he sensed loyalty in the Mahdi's followers, its roots had already struck him as decidedly contingent. And the SAS men; all he felt for them was empathy, he was no more important to his country than they were to theirs, all of them sent here for Allah knows what.

As for the training of Artay, if the boy did not have the stomach to do as he was told, there would always be some state sponsored animal who would do it for him, beat and break anyone who withheld information in the misbegotten belief that there was some part of the soul that coercion could not reach. Nineteen Eighty Four, his favourite book during his English Summer, had not been a dystopian nightmare, more a training manual. At this very moment there was a cell in Tehran they were helping secure the walls of, the blood shed here no different to the kind Golem had wiped off a post after commanding his first firing squad. This is what it was to pursue the interests of a state, and their enemies were no different, only slower off the mark...this is what he had to believe. Golem bit his lip, overcoming a stronger than usual urge to kill himself, 'So now you know. Know what we are and what we do.'

Artay lowered his eyes and nodded, 'thank you.' His tone was cautious. 'I came here for this experience, I apologise for not realising sooner that you were the right man to provide it. I suppose I did not care what you thought of me, because I did not respect you, that led me to think and act immodestly, and I am sorry for it.'

Golem eyed him disbelievingly, 'it doesn't matter now, it didn't matter then, it is normal for men in our position to not get along, it is alright so long as we understand one another, go to the front, you can be the first to see the camp of our great ally, I'll take the rear.'

* * *

The track had grown wider, and as they felt their way underneath trees and below branches it slowly began to look as though they were proceeding down an African boulevard, the clearing at the end of which opened up to reveal the back of an old and worn slope. 'Monkey Mountain,' declared General Amnesty portentously.

'Why Monkey Mountain?' asked Artay, squinting like a disappointed tourist.

'Because of the shape of its head,' said Amnesty, pointing to a large and lonely rock near the summit.

'That's the head of a monkey?'

'Yes, I did not give it its name.'

'It looks more like a flattened Squid.'

'Listen,' said Amnesty, eager to change the subject, 'can you hear them?'

A slow and ghostly rumble was coming from the far side of the mountain, echoing through the trees, the tone monosyllabic and powerful, one word being repeated again and again, *"MAHDI, MAHDI, MAHDI, MAHDI, MAHDI..."*

Artay shuddered, the tone was aggressively unwelcoming.

'Behind that hill is the temporary headquarters of the Mahdi, we will stop now and begin again in the morning.' Amnesty's sober face looked sad to be at the end of the journey, like one who had not really been looking forward to coming home.

Though it was still light Artay could see the sense in stopping; late as it was the afternoon was becoming hotter for the walkers and there was no wind, 'it doesn't look far to climb.'

'It may look like nothing more than a hill to you but the slope is higher than you think. With the President killed, the Mahdi's journey to the capital should now be just a formality. We will join him in the morning and then make it there together.'

Artay feigned a scowl and looked over the hill disapprovingly, the others were drawing near and he could sense what they were thinking without so much as looking at them: no one wanted to get to the other side of Monkey Mountain. The African leadership had lost the swagger they usually comported themselves with and were exchanging uncomfortable glances, the Europeans knew that they were a stage closer to imprisonment and Artay had his own reasons for wishing to prolong the climax of their mission. The chanting was becoming frighteningly inhuman, droning on without variation or interruption with none of the transcendental exoticism of the call to prayer, or reassurance of church bells. The dull and remorseless song to the jungle leader bore no relation to religion as the foreigners conceived it, the high pitched exclamation on the "*i*" in "*Mahdi*" erupting like a nervous catamite howling out in pain, the Africans in their number looking round hesitantly rather than joining in, as Artay thought they would. What had until now been too abstract a matter to consider, that is, the nature and character of the Mahdi, was a bellowing reality. Wiping a fresh line of sweat from under his turban, Artay said to Golem, 'I hear no beauty in it.'

'You are not meant to.'

Whatever ill will they bore the Mahdi was present in their faces for others to see, this was the esoteric purpose of the chant Golem decided, to strip not just the chanters, but all those who heard them, of their individuality and privacy.

'Very, very ugly on the ear.'

'I don't understand how this man can think he has any connection with God. Unless they're right and he is mad. This noise is inhuman.'

'Which is the point about God, he isn't human, we've made religion *too* human, when the truth about God is that he is meant to be *inhuman* and unfathomable. It may be that this is how all primitive religions began, banging drums like monkeys do. Look around you though, I don't see devotion in the faces of these men, they are scared, this Mahdi of theirs rules more through fear than devotion. The whole display, the mountain, trees, invisible disembodied voices, it is all theatre designed to tap into our oldest fears, mountains that speak, spirits that know, hearts that can be read. Don't allow yourself to be spooked, it is all part of the show.'

'You're right. He has to unite all his factions. What do the devout ones,' Artay pointed at the men with beards in Arabic style smocks, 'what do they have in common with the jungle pirates like War Boss and freaks like Amnesty? The Mahdi has to convince them of his extra sensory importance or else his coalition would never hold. These men are not simple savages, they are independent minded too. But he would make savages of them.'

'Perhaps that is why he created the myth. We'll know soon enough.'

'Then you think there was never meant to be a Mahdi, the scriptures are wrong?'

'Like the arrival of Christ the saviour, I would have to be there to know. So far as this trip was concerned I never entertained any great hopes.'

'How will you address the man when we meet him then?'

'I will take him as he wishes to be taken, try and see him as he sees himself. The same way as I would with any other head of state, which is what he is now as good as. My guess is that he may overcompensate for his unconventional political career, by needing more humouring than most.'

'Evidently. Are you alright, you look a little ill?'

'Tired, only very tired.'

The chanting had slowed down into a low moaning groan, a dying creature asking to be put out of its misery, 'this is like something out of The Lost World', said Beasley throwing himself onto the floor, 'you've got to hope they knock it off for dinner.'

'They will,' said Francis, 'everyone has to eat.'

'Was your old mate always so insecure Francis, needing a camp full of loonies to sing his praises?'

'No, he was very charming, one of these, "if you like my ideas you'll like my sexual organs" kind of men…'

There was laughter; Francis seemed to have reconciled himself to whatever his fate held in store for him, 'always very successful with women from the beginning…' Francis hesitated, and seeing Foy was not listening continued, 'he was a very good salesman too, good with all kinds of people. He could probably have succeeded at anything he put his mind to. Had he been English who knows, he might have sat on the board of one of your mobile phone companies ordering Shimbite from the same mines his followers have deserted to follow him from.'

'Swings and roundabouts eh, you make him sound like an all round good guy.'

'I would not go that far, I never trusted him, but then I had no need to, it was enough to obey him. From the time of his visions he changed, the army militia became more like a cult, and he became more mysterious and private about his ways. That it should have ended up like this does not surprise me.'

'What do you think he'll make of our presence in Shimba?'

'He is a megalomaniac so of course he will think that you have come here for him, it would not cross his mind to think any other way, whatever these Iranians might tell him. And of course, he's right.'

'And what the hell are they doing here anyway, had you ever heard of an Iranian connection in this place?'

'They send him guns, that we have long expected.'

'We should be glad we ran into them' said Pagan joining the conversation, 'they've made life considerably easier for us. Taking us right up to the Mahdi, with a promised personal introduction, perfect.'

'Are you honestly still thinking about the mission now Captain Pagan?'

'Why not Francis, these two Iranian fellows seem quite nice, at least the older one does, more bark than bite and they clearly think we're a busted flush. And your old Warlord pals have been very sweet to us too, so with the exception of those pygmies and Elder, God rest his soul, we've had a cushioned ride, practically mollycoddled when you think of it, which is the key, everyone has their own fish to fry and angle to pursue, they've forgotten or just plain underestimated us.'

'All power to you for staying frosty Sir, but won't it be enough to try getting away point blank without taking their precious Mahdi with us. They'd give us a bit of hot pursuit at the least, fanatical chanters no less, a touch of bloody suicide about the idea you have to admit.'

'If we can find a way of doing it we should, because we're back at square one, we have surprise on our side, just not as much of it as before.'

'It's exhausting, isn't it?' said Beasley looking at Foy, 'it's not enough for us to be taken prisoner, we have to avenge the slight by turning the tables and taking this mad fellow,' he beckoned at the mountain, 'to the cleaners.'

Francis clicked his tongue, 'it's not impossible, by all reports the Mahdi has become slack, autocracy is no longer a tactic for him, it has become a matter of temperament. He would never dare to entertain the idea that men would come to his own camp to grab him as a prisoner. Especially now, the moment of his greatest triumph…'

A thundercloud was forming, its black hand stroking through the sky, other colours, as if from other worlds, visible behind it, slow purples and serene pinks, receding like outcasts.

'Beautiful isn't it?' said Foy.

'The benign indifference of the universe,' said Beasley.

'No, nature asking us to be more like it,' said Pagan, 'powerful.'

Foy felt a warm push, as many parts loving as lustful, swill round her belly. Taking care that Beasley had gone back to talking to Francis she asked Pagan, astonished at her own boldness, 'are you married?'

'I'm sorry?'

'Are you married? I apologise in advance, I know it's the kind of thing you expect to be asked by a woman with no time to spare in Bangkok airport, I guess my position isn't so different from her though.'

Pagan was not sure what she was driving at, or although

nearly sure, could not quite believe it, 'I appreciate your directness, I'm not married to anyone now. I was, still would be I guess, if she hadn't ended it.'

Foy pursed her lips, no longer quite sure of what image of herself she possessed, 'so no love in your life?'

'I...I guess I try and avoid hatred but I'm not a great one for love...' as he said this he recognised his understandable attraction to Foy *was* slightly wayward, veering away from simple desire towards an undefined yearning. Quickly he added, 'and your love life? If I was your boyfriend I wouldn't have been mad enough to allow you out here on your own, or at all.'

'My love life? You've seen all there is to see! Mainly restricted to how those pygmies and that creepy young Iranian are looking at me! Though from what I gather, it's all about to get a hell of a lot more complicated.'

'You mean all this about you becoming this Mahdi's wife? Why those psychos kidnapped you?'

'That was what I meant, yeah. My four days of fun in the great outdoors. You should have seen me, I was the star turn, honest.'

There was a lightness about Foy, only noticeable when she relaxed, an awkward grace in her movements that was girlish in a way that did not irritate him. For a tall woman she dropped her shoulders and had obviously never been taught about posture or how to walk properly, all stuff Pagan assumed the rich took care of in finishing school. The clumsy way her beauty fell off her settled it. Compared to her strength and adaptability, Foy's surfaces were nothing to him. Or at least, to Pagan's astonishment, a quality he could see past.

'I really don't know what to make of you Foy, and nor, would I guess, will the Mahdi. He'd be a foolish man if he thinks just because he's got a ring on your finger, he'll be leading you up the aisle.'

'Should I tell him I'm already spoken for?'

'No need, we'll get you out of this before it comes to that, come on, you must have noticed our extraordinary military prowess by now!'

'Oh yes, our guards...'

'Are shitting themselves,' Pagan laughed.

'Keep your voice down Sir, we've company,' said Beasley giving a thumbs-up sign to Golem, as he walked towards them with a bent tray of tin cups.

'Tomorrow we hand you over to the Mahdi, you know that, so this will be our last chance to talk. And first. This is *chang'aa*, not porridge' Golem handed Pagan a tin cup. They had walked a few metres away from the rest of the group and were sat beside a ditch of pretty weeds.

Pagan stared at the offering with suspicion; '*channg'aa*...Shimbali for "oblivion".'

'Correct Mr Bond.'

The liquid smelt of pilfered jet fuel, with a hint of embalming fluid and methanol.

'It's not a truth serum, Banana Gin, our African partners swear by it.'

Pagan hesitated. For a second Golem eyed him with the fear and suspicion drinkers have for non-drinkers.

'Goodbye Mother.' Pagan downed it in one.

'More?'

'Thank you.'

Golem waited a moment. 'I'm glad you aren't embarrassed with silence.'

'This isn't a dinner date and you're not a pretty girl.'

'No, but I may be about to torture you.'

'True, I can't discount the possibility.'

'You don't feel it in your bones though?'

'No.' It was true, Pagan's sixth sense for violence, usually keen enough to pick up on the faintest tremor of menace, was mute. He was not in a threatening situation, or even an interrogative one. If anything, it was Golem who appeared to be the keener to talk, to tell Pagan everything. It was possible that the Iranian had come down to this level of operation from something bigger, an important desk job in Tehran or a Bureau of his own, because he looked tired of it all, well on his way to absolute unbelief, thought Pagan, 'any more of that in the flask?'

'How rude of me. Yes, you are not wrong. Your head is unlikely to appear in that ditch, whatever information it may hold. I am not interested.'

Pagan turned to look at the speaker, with interest now that he knew he was in no danger. Golem had allowed his eyes to close and head to droop, almost dreamily. Though it seemed unlikely, Pagan was sure that Golem was on the verge of crying, or at the least, very much wanted to. The tremendous sense of exhaustion packed into his last remark aroused a pity Pagan was careful to notice but not give in to. In spite of his role as the captor Golem was lost and friendless, whereas Pagan had Beasley, Francis and, yes, Foy, to talk to and be inspired by. It was a small thing viewed from above, a handful of human beings dressed like shipwrecks exchanging remarks of dubious validity, yet together they were the difference between a pain suffered and one shared. Golem was the true captive, kept under arrest by thoughts he could not air. Pagan watched him stretch an arm and mechanically fill his cup, his eyes still closed. Mechanically he filled the cup to the brim, spilling not one drop. Golem's secrets were a greater restriction on him than the people he kept them from, his junior officer an untrustworthy rival and his African partners loyal only to success. Of the two Iranians, it was the scowling Artay who was still full of beans, back in the camp chatting to the po-faced Islamicists, which gave Pagan an opening, 'your number two, he's making the most of it with those Al Qaeda types, it often surprised me that your two sub sects of Islam don't find more in common with each other. You both hate us for a start.'

'We probably would if this lot gain control of a state, or better still, a Continent.'

'Détente?'

'Superficially and for a little while, maybe. The different strands of the Mahdi's grand alliance look to be getting on, all happily wrong together, so long as there is an obvious enemy to define themselves against. And of course, a Mahdi to lead them. Once they gain power however, they will fight each other, even us, like the different Communist countries fought each other and the different Christian ones did before that. In the historical battle between belief and tribe, tribe trumps belief, local interests over universal brotherhood, I'm sure you know the story.'

'Belief has its moments.'

'I'm surprised to hear you say that. I assumed you would be a typical English pragmatist of few words and few ideas. Yes, belief rises to the surface from time to time, gains the ascendancy, but it is a sprinter and not a long distance runner, it can't last the distance against habit, against blood. Nations are like families, you care about yours first, even if you hate its guts.'

'Nothing like travel to broaden the mind. I thought you Mullahs were all ideologues. I'm glad to find I'm wrong about that. Where did you pick up your English? It's word perfect.'

'London. When I was younger I thought I might live there.'

'Never say never.'

'Please don't get any hopes up that you can turn me into a double agent. I'm tired of all sides.'

'Not only you, but I'd still rather be used, exploited and left to die by my side than yours.'

'Why, what difference does it make if you die?'

'Because it's mine. It isn't all about outcomes, its about the stuff that comes before them that influences whether you think your career in international violence was worth pursuing or not. My guess is you've had a road to Damascus style experience out here, it would have come wherever you went, because you've aligned yourself with a band of life-hating maniacs, but it happened out here because this is where you are. I won't insult you by any further analysis. Will you let us go?

'No, of course not. This isn't bloody Christmas.'

Pagan looked to see how far they were from the nearest armed guard. The moment to overpower Golem and make a run for it had passed, he had squandered it by overplaying his hand and underestimating the tongue loosening effects of Banana Gin on an empty stomach. Maybe Golem was the cannier player of the two of them, after all.

'I will not let my assistant kill you either, which was his intention, so it is not all bad news for you. You can enjoy the difference between life and death for a while yet.'

'Enjoy the difference?'

'Yes, the difference between life and death, the difference between tasting tuna fish or not.'

'I had thought brutal questioning was going to be more the order of the day, if you passed on the killing option.'

'A broken finger for a name my Government already knows, a gouged out eye to discover that Shimbite is important to your country's commercial interests? Really, what truly new thing could torturing you or the Sergeant tell me? Neither you nor he would talk, of that I'm certain, so I would end up having to do you to death, if only to remain consistent to my purpose. Interrogation is useful in revealing enemies you don't know, the ones who would stab you in the back, which is why we use it against our own people, the enemy within. You are not that. We know where we stand with the external threat. With you there is no burning fuse that pulling your fingernails off will put out, so for me, why bother with you? Ideology would have inspired me in the past, yet as you know, I have no use for it at present.'

'Aren't those the kind of tricks that make interrogators tick, not that I'm in a hurry to lose a fingernail. Personally I never thought torture was *for* anything, just another penalty to give you a greater incentive not to be on the losing side.

Counterproductive when you look at it from a neutral point of view.'

'That is an admirably practical way of understanding the phenomenon. Yes, I must be losing touch with my calling. I have a wife and child at home, even if I succeed in my mission, and it is not at all clear I will as my mission is not at all clear, I have a growing, let us call it adumbration, that all will not be well for them, or me, when I return home. So in the spirit of a drowning man I have no wish to take any more people down than I have to. I still believe in God you see and I don't want to add any more harmful acts to those I've already committed. You will still be left with the Mahdi, which may be bad enough, I cannot tell. I, however, hold no dire intention towards you or your companions, and am sorry for the one that is already dead, and those that were killed earlier. Don't worry about the girl, she will safely disappear, you have my word on it. That is all I have to tell you.'

It was in Pagan's nature to take advantage of an opponent letting his guard down; here he saw he did not need to. It reminded him of being on the receiving end of an apology and how difficult he found it not to rub the apologiser's nose in their own remorse, to gun for victory rather than a humble truce. Golem was not the only one losing touch with his calling.

'Thank you,' he said, and offered Golem his hand.

Golem allowed Pagan to walk a few steps in front of him, like a teacher anxious not to damage a wayward pupil's credibility, aware that by the standards of International Espionage, he had as good as incriminated himself in a plot against his own interests. The camp was preparing for sleep, an easy-going conviviality creating a false impression of universal brotherhood. Straining his ears Golem tried to pick up the odd remark from the different fires, staggered pockets of noise from the pygmies, a closing quip from Beasley, 'where I come from the norm is the exception', for the benefit of Foy who giggled coquettishly, and dark, joyless muttering from the bored fanatics whom Artay had taken his place with, again. It would seem that his bonding with Artay might have heralded a false dawn, especially as it was based on a false view of himself, sold to his junior as a way of appeasing him. Any warmth between them relied too heavily on misperceptions, the effect of which could last a day or two, until some major decision gave Golem away as a doubtridden apostate.

'Good evening to you both.'

Below him sat War Boss and Amnesty, huddled together in conversation with Francis, nominally their prisoner, yet by appearances barely put out by the fact. Golem had delayed this encounter for too long. 'If you'll excuse me' he said addressing War Boss and Amnesty, 'I would like to ask the prisoner a few questions, in private.'

The two men sloped off sheepishly, as if they had been caught out, Francis staring stoically at the small fire, a tolerant smile on his lips.

'I'll come to the point. I lied, it's not what I want to ask you, it's what I want you to know I know about you, and have known before I arrived in Shimba.'

'I beg your pardon?'

'The files I read in Tehran told me all about you Francis Leslie, you are known to us, though judging by your current predicament, I'd say our intelligence is rather out of date.'

'That is surprising and flattering' said Francis, displaying neither surprise nor the look of one who might be flattered.

'Why has a man of your intelligence and experience ended up as an assistant to a corrupt, and now dead, quasi Dictator?'

Francis hesitated.

'Speak frankly with me.'

'What for, if you know my history anyway?'

'Because I want to hear it from you, on paper it puzzles me, coming from your mouth it may make sense.'

'As you prefer. When I was fourteen I fought with the Shimban People's Army, to establish a Marxist Republic. We killed the King, his family, and then each other. Next I embraced secular Socialism, the gospel of human rights, the cooperatives and communes; later I even accepted the market reforms, the IMF, foreign investment as the future. Where I drew the line was at religious revelation. I did not want to try on every hat in the shop.'

'You feel that way about the Mahdi's religious turn?'

'Yes.'

'That's a pity, a man with your enquiring mind would have been good for religion, a religious movement at least could use you. I was instructed that if I made contact with you, you would be a good man to talk to, to do business with, trapped as you are between two different tendencies in this country. I have a proposition for you. There is nothing about your background that should predispose you towards suicide, which is what continuing on your present course would amount to. We know you have fallen foul of the Mahdi and tomorrow he will probably kill you, horribly no doubt.'

'No doubt he will. I have been preparing myself for it.'

'So it would be a terrible waste for you to die like that. You are perfectly posed between the Mahdi and the old Regime, there is so much you know about this country and its leading players that we in Tehran don't. In the circumstances it would not be impossible for me to find a way of getting you out of here, back to Tehran, cut a deal of some kind, you understand?'

Francis nodded.

'We could use an indigenous African expert, one with your wide and varied background. You would not be betraying your English friends; they and their country have no future here. Besides, if you stay here you will be killed, the Mahdi will not give you a second chance, you must know that. These fortuitous coincidences, my being in charge rather than my assistant, your old friends Amnesty and War Boss deciding not to kill you, these coincidences are all Allah's way of keeping a low profile. You would be a fool to not take advantage of them, and one thing I know you are not, is a fool.'

'I know.'

'Then think about what I've said, and tell your friends War Boss and Amnesty, who I know are not the type to turn down a good offer, tell them that they will be rewarded if the English girl somehow loses her way to the Mahdi's nuptial chamber, and ends up on a plane to Arusha.'

A handful of flame flickered over Francis's face, showing only the lower half, making it hard for Golem to know what kind of impression his words had made.

'Stay close to me tomorrow. I know you enjoy being an enigma, now might be the time to declare your hand.'

'I will,' said Francis, meaning something very different from what his captor had in mind, though not so clear for him to even know what it was yet.

CHAPTER ELEVEN

The prophet armed

The next morning
The mood in the Mahdi's camp was edgy, and not only because the close cycle of praise and blame was too severe for the praised to enjoy it, or the blamed to feel it was deserved. Irrational leadership techniques worked when there was a strong leader visible. The problem for the timid and far too emotional General Strike, acting commander of the army, was that the Mahdi had not been well enough to appear in front of his public for over a week, missing his moment of triumph, the death of the President. The stalling tactics, body doubles, talk of the Mahdi returning to his roots in the wilderness and endless incantations and chanting had not disguised the void left by his absence. No one was more sensitive to this than General Strike, a five foot two ex-librarian, hopelessly short sighted, given to tantrums and a crying fits, chosen for his devotion which bordered on the idola-trous, and now hopelessly out of his depth. Only that morning he had overheard soldiers say that they would die for the Mahdi but they'd be damned if they'd die for the faggot Strike, fairly well encapsulating the strength of his personal following. This did not mean he was a fool, only a weak man promoted above his ability because of the Mahdi's rampant distrust of anyone perceived as a threat or potential leadership rival. In happier times this was an arrangement that worked well, Strike had shown a talent for the kind of logistical and administrative work that bored the Mahdi; what he could not do, was address a crowd, though nor for the moment could the Mahdi. His Doctor had diagnosed him with a rare variant of Jungle Flu, carried by a flesh-eating parasite, the effects and duration of which were

indeterminate. Practically this meant that the Mahdi, Lord of Shimba, lacked the fortitude and energy to go to the lavatory by himself, hardly able to project his voice further than the huddle of minions collected by his bed, desperate for orders and commands to pacify a potentially directionless army. On the positive side there was little doubt that the Mahdi, with rest and the modern medicine, would live, on the negative, it would be months, if not longer, before he made a recovery. Strike had no idea how his reign would last another day, the impatience surrounding his obfuscations growing hourly. If only he had the wit to explain that some aspects of the Mahdi were human and therefore fallible while others were not. The propaganda machine had long since taken on a life of its own and there could be no way of admitting that the Mahdi bled blood, far less emitted human, all too human snot every time he sneezed.

Strike's most pressing concern, that morning, was the arrival of Amnesty and War Boss, two backstabbing opportunists who had always had it in for him. With them was the Iranian delegation. If this was not enough, they were also in possession of two British prisoners, one of the President's lackeys and the Mahdi's white bride to be. This last personage caused Strike the greatest distress, his master already had six beautiful Shimban wives, and two Nigerian and Ugandan ones, so what did he want with a milky infidel filly? The whole business involving the disgusting British mercenaries, who had not come cheap, was inexplicable to him, War Boss's suggestion that the Mahdi might be something of a pervert earning the stiffest rebuke. It had, however, planted the only seed of doubt Strike dared entertain against his overlord, not helped by a suitcase full of erotica he stumbled upon whenever they moved camps.

The commanding heights of the cave-mouth Strike stood at overlooked a small and desultory courtyard, carved into the mountain by one of the ancient tribes. The impression was one of a modest castle keep, the surrounding holes in the wall housing the Mahdi's various wives. The main cave, a quarter of a mile deep, acted as the headquarters of the army, map room and the Mahdi's private residence and hospital. Strike's defensive posture, his short legs spread-eagled and arms aggressively folded, was more than symbolic. He was under instructions to not allow War Boss or Amnesty into the dwelling until the Mahdi woke and was in proper possession of himself, nor was he permitted to suggest that the Mahdi was in anything less than full health. The Mahdi, even in the throes of illness, recognised that God helped those who helped themselves and the admission of mortal frailty, even to cynics like War Boss, could cost him his army.

Leaving their prisoners on the other side of the stone tunnel that separated the yard from the main camp, Amnesty and War Boss strolled up to the rock staircase, guarded by the agitated Strike, his fluttering eyes critically assessing the situation.

'You're late' he shouted from his platform, 'you were expected over a day ago.'

War Boss laughed out loud, conscious that he was not being accused of a particularly unique kind of disciplinary lapse.

'We are here to see the Mahdi, not you Strike; it would be best if you returned to your charts and ration cards.'

'Change your tone when talking to me, I'm not one of your slum blacks to be ordered around.'

'It was a long journey with plenty of incident, tell the Mahdi we await him.'

Strike felt his blood surge with an intensity that made him dizzy. This happened regularly enough for him to know that if he started shouting his voice would raise an octave, lending him a female tonality. Controlling his rage, he squawked with as much authority as he could muster, 'who are you to demand an audience with your commander, he who made you and lifted you up from bondage?'

'Save the Old Testament stuff Strike, and all your talk of

bondage, we don't come to you with our problems,' replied War Boss with a wink, 'you confuse us with yourself, no one raised us up.'

'Your nerve is astounding! Have you any idea how far I go out of my way to protect you?'

'What you add to the truth, you take from it Strike; where is the Mahdi, what is going on here? Already I'm hearing stories, people are talking.'

At times like this Strike consoled himself that his enemies' motivation could make their negative feelings towards him easier to bear. The two Generals were jealous of his relationship with the Mahdi and felt ill-used, having spent too much time at the front. Still, each time they returned their insolence and swagger seemed to increase exponentially, and a dressing down, one that involved chains and a public recantation, would be useful when the moment allowed it. Sadly, that moment was not now. Doing his best to imitate the Mahdi's regal manner of speech, Strike continued, 'don't confuse your impertinence with that of the human race. Go back to your prisoners. The Mahdi will see you when he is ready and only then. You appear to forget his position and overestimate your own...'to his relief War Boss and Amnesty took a step backwards at these words, 'go and take a wash and bring the Iranians in, they are our guests and should be treated with every courtesy. And please, let us stop talking at cross purposes, we are on the same side.'

War Boss and Amnesty bowed their heads a little mockingly, obedient yet unconvinced. Clinging to his successful display of leadership, Strike doubled back in to the cave, hoping that further instructions awaited him, the burdens of command too existential a wager for a man who wished to live in the shadow of a greater one.

Foy had stopped thinking, it was the only way she could clothe her fear. She had, in effect, become two people, one was still able to talk, smile, give and share compliments, the other too terrified to declare itself. If she allowed this second person supremacy, or even listened to it, her knees would give way and the earth would swallow her. So instead she kept calm and carried on, finding that, in continuing, things worked well for her, Beasley made her laugh, Pagan was still causing shivers and even the attentions of Artay were endearing. There was no denying though, that she had come to the end, or near to the end, of her journey. The nastiest aspect of entering the camp, a cross between a community centre and hastily convened festival, was that everyone knew why she was here and looked at her with a mixture of curious sympathy and knowing contempt. Everything she had experienced in life before Shimba was academic compared to this, how she wished she could have had all this meaning without the danger, endless profundity without the feeling she was about to die.

'They will be trying for an audience with the Mahdi,' said Francis, 'he likes to play games with people, do not be surprised if we have to wait here for hours...'

'This feels like someone pissing in the wound after the salt has run out' said Beasley, 'times you wish the buggers would just hurry up and do their worst.'

'I can wait,' Foy somehow mustered.

They had brought her here for sex; that was what the whole escapade amounted to. Foy had always felt that sex brought out people's selfish sides, and what could be more selfish than reducing someone's existence to kidnap, torture and bondage. Having forbidden herself to think at all about the Mahdi as a person, rather than as a situation, Foy now faced the prospect that a flesh and blood being was responsible for her predicament, and that in the event of their meeting, she was unlikely to like him very much.

'What are you laughing about?' asked Beasley.

'I can't believe this is happening to me, it's so wrong, I can't help it, laughing, if you can believe that.'

'You're laughing, so yeah, I can.' Beasley surveyed the veiled women trading lumps of Shimbite, scowling teens practising small arms drill, and the general stench of shallow latrines, then shook his head, 'not much cause for humour but to hell with it, why not.'

'I know laughter is the most obvious defence mechanism in the book, but I can't think about what's going to happen to me, if I did I wouldn't be able to stand. I mean it.'

'Tell me about it, it makes me nostalgic for the jungle. What are all these blind people with sticks wandering around here for Francis?'

'It's the Mahdi's preferred form of punishment; eyes are burnt out for "infractions of discipline". We should have made our break for it last night,' said Francis, 'to hell with whether they killed us or not, at least we'd have had a chance.'

'Cheer up, we still do. It's late, I know, to talk of how we're going to get out of this disaster,' Pagan intervened, 'and after what you've been through you'd be entitled to not believe me anyway, but things will work out well for us, especially for you Foy.'

Foy examined his face for sincerity, and on finding it, said 'thank you, I don't know how you know but thank you.'

Pagan was about to tell her about his conversation with Golem, as the night before he had been bound on his own, when War Boss and Amnesty emerged from the tunnel and beckoned to Foy.

'My time has come' she said and, brushing deliberately against Pagan, walked towards them, not wishing to be dragged kicking and screaming to her fate, hopeful even now of a miracle.

'It's going to be okay,' called Beasley, slightly less confidently than Pagan who yelled the same thing, *it's going to be okay, don't worry.*'

Golem watched Foy disappear into the tunnel, Artay

otherwise distracted with the bearded gunman who now seemed to be acting as his personal bodyguard. To Golem's surprise Foy did not turn around, heading directly into the tunnel with dignity and restraint. He had his own reasons for supposing the English were correct and that she would be "alright" and wondered whether she already knew, or if this was a rare display of stiff upper lip. At least she was free of responsibility, with as little say in his plan to free her as she had in the Mahdi's to make her his wife.

'Take care of the girl,' he called. Golem was fairly sure that he would be judged on what was best for Iran, getting involved in sordid stories involving white slavery would bring no glory on him or the regime. Therefore it was best to get the girl out of the picture as quickly and quietly as possible. Weirdly, and if he was honest with himself, he would rather perform this service for the girl than for his country, or his own reputation. Why he should care so little about his own fate was a puzzle. He had always suspected that a life lived on behalf of others, whether it was his family or country, would not be enough to sustain a selfish decadent like him. And though he loved his family, and his country, taken together, both fell short of inspiring him to great deeds. A spiritual lethargy, so long hinted at on the Monday mornings that followed his Sunday nights, was on him with a vengeance, crippling his zeal without, peculiarly, affecting his confidence. It was a confidence based on a strange premise, a liberating lack of care as to what might happen to him now they were in the Mahdi's hands. To care so little was a mixed blessing, and Golem felt a little like a madman taking perverse pride in emptying out the contents of his own brain for a bet. Care was what had kept him alive, bestowed him with preferences and provided him with a moral outlook. Jettisoning it could leave him hung out to dry in the long run which was the point; Golem had stopped thinking about the long run, a finality imbuing all he sensed and saw.

'Looking pleased with yourself,' said Beasley, 'it can't be good working as a pimp.'

Beaming at him as though he had been complimented, Golem delivered Beasley a sharp upper-cut, a jet of warm blood rising like freshly struck oil from the Sergeant's nose.

'I had that coming' Beasley laughed, taking a step back to acknowledge the impact.

Golem offered him a handkerchief, 'I'm sorry, your remarks are usually amusing. That last one wasn't. That girl will be looked after, and not in the way you're afraid of…'

Neither War Boss or Amnesty said anything, they did not need to, Foy was well aware that they had no intention of taking her to the Mahdi. Furtively, glancing up at the cave mouth to make sure they were unseen, War Boss took Foy by the hand and ushered her into a hole in the wall. Inside was a storeroom of sorts, cans of soda water stacked in piles next to canned meat that had gone astray from the aid organisations that had purchased them.

'Quickly' said War Boss, brandishing a pair of old overalls, 'change into these.'

'This doesn't look like a wedding dress to me.'

'It isn't, we're going to smuggle you out of here, and from here to the Tanzanian border. There will be no wedding in Shimba for you.'

'What will you tell your Mahdi?'

'Leave that to us.'

Which would have been a good way of leaving it had not General Strike entered the room in search of something.

'What are you all doing here?' he said, more puzzled than suspicious.

'Getting a drink man, we're thirsty.'

'Well hurry up and get one then, the Mahdi wants to see you.'

'See who?'

'To see all of you, the girl, the British, the Iranians, all of you at once. Get me a drink while you are at it too, the dust is murder.'

War Boss looked at Amnesty with dismay, an expression mirrored by Foy. Strike had a nervous harried look, 'as you may be aware, the Mahdi hasn't been in the best of health. You may find him somewhat...different, changed...quieter than before. You must not be alarmed.'

Amnesty glanced at Foy and shrugged his shoulders as if to say he had done his best. Foy focused on a large white moth, a feeling that her last chance had passed her by, and there would not be another coming, summed up by this static Lepidoptera, consoled only by the thought that whatever was going to happen, would happen soon.

'What do you think Sir, we going to the scaffold quietly or going for the full Danton, kicking and screaming our way to the scaffold as we go?'

Pagan had to concede that Beasley's question was as well posed as it was relevant. The party had been herded into the main cave, unbound from their cuffs, and assembled in a line, a parody of courtiers awaiting royalty. The affect of this, other than bringing attention to how dishevelled they all looked, was to introduce an equality to the proceedings, with prisoners, Iranians and Shimbans all on the same level, that is, one substantially below that of the man they awaited.

Strike cleared his throat loudly, the grating catarrh echoing upwards. Hopefully he looked towards the stairway that led into the back of the cave and the Mahdi's chamber. Wisps of starchy white light percolated through the gloom, pouring out of holes high in the roof of the cave. A large crimson drape had been hung like a curtain over the entrance to the second chamber, burning urns mentholating the air, the atmosphere uncomfortably feral, better suited to a convalescing animal than a new head of state. Not showing any signs of nervousness, or interest in his surroundings, Pagan whispered back to Beasley, 'be prepared for anything. This place is a fucking madhouse straight out of a Kurtzian wet dream.'

'You're being generous Sir.'

Foy, who had been brought to the far left of the line, was sobbing gently, 'I'm sorry,' she coughed.

'Don't be,' said Beasley.

'Shhhh!' Strike held up a hand ceremoniously and then thought better of it, 'he is here, the Mahdi, all kneel, all kneel.'

Francis choked with indignation and looked sideways in disbelief at War Boss and Amnesty who, along with the other guards, had obeyed the command.

'All kneel, all kneel? Has Julius completely lost his mind?'

'You had better do as you're told Francis,' hissed War Boss, 'it'll be easier this way.'

'Not you' Strike waved his finger at Golem and Artay, 'or you, just bow a bit, like this', Strike lowered his head like a practised courtesan. Both Iranians ignored the instruction and held their bearing upright. Golem noticed Artay was shaking, shaking so involuntarily that he was not bothering to disguise it, his eyes eagerly awaiting the Mahdi with something approaching panic. A strange boy, thought Golem, perversely wedded to those things he professed to dislike. Foy was shaking too and Golem guessed that whatever plans his confederates had for her had been foiled by the speed at which they had been granted an audience with the Mahdi.

'The Mahdi' said Strike again, a little louder so that whoever was stood behind the curtain could hear him and raise the thing. A gong was sounded and another cloud of mentholated smoke floated over the top of the partition.

'Behold the Mahdi!'

'With that build up I'm not surprised he's stalling,' Beasley sneered between his teeth, 'perhaps the magic carpet got stuck in traffic.'

Pagan, who was standing next to Foy, squeezed her hand, an image of a sunflower shored up by a brick triggered by the touch. It was not usual for him to experience mental pictures like this, and in an attempt to compensate for it, he said,

'I've my eye on the bastards, stick close whatever happens and we'll be out of here, alive and with your life ahead of you. Hold onto that.'

Golem raised his eyes patiently. There was no doubt that they were being served up the moment they had all been waiting for with oak cured ham and a generous portion of cheese; hence if a two headed Griffin had flown out of the cave it would still be anticlimactic. No creature could possibly live up to the kind of mythic hyperbole the Mahdi had enjoyed, which explained their collective shock as a crooked man, leaning on a plastic crutch, slowly emerged from the shadows. That it was the Mahdi, there was no doubt. He was dressed not in robes, turban-less and clean shaven, and Pagan's first thought was of a retired officer from the Kenyan Army who had lectured at Sandhurst, Foy's of a crabby Nigerian minicab driver who had let her off a fare, Golem's of the great and mighty Oz, another bastard human who relied on smoke and mirrors. It would be wrong to say that this infirm figure was, when taken on his own terms, underwhelming, as without looking like a prophet in the Koranic sense, his appearance invited a second opinion. The face was interestingly ageless, not young, rather one that had not lived in time or looked to have any relationship with chronology. There was a jarring neutrality about it, as though it could, in its unformed plasticity, have access to any face it wished to pull or imitate, a contortionist caught off guard, or one about to pounce, Golem could not tell. Granted the Mahdi was a performer, one who gave the air of being possessed by his material, reflected in the confidence, or complacency, with which he dressed. Stocky, despite his illness, and of average height with a narrow shaven head, the Mahdi wore a purple cardigan pulled over his shoulders and mauve Henri Lloyd vest, with large Firetrap shorts and orange flip-flops. These clothes were worn as a challenge to, rather than confirmation of his status as an otherworldly being. Whether they had simply surprised him at home, or this informality was part of his plan to confound expectations, was answered in the whites of his eyes. For that is what they were, titanium white like a blind man's, expressionless, dead, enigmatic, the only colour in them the faintest hint of red. The large sunglasses that formed part of his public appearance had been discarded in this world of the cave, and his voice, a deep squeak if that was possible, made him sound like a giant mouse. This, and his clipped moustache, would have been funny if humour were an instinct as strong as fear. Golem had expected the Mahdi to be ridiculous, and this he was, but the sheer sinister bearing of a man who shares his jokes with God and not fellow mortals, was something he had not considered until the Mahdi spoke, the air souring instantaneously. 'None of you look like you would mind very much if you died. Brave men to come here.'

Letting go of his crutch, the Mahdi raised his hands, picking up some invisible object, and threw it over the heads of those assembled.

'God is great. Obey me. Obey him. Disobey and join the eyeless ones. One eye for me, one eye for Allah. *I am the Mahdi.*'

It was, thought Foy, a silly yet terrible thing to say, terrible in the high old meaning of the word, one that would make her think about what that word meant for a long time after.

'There is so little of it left, Strike. Time. It goes, goes so fast. Down these steps, my doctor says I must rest, this I know, let us make these minutes count then, for there is little of it.'

Strike bounded up the crudely constructed platform with the aplomb of an eager puppy keen to show he was his master's favourite.

'What a nutter, he can't even speak properly,' said Beasley under his breath, 'what do you think?'

'A black Transylvanian,' answered Pagan.

'I knew they were after our blood.'

Ignoring his generals and the Iranian delegation, a faint twitch stirring over his redder eye, the Mahdi allowed Strike to lead him down the stairs, level with his audience. Leaning against Francis's chest he said a few words in Shimbali.

Answering in English Francis said, 'yes, she is really English. I can't answer for her virginity.'

Trying to ignore this frank declaration of the Mahdi's priorities, Golem stepped out of the line only to find that Artay had vanished from his side. Before he had time to take in the fact, or to see where his assistant had gone, the Mahdi had signalled to a guard to lead Foy away.

Beasley and Pagan watched her go, presumably weighing up the options of what could be achieved by a suicidal intervention. Discomfortingly the Mahdi, smelling strongly of Fahrenheit 451, was looking at them both in way that might possibly be construed as amorous, or friendly in a way that bore them no good.

'British Army. Here to parley or kill, I wonder…always the same tricks,' the Mahdi sighed disappointedly, 'it has been a while since an African leader has had the courage to take the lives of white prisoners…what to do, what is to be done, always, what is to be done…'

'Mahdi' interrupted Golem, 'we have come a long way to see you…' he immediately regretted his choice of words, reminding him of the kind of thing a tourist might say to Mickey Mouse in Disneyland. 'Would I be wrong in thinking you calculate the interests of British prisoners over those of the Iranian state? I am here as its representative.'

For the first time the Mahdi seemed to notice Golem, running his tongue over his sweaty moustache. With an expression that could be described as bashful, though with words that were anything but, he said 'men that aren't calculating live in fear of decisions they did not have the intelligence to make. I know who you are. I give no more of a dog's cuss for you, Persian, than the British pair. You were lost in the jungle, and back into her you will go. I accept your nation's arms but not her envoys.'

'That is what I thought,' said Artay, walking back in to the chamber he had so recently vacated with four of the bearded holy warriors at his side, 'I know you for what you are, "*Mahdi*". '

The Mahdi registered no surprise, not until the bullet hit him, at which point, Golem guessed, he had expected someone to stand in its way, or perhaps a heavenly power to divert it. The bearded warriors, doubtless at Artay's orders, had formed a ring round the cave-mouth and were trying to disarm the guards. Artay went forward like a train, firing off another bullet that reached its intended target with ease. Folded up on the floor, the Mahdi tucked in his legs and smiled to himself, as though overhearing a secret, a burst of machine gunfire from one of the beards cutting down an open mouthed Strike who fell over him with a thump. Both the SAS men, War Boss and Golem had dived behind a stone alter, Foy taking advantage of the chaos and breaking from her guards in an effort to reach them.

'Get down,' shouted Pagan, 'lay down where you are!'

Golem felt for his pistol. Artay was leering wildly, ecstatic, this assassination worth a thousand validations. 'Help me' called the Mahdi hoarsely from his place on the floor, blood collecting round his twitching body, so nearly a corpse, 'I feel the blood leave my soul.'

'There was always, don't you think, an unnoticed possibility to this situation,' Artay spoke breathlessly to Golem, tormented by his own excitement, 'something I knew that you did not, did you not wonder? Drop your gun Mahmoud. This mission was not about interpretation. This was never a trip you were meant to come back from. The state will look after your family, you need not worry about them.'

'Jafari's orders?'

'I was his insurance if you lost your way. You did.'

Golem saw it too late, the loose ends that could only have been tied if he had the nerve to recognise his own total unimportance, to see that his life was not singular or meaningful but a statistic and over. Artay was the mole Jafari had lumbered him with and the mad fanatic's next bullet was meant for him. Except it did not play out that way. Instead of the bullet he anticipated, Golem watched Pagan break a boulder over Artay's head with such force, that the skull cleaved into two perpendicular halves. The bearded assailants, surprised at this unexpected turn of events, lowered their rifles, fatally for their tactical advantage. War Boss, Amnesty and Francis were on to them, Beasley breaking the neck of the one closest to him with a heavy yank. From outside, a volley of randomly discharged lead arrived, fired by frightened guards ready to hedge their bets.

'Please,' whispered the Mahdi, 'I will share all this with you, power...power.'

Moving decisively towards a destiny he could at last be proud of, Golem walked up to the wounded man and, looking into his snowploughed eyes, emptied a chamber into one, and then the other. War Boss, rather than rebuking him, called out, 'you, you are in command now.'

'No,' said Golem pointing to Francis, 'he is', and without waiting for a reaction stuck the revolver in to his mouth and blew his own head off.

'Win some lose some, its all the same to me. Jesus, what a mess,' groaned Beasley and collapsed to the floor, a stray round having entered his back on a ricochet.

War Boss looked at Amnesty and then at Francis, 'what should we do?'

Showing no emotion whatsoever Francis strapped on an automatic rifle, and turning to Foy and Pagan, shouted, 'go, Mr Beasley is dead, go now you can...'

'What will you do?'

'Haven't you heard?' laughed Francis, 'I am the man who would become King!'

They did not need a second invitation. Through to the end of the cave, and out onto the back of Monkey Mountain they fled, looking one way only. It was not quite the end that Pagan had foreseen, running away was shabby and he and the nation he wore the uniform of had done a lot of it of late, running in Iraq, Afghanistan and now here. Of course, they called it different things, strategic redeployment, tactical retreat, letting the Americans have their turn, but it was the same old running away that was common to each situation, and at present there was no elaborate jargon to disguise the reality of what he and Foy were doing. Who cared what sort of country this made England or person it made Pagan? There were more important things in life than to discover what happens after death, and at least if he were killed now it would be for a reason. Foy. England, and standing your ground, like all useful ideas, would crop up again in some form or other.

Clearing the hill the two fugitives flung themselves on to a dried up river bed which led back into the jungle, the firm floor able to support them and on the far shore clumps of weed to hide behind if Francis turned out not to be the man who would be king after all. It took Pagan a moment to notice they were kissing passionately, the breathlessness of the run not making the slightest difference to the length and firm application of Foy's lips. For a giddy instant it felt like this was all they were going to do. Expecting that he was going to say something mildly humorous or wry, Pagan elected to say nothing, instead breaking off and saying 'I'm making up for the days and months I've wasted in these minutes, with you.'

'You mean it?'

'I do, who am I protecting? You need to know Foy.'

And with that they were on their feet, running again, not

running away, the ghosts of Agincourt, Waterloo and Mons covering their retreat, or so it would seem as a mist fell behind them and the two bodies entered the jungle and disappeared from sight for good.

Epilogue

The Headmaster did not know how to begin this one, accepting, as he did, the impossibility of passing it off onto someone else. He knew the man and his son personally, and had done so for years. It was his duty to do it himself; failing to would be a damning reproach to live with.

The sign saying 'Beasley Stores' needed repainting, in fact, the whole shop did. The Post Office concession had closed and with the food all out of date or from another time, there was little reason for anyone to go in, only sympathy for the old man, of which there was plenty. A pint of milk, a plastic cherry and the Sunday papers, on this little trade Morris Beasley survived, that and his inordinate pride and love for Ian, his only child, the centre of his life and entire reason for existing. It was impossible for anyone to enter the store, especially the Headmaster and his wife, without hearing about what the boy was doing, or in the Headmaster's case, being asked with a knowing wink what the boy was *really* doing. From the time his son had joined the army, to his graduation to The Special Air Service, the army and Ian's place in it was all that mattered to the old man. And now the boy was dead and the old man's reason to live with it, another casualty of the conflict killed off the battlefield, away from the official statistics and plinths. Or at least, this would be the case, once the old soldier heard that the young one had disappeared on a mission too covert to bring a body home from. And he would try and understand, and nod manfully as he had taught his son to, once a soldier himself, and wait until the Headmaster had left before he smashed the shop to pieces or drank himself into a coma.

Ruefully the Headmaster watched Maurice turn the tatty sign round from "Closed" to "Open", the resemblance to his son stronger than before, now that there was no one in their prime to compare him to. It was like playing God, watching the man live, not knowing yet, and though it would be cruel to not tell him, it was crueller to tell him right away and destroy these last few minutes of life he still had. Certainly the Headmaster could do nothing until he reigned in the ludicrous fit of sobbing he was in the grip of. He did not *feel* the man's pain, he *was* it, this is what he wanted to say: "I am you, I know what you know, I am the very same thing", which was nonsense, or would at least sound like it and not help anyone.

Maurice Beasley propped opened the door with a tray of empty milk bottles and squinted at the Volvo parked opposite his shop, his hand held over his eyes in an effort to see who his first customer of the day was. There was a perkiness about his movements typical of one who enjoyed the mornings, he was in the world now, ready for anything. The Headmaster pulled a bottle of Scotch out of the glove compartment. It was easier to tell sons about their dead fathers, that was what he had been used to doing, cheering up small boys. The natural order had turned and all he could think of was the line of Kipling about sons dying because their fathers lied. The Headmaster got out of the car and crossed the road, walking towards the old man, the world still there, only less so, less so than before.

ACKNOWLEDGEMENTS

Publishing has changed from my working with professionals who sometimes became friends, to working with my friends who in their proof reading, copy editing, design and photography and even marketing, attain a professionalism that is indistinguishable from the real thing. Thank you Johnny Bull, Vicky de Cervera, Emma Goddard, Margaret Glover, Matt Hobbs, Ian Hartshorne and Hugo Stewart.

Also The Royal Literary Fund, Eugenie Furniss and Claudia Webb at William Morris and the small but plucky workforce of zer0 and O-books, you are all players!

Contemporary culture has eliminated both the concept of the
public and the figure of the intellectual. Former public spaces –
both physical and cultural – are now either derelict or colonized
by advertising. A cretinous anti-intellectualism presides,
cheerled by expensively educated hacks in the pay of
multinational corporations who reassure their bored readers
that there is no need to rouse themselves from their interpassive
stupor. The informal censorship internalized and propagated by
the cultural workers of late capitalism generates a banal
conformity that the propaganda chiefs of Stalinism could only
ever have dreamt of imposing. Zer0 Books knows that another
kind of discourse – intellectual without being academic, popular
without being populist – is not only possible: it is already
flourishing, in the regions beyond the striplit malls of so-called
mass media and the neurotically bureaucratic halls of the
academy. Zer0 is committed to the idea of publishing as a
making public of the intellectual. It is convinced that in
the unthinking, blandly consensual culture in which we live,
critical and engaged theoretical reflection is more important
than ever before.